Praise for *Mistress of the Storm*

'A really gripping magical debut with
a strong girl heroine' *The Bookseller*

'A convincingly magical world . . . The final few
chapters are thrillingly tense, and very exciting.
Just very occasionally, when you have a new book to
read by a new author, you find that you have come
across a book that deserves to become a classic.
This was definitely one of those books. I loved
it all the way through, from start to finish, and
would highly recommend it' *The Bookbag*

Praise for *Heart of Stone*

'Both sweet and magical . . .
Highly recommended!' *Fluttering Butterflies*

'With a fantastic cast of characters, some thrilling
adventure, a pinch of mystery and a budding
romance, Verity Gallant's adventures are
a must read!' *Portrait of a Woman*

Melanie grew up on the Isle of Wight and lives in Suffolk with her husband Lucien and their two sons, Joe and Ben. *Heart of Stone* is the sequel to her first book *Mistress of the Storm*.

# Heart of Stone

## of

### A Verity Gallant Tale

# M. L. WELSH

David Fickling Books

OXFORD · NEW YORK

31 Beaumont Street
Oxford OX1 2NP, UK

HEART OF STONE: A VERITY GALLANT TALE
A DAVID FICKLING BOOK 978 1 849 92050 6

Published in Great Britain by David Fickling Books,
a division of Random House Children's Publishers UK
A Random House Group Company

Hardback edition publisged 2012
This edition published 2013

1 3 5 7 9 10 8 6 4 2

The Random House Group Limited supports The Forest Stewardship Council® (FSC®), the
leading international forest-certification organisation. Our books carrying the FSC label are
printed on FSC®-certified paper. FSC is the only forest-certification scheme supported by the
leading environmental organisations, including Greenpeace. Our paper procurement policy
can be found at www.randomhouse.co.uk/environment

DAVID FICKLING BOOKS
31 Beaumont Street, Oxford, OX1 2NP

www.randomhousechildrens.co.uk
www.totallyrandombooks.co.uk
www.randomhouse.co.uk

Addresses for companies within The Random House Group Limited
can be found at: www.randomhouse.co.uk/offices.htm

THE RANDOM HOUSE GROUP Limited Reg. No. 954009

A CIP catalogue record for this book is available from the British Library.

Printed and bound in Great Britain by
CPI Group (UK) Ltd, Croydon, CR0 4YY

*Hello Joe and Ben.*
*This is a secret message just for you.*
*Lots of love from Mummy xxx*

# Prologue

*I*t takes a long time to reach this stretch of coast, but when you do, the sight of its emerald-green ocean can lift even the darkest soul. Here lies the farthest-flung outpost of this great land we call Albion: the famous town of Wellow. Its houses cling to the curved cliff-face, larger and more ornate the higher up they reach.

Continue past the town and travel along the south-westerly shore. Here the sandstone cliffs turn to brilliant white chalk. The sea is clearer still. And as the sun beats down, the only vessel to be seen on the water is a small, well-loved wooden dinghy, with a faded red sail.

She is moored at present. Two children sit in her. One, a girl, is tall for her age with long brown hair that *strays from its clasp in an unruly fashion. She is nut-brown and freckled. Her friend, a small sandy-haired boy, is gazing up at the sky.*

*They are happy. But there are souls in the world who wish to put an end to happiness. For them, each happy-ever-after is an insult that must be corrected.*

*Book One*

# *The End of Summer*

# Chapter One

'It seems to me,' said Henry Twogood, 'that if a person was particularly fond of their catapult, they wouldn't leave it on the kitchen table.'

Verity Gallant lay at the other end of the dinghy. The hot sun warmed her cheek. Her eyes were half closed. Rainbow circles of light fluttered in front of her.

Henry paused to shift his legs over the side. He was lying in the bow with a rolled-up spinnaker for a cushion.

'And as for it breaking, surely that's got to be down to shoddy workmanship in the first place?'

Verity looked at her sandy-haired friend and grinned.

He took another bite from his sandwich and frowned. 'This cheese is floppy.'

'The sandwiches have been out in the sun all day,' she said mildly. 'They're probably past their best.'

Henry considered the point, then took another bite.

Verity gazed up at the sky. It stretched above her, acre after acre of intense blue. The weather had been like this for weeks. Every day was glorious. Each morning she bolted down breakfast so she could run to meet Henry and go sailing in his family's dinghy, *Poor Honesty*.

A gentle breeze kissed her forehead. The air smelled of salt and freedom.

'I can't believe it's the last day of the school holidays,' she said.

'I don't know where the time goes,' Henry agreed.

Verity thought back to her life just twelve months before. In her mind she remembered herself as the lonely little girl who had walked into Wellow library to find a tall, dark stranger sitting on the floor, in tears. She could hardly believe her life had changed so dramatically since then.

From the arrival of the famous smuggling galleon the *Storm* – and the terrifying woman who insisted on being called Grandmother – it had been just a short while to the discovery that her grandfather, Rafe Gallant, had been the renowned leader of the world-famous band of smugglers known as the Gentry.

She had no idea how her parents had managed to keep their past hidden for so long, although Henry insisted that she walked round in a dreamworld most of the time.

Despite the heat, Verity couldn't stop a shiver. Her own grandmother – or at least her grandfather Rafe's former wife – was the Mistress, one of the four Keepers of the Elements. A fearsome witch whose power knew no bounds.

She looked towards the shore. The white chalk cliff hurt her eyes.

'Have you ever been in those caves?' she asked.

'There aren't any in this bay,' said Henry, as he ferreted for the last orange.

'Well what's that?' asked Verity, pointing in

the direction of a large cave entrance in the cliff.

'That didn't used to be there,' said Henry.

Verity smiled.

'I'm telling you. That cave was not there two weeks ago. I was here fishing. Bertie let me go with him, well, Mum made him take me. But I was here. And that cave wasn't.'

'Let's have a look,' said Verity excitedly.

'What a great idea: a sea-bound cave that's appeared in the cliff-face, miles from home. How could anything possibly go wrong?' said Henry sarcastically. 'Caves don't just appear in the cliff.'

'That one did,' said Verity.

'I mean, if the cave appeared quickly it must be unstable.'

'It can't hurt to look,' said Verity, pushing the rudder to move *Poor Honesty* in the direction of the cliffs. The dinghy sailed in one swift reach towards the shore, the wind straight behind her.

'I'm waiting here,' said Henry as they neared the beach.

'Fine,' said Verity, scrabbling in the hold for the anchor, then taking off her very shabby and much-loved deck shoes. She hopped over the gunwale.

Henry swore. 'Obviously I can't leave you to go in there on your own,' he grumbled, following her.

Verity smiled. She had never been in a sea cave before, despite her Gentry heritage. She peered around the entrance, gazing up at the chalk walls. The pale white sand was still damp from a receding tide.

Henry strode forward, staring intently at the interior. He frowned, rubbing a piece of the chalk cliff.

'This appears to be a solutional cave,' he said.

Verity crouched down to pick up a pretty white shell. Henry knew perfectly well she didn't understand a word he was saying. 'So it's been created by rainwater dissolving the limestone,' he continued.

'Right,' said Verity, turning over the shell. It was very delicate, almost pearl-like.

'Which isn't possible,' said Henry. 'Caves that have been created by dissolving limestone don't just appear overnight.'

The cave wasn't all that big, perhaps fifteen or twenty feet long, although taller than both of them.

Verity stepped further inside the solid mass of rock. Instantly everything seemed quieter. In the silence she heard a low hiss, or perhaps a rustle. Something dusted her hair. Verity flapped at her head. She hated bats.

From nowhere came a boom of noise that ricocheted around the cave.

Verity shrieked, jumping backwards.

'What the hell was that?' said Henry, creeping further in to investigate. Then he grinned. 'It was air being pushed down here: this explains a lot,' he declared triumphantly, staring at the ceiling. Above him was a round hole in the rock, about a foot in diameter.

Verity walked over to the same spot and looked up. 'I can see daylight,' she said, astonished.

'Goes all the way to the top of the cliff,' said Henry. 'I think it's the wishing well.'

'The hole in the cliff, that was supposed to grant wishes? Did that really exist?' asked Verity.

Henry looked surprised. Verity's parents had always discouraged her from learning about Wellow's fables.

'I read about it last year,' she explained. 'People would shout their desires into it, and they came true. Except most people messed up the wording. Or asked for the wrong thing.'

Henry nodded. 'Asking to be rich, then inheriting money from the death of someone you loved.'

'Wanting a handsome husband, but forgetting to mention anything about him being intelligent or kind,' said Verity. 'So the townspeople filled it in, to stop it being used. And that's it.' She craned her neck back.

'Obviously in real life it doesn't actually grant wishes,' said Henry. 'But yes, there's a pothole in the cliff, and it's always been plugged up. A rockfall must have opened it again, and the entrance of this cave too. Another bit of Gentry nonsense,' he said briskly. 'They were just trying to keep people away from one of their prime smuggling spots.'

Verity looked down at the ground. The pale white sand glistened in the half-light.

With a hissing scrabble, a small flurry of rocks and sand fell from the cave roof. Verity yelped in pain as something sharp hit her head. Henry grabbed hold of her arm and pulled her outside.

Verity sat on the sand and rubbed her head. She felt a bit dizzy. 'I think I might have cut myself,' she said.

Henry crouched down to take a look. 'You are such an idiot,' he scolded.

Verity squashed down a pang of fear. Henry always got cross when he was worried.

He gently parted her hair to inspect the cut. 'You're fine,' he said gruffly. 'Just a scratch. I expect your parents won't even notice.'

'There's still a lot that passes them by,' she said.

'Aren't you supposed to be seeing your grand-father for tea?' Henry asked.

Verity looked at the position of the sun in the sky and gasped. 'I can't be late again. Mother arranged it with Poppy.'

'I'll drop you off,' said Henry. 'You can walk up the cliff-path: that'll save time.'

Verity ran across the sand and began pushing *Poor Honesty* back into the water.

Henry watched her. Her long brown hair was even curlier than usual today from the salt spray.

*12*

'Come on, aren't I supposed to be the day-dreamer?' she called back.

Henry snapped out of it. He jumped into the dinghy and took his place at the tiller, ready to start filling her sails with wind.

They began to tack back. The gentle breeze was like a tonic. Verity enjoyed the quiet splash of the ocean against the hull. At last they reached the beach owned by her grandfather. The cliffs towered protectively over them, covered in trees.

'Can't be bad, can it?' said Henry, nodding at the enchanting view. Verity smiled awkwardly. She felt awed herself by Rafe's wealth.

Verity slipped over the side of the dinghy and dropped into the clear shallow water. It was silky cold, the sand soft underfoot. She turned to smile ruefully at Henry. 'See you at school tomorrow.'

'Course,' he grinned. 'I'm not going anywhere.'

When she reached the wood that lay at the foot of the cliffs, Verity turned to wave. But Henry was already at the entrance to the bay.

She stood silently for a moment. The wood was humid today: fresh and rich. The damp rock removed all echoes. Verity placed a steadying hand on the old stone wall that ran through the trees. Its angular shape looked distinctly out of place amongst the fluid lines of leaf and branch. The wood seemed to agree, and had covered it in a thick blanket of velvety lichen.

She walked along the twisting mud path, ducking to avoid low branches, then began the ascent to the top. Occasionally she paused to glance at the view through gaps in the trees: the clear green sea rippled away to the horizon, meeting the sky in a hazy line of white.

It was so pleasant here: quiet and calm. Finally she reached the break in the stone cliff, a signal that there were just a dozen or so steps to the top. The cold dark rock towered over her. Even on this hottest of days, the fear still flickered through her mind, just for a second, that it might close in and trap her forever.

She remembered coming here for the first time with Jeb Tempest. He had brought her here when the strain of dealing with the Mistress had become too much. She'd been so grateful to him for his friendship. And a mischievous part of her had delighted in the envy it aroused amongst many of the girls at her school.

A fleeting memory of the way his bright green eyes had locked with hers flashed through her mind. Verity brushed it aside. He was gone now: travelling the world, seeking adventure. Not that she could blame him. She'd do the same if she could.

At last she reached the top. Verity paused to catch her breath, gazing at the lawned garden which surrounded her grandfather's house. She still found it hard to believe he lived here.

Wellow Manor sat at the top of the town's upper cliff. And although it was not over-whelmingly luxurious, nor particularly large, it was nevertheless a landmark of the area. The entire house was constructed of stone. Even its window gables and roof tiles were made of the distinctive quarry material, so popular in Wellow for those who could afford it. The glass windows were leaded in a diamond lattice.

Verity spotted her family outside, enjoying the

weather, a hazy vision in the heat. Her mother, Felicity, so pretty and fair, held Verity's baby sister, Olivia, on her knee. Her other sister, Poppy, was at a garden table drinking elderflower cordial and chatting animatedly to their grandfather and father. Verity smiled. It didn't matter where Poppy went, she was always the life and soul of the party.

Verity strode silently across the grass. Her grandfather stood up automatically, smiling. Verity looked with slight wonder at the man she still knew more from history books than personal experience.

He had obviously once been very handsome, and was still good-looking now. But it was his eyes that really caught the attention: their cornflower blue was so vivid, they seemed to have an inner light. When he looked at you it was entrancing. Verity could quite understand why he had held the fascination of so many.

'A good day on the water?' he asked warmly, holding out both hands in greeting. Both he and his son, Verity's father, were dressed in linen suits with Panama hats for shade.

'Yes, another one,' she said, kissing him and then

moving to say hello to Olivia. The baby girl smiled instantly at the sight of her. Her bright blonde hair was starting to curl. Verity grinned back happily. She held out a finger for Olivia to grasp in her chubby little hand with its tiny tapering fingers and minuscule nails.

Verity stared adoringly into her sister's beautiful blue eyes and, as always, Olivia looked straight back as if she could reach out and touch her soul. Verity kissed a round fat cheek affectionately.

'Nn-nn-ma-ma,' said Olivia, shoving Verity's finger in her mouth.

'Dirty Olivia,' said their mother, instantly removing the offending item.

Poppy jumped up to fetch a chair for Verity. The long school holiday had bleached her hair platinum. She was wearing a whitework cotton sundress that made her look even prettier than usual.

'Just astonishing how brilliant you've become at sailing in such a short time,' she said.

'The Gallant instinct,' said Rafe proudly.

'Such a good job Verity has it. It would have

been in danger of dying out entirely, left to me.'

'Poppy, you have more than enough gifts for one young lady,' said her grandfather.

Poppy burst out laughing. 'Oh Grandfather, you are funny.'

The air was still balmy and hot, even though it was late afternoon. Verity accepted a cool drink of freshly squeezed lemonade and gazed round happily while her family chatted. Her father had a newspaper on his lap. His amiable handsome face was a gentle brown, his wavy blond hair escaping from under his hat.

Verity had not been party to his reunion with Rafe. No one had. Sometimes she wondered what had been said, what could be said to explain a lifetime's absence. But he was happy now.

By the time they'd finished dinner, the sun was beginning to set. Olivia had long since been put to bed in her pram.

While Felicity fussed and tidied, Verity and Poppy carried a stack of plates each across the lawn to the kitchen door.

'Shall we go for a walk?' said Poppy. 'Even in someone else's house Mother doesn't like too many people getting in her way.' Verity grinned.

The sisters wandered idly, breathing in the early evening scents. The garden was packed with plants; clematis, honeysuckle, white rambling roses with small, closed blooms. Rafe had left the Manor empty for decades, and although his loyal friend Isaac, Jeb's grandfather, had done an admirable job of maintaining the house, the gardeners were only now getting to grips with the grounds. Verity loved their ramshackle appearance nonetheless.

The walled kitchen garden was a particular favourite. And now, the twilight made all the colours more vivid: the grass was richer and more lustrous, the sky a swirl of purple and crimson. The scent of herbs was heady.

'I love how secret this feels,' said Poppy happily as she hopped onto a low wall that marked out an asparagus bed, balancing on it as she walked. The sandy soil was pale in the evening light.

She jumped once more to the ground.

With a terrifying *crack*, the earth underneath

Poppy split in two and she dropped several feet in seconds. She screamed, her pretty face a mask of terror. Without thinking, Verity lunged forward and grabbed her sister as she fell.

Poppy flung both arms around her neck and clung on for dear life. 'I can't feel anything under my feet,' she whispered.

Verity's stomach churned. 'Don't let go of me,' she instructed, trying to pull Poppy up.

Her sister flinched. 'I think I'm stuck,' she said.

Verity felt lightheaded with fear. 'Help,' she shouted at the top of her voice. '*Help.*'

'My ribs are hurting,' said Poppy.

Verity's heart pounded. 'Can you feel the ground below you?' she asked.

'I'm not sure,' Poppy replied, her voice trembling.

Verity held on to her with one arm. Using the other she leaned forward and brushed away some of the soil near her sister. She could see now that Poppy had jumped onto a large concrete covering, which was split in the middle. All that held it together were two rusting spokes of iron. She could just about make out a glimmer of wet stones. 'It's a well,' she said. 'For the kitchen.'

Poppy let out a sob of fear.

Verity gripped her sister tightly. A trickle of pale sandy soil hissed through the gap into the space below.

'You're going to be fine,' she said, with more confidence than she felt. Then held her tighter still.

Felicity and Rafe ran into the garden.

Their mother gasped at the sight of Poppy half-swallowed by the earth. 'Oh my goodness.'

'That blasted pump,' cursed Rafe. He dropped down to sweep away the sandy earth, inspecting the broken cover, then started to clear the rest of it away while Verity held onto Poppy. A piece of concrete had shifted and was pinning her in.

'Hold your sister tight,' he said, straining to push it out of the way.

Poppy screamed as it moved.

Felicity shrieked, holding her hands to her mouth.

'There's nothing supporting me,' Poppy whimpered.

'I've got you,' said Verity firmly. She closed her eyes, blocking out their mother's wails. Felicity was the last person you wanted near you in a crisis.

Verity's arms were starting to ache. She banished the thought from her mind. Her mouth set into a determined line. There was no way she was letting go.

'There's enough room now,' said Rafe. 'I daren't drop this. Can you get Poppy out?'

'Of course,' said Verity. She held on tight and steeled herself to lift her sister up. She heaved, but the angle made it difficult, even though Poppy was so light. She could see her grandfather straining to hold the slab.

Felicity was sobbing now. Verity focused on clearing her head of the noise around her and pulled with all her might. She fell backwards onto the earth as Poppy landed on top of her. Both girls laughed hysterically with shock and relief.

Verity brushed Poppy's fringe out of her eyes. 'Are you all right?' she asked.

Her sister nodded, unable to speak just yet.

Rafe dropped the broken slab, then crouched

down to inspect both his granddaughters. 'No broken bones, no cuts,' he announced. He peered down the well. 'It's not actually that deep,' he said, in relief.

Felicity sat on the ground. Poppy ran to give her a hug, then her grandfather.

'We stopped using this well years ago, before I left Wellow,' Rafe explained. 'It couldn't supply the house. And I had concerns about the quality of the water. I'll close off the garden and make sure the well is capped properly tomorrow.' He shook his head. 'What fool thought this would cover it safely?' he asked. 'How could I have been so neglectful?'

'YIt's not at all your fault,' Poppy insisted, quite herself once more. 'I'm absolutely fine. And I wouldn't have been badly injured, even if I *had* dropped.'

Tom appeared at the garden gate. 'There you are,' he said, oblivious to what had just happened. 'It's lovely to see you all so happy here.'

Poppy flung both arms around her father. 'Shall we go indoors?' she asked.

Verity watched them with a fond smile. Looking around, it dawned on her that life was exactly as she would like it to be. Her family was happy, she spent her days sailing and having fun with Henry. For so many years she'd felt like a spare part. And she didn't any more.

The light was fading fast, and as the final sliver of sun disappeared beneath the horizon, the air turned chill. Verity shivered.

She stared anxiously at her family. Deep in her soul she wasn't sure she deserved to be so blessed.

Taking a deep breath to calm herself, she slipped off her sandals and splayed her toes on the cool grass. Her feet were gritty from the beach. She bent over to brush away the pale white sand that had stuck to her legs. It made a soft rasping noise as it fell to the ground. *The sound of unhappiness*, a little voice whispered in her head.

She stood up straight. You're being silly, she told herself firmly.

She was wrong, of course. And she would discover this in time. But for the moment, at least, Verity could believe her worries were unfounded.

# Chapter Two

Verity often found the first day at school particularly turbulent. Priory Bay this year was no different. Dozens of small bewildered children could be found trailing – timetable in hand – down long unwelcoming corridors that echoed with noise. Each one obviously wondering how they would ever become like the confident older pupils who strode about purposefully.

Verity watched a new girl being buffeted by the crowds. She was clutching a particularly large bag to her chest.

'Remind you of your first day at school?' asked Poppy.

Verity smiled. She had been absolutely terrified at the time. So alone, so out of place:

and little had improved for several years.

The sisters stood side by side, kitted out entirely in new uniforms. Verity had fared less badly than usual - this winter's skirt was almost flattering.

'Wasn't it this time last year you met Henry?' Poppy asked.

Verity said nothing, remembering her first proper encounter with her friend: he'd saved her from the bullying Blake brothers. As the youngest of seven sons, Henry was pretty fearless.

'You're lucky to have him,' said Poppy, 'I'm really quite envious.' Someone waved on the other side of the playground. 'Better dash,' she said, giving Verity a kiss.

'*Verity*,' a familiar voice shouted.

Verity swung round. '*Martha*.'

They hugged. They hadn't seen each other since the start of the summer holidays, when Martha's parents had announced they would be taking their daughter with them on an academic sabbatical.

'I missed you so much,' said Martha joyfully. Verity's friend looked less pale than usual. The freckles on her round face were so prolific they had merged together to give her a distinctly sun-kissed look. But the sleek dark bob and round gold-rimmed glasses were still the same.

'You're taller,' said Verity.

'I was just thinking the same thing about you. You look as if you've been stretched,' Martha giggled.

'So what was it like?' asked Verity.

'You know, it was fine,' said Martha, tucking a lock of hair behind one ear. 'I think being absorbed in their work distracted my parents from fighting.'

'You've caught the sun,' said Verity.

'We were on an archaeological dig,' said Martha, raising her eyebrows.

'Wow,' said Verity, thinking this sounded pretty impressive.

'It's actually quite dull,' admitted her friend. 'But you do at least get to work outside, instead of being stuck indoors with loads of books.'

'In a library, for example,' said Verity, referring to the many hours they'd spent together trying to find out more about the Mistress.

'Precisely,' said Martha. 'Although I think it adds a certain something to research when your life's under threat. I can't believe how much I missed Wellow,' she added, looking around her happily.

'It's been a glorious holiday,' said Verity.

'You look like you've spent the whole time on the water,' said Martha enviously, brushing sand from Verity's blazer.

'Pretty much.'

'Wotcha,' said Henry, appearing behind the two girls and gently knocking Martha's legs with his bag. Martha grinned in reply, then gave Henry a hug.

'Easy,' the youngest Twogood protested affably. 'You must be the only person who's pleased to be here.'

'Well you should thank your lucky stars your parents don't drag you off to the middle of nowhere,' said Martha.

'We *live* in the middle of nowhere,' shot back Henry.

'Yes, life in Wellow can be so uneventful,' said Martha dryly.

Henry laughed, pleased to have his old sparring partner back. 'This summer's been quiet.'

'It's been wonderful,' said Verity.

'*Crikey*,' Henry exclaimed, his eyes widening. 'Isn't that Miranda Blake over there?'

Verity and Martha swung round to stare in the direction Henry had indicated. Verity's jaw dropped. Henry was right. The unmistakable Miranda Blake was wearing a Priory Bay uniform. Flanked by her oversized brothers George and Oscar, she didn't seem to have grown at all. If anything she looked smaller. Certainly her pinched face was thinner than before, her eyes more bulbous still.

'What's she doing here?' asked Martha.

'Nothing good,' said Henry.

Miranda looked in their direction, noting their confusion with amusement. Murmuring something to George, she walked over confidently. 'Surprised?' she asked. Miranda had always previously attended Whale Chine School: sworn enemies of Priory Bay.

'Saddened and dismayed,' said Henry. There was no love lost between the Twogood and Blake families.

Miranda stared disdainfully at him. It was astonishing, thought Verity, that such a short girl could still manage to look down her nose at all she surveyed.

'To think it's come to this,' said Miranda. 'Going to the same school as a Twogood. Lucky for you they offer scholarships here.'

'Lucky for *you* they take fee-paying students,' retorted Henry. 'You'd never get in on brains alone.'

'You can thank your little intervention for my presence here. Mother had to look for a more economical option after you got rid of the Mistress. She was livid,' said Miranda. Her eyes were dark, and bleak. For a second Verity felt just the tiniest flicker of pity.

'I'm sorry your mother took it out on you,' said Verity, genuinely, 'but you can't blame us.'

'Oh I can, Gallant,' said Blake lightly.

'Watch your step, you poisonous little peanut,' said Henry.

'I'd expect you two to side with her,' said Miranda. 'After all, the Twogoods have nothing.

And you,' she continued, looking at Martha, 'your family are nobodies.'

'Who do you think you're talking to?' asked Verity icily, pulling herself up to her full height.

Miranda smirked. 'The Gallant spirit,' she lisped. 'You have it, after all.'

Mercifully the break bell sounded. Miranda sneered, then glided away silently.

'You're nothing like her,' said Martha, slipping an arm into Verity's as they headed for class.

'Not at all,' said Henry. 'Didn't she look smaller? I think all that spite has shrunk her permanently.'

'You're not usually so chipper when there's double chemistry looming,' said Verity with a twinkle in her eye.

'Ah yes, but I have it on good authority that there's a replacement teacher,' said Henry. 'Mr Ford ran off to join the circus last week. Always wanted to be a trapeze artist apparently. Mum told Auntie Violet when she thought I wasn't listening. Anyway,' he continued gleefully. 'Everyone knows that part-time teachers are an easy ride.'

'We're here to learn,' said Martha reprovingly.

Henry cheerfully made a rude gesture in her direction.

All three children stopped short at the classroom door. It was chaos. A hastily-made paper plane shot past Verity's nose. Henry caught it in one swift grasp.

It took a few moments for Verity to realize that there *was* a teacher at the front of the room. The man was tall, but practically skin and bone. His short white-blond hair stuck out in dishevelled spikes, his eyebrows were so pale they could hardly be seen and his eyes were a very pale shade of grey. His lips were full and pink, bunched permanently in an unattractive pucker.

The teacher pulled a chair towards him and stood on it, waving his arms in the air. He wore a polo neck jumper and a baggy green corduroy jacket.

'That's seen better days,' muttered Henry.

'Quiet, please,' shouted the teacher at the top of his voice, which was still not very loud. He looked as if he would rather be anywhere else in the world than here. The pupils continued at full throttle.

Verity, Henry and Martha shuffled through the scrum to three empty seats at the front.

'If you could, er, just hush up now.'

One of the pupils had broken into the supplies cupboard and was dishing out contraband. His friend had taken first dibs on the sodium and a tin beaker of water. It hissed and fizzed angrily. A couple of girls screamed.

The teacher gave an anguished squawk and hurried over. With a great flapping of hands he tried to put an end to the experiment, but managed only to singe both eyebrows as it exploded in a shower of sparks. The room resounded with shrieks, and howls of laughter.

'We're entering the Heartsease Cup this year,' Henry shouted to Martha above the din. 'How about you crew with us?'

'You must,' said Verity excitedly. 'It'll be brilliant.'

'But that's the biggest race of the year,' said Martha. 'You need someone better than me, surely?'

'You'll be fine,' said Verity. 'And it'll be more fun.'

Martha looked with exasperation round the class. 'How is the teacher supposed to start with this racket?' she asked. Another pupil had found a roll of magnesium strip and set fire to it. It flared with a piercing white light. Martha looked pleadingly at Henry. 'Can't you do something?' she said.

Henry shrugged. 'I'm sure I could, if only I knew who I was racing with in the Heartsease Cup. It's preoccupying me.'

Martha huffed. 'Fine, I'll crew for you. Happy?'

Verity grinned.

Henry put two fingers in his mouth, and blew a piercing wolf whistle. Finally, with a couple of jeers, the class settled down into an excitable approximation of silence.

The teacher stared at the assembled children in astonishment, then gulped and did his best to resume control.

'Your spirits are commendable,' he said, with an anxious smile. 'But we should get on with the lesson.' He turned his back to the class to write his name in chalk on the board. 'No harm done, no harm done,' he said. 'I am Brother Povl – slightly unusual Nordic name – of the Usage family. Whom you might have heard of.'

Verity stared in astonishment at their teacher. The Usages were a prominent family in Wellow, known in equal measure for their greed and aggression. How had they produced such a skinny, frightened man?

Povl scanned the class nervously. 'Who will tell me where you got to last term with your studies? Ah, yes, you—' he pointed to a pupil.

'Miranda Blake.'

'The Blakes,' said Povl, stuttering. 'An esteemed Gentry family.'

Miranda stared coldly at the teacher. 'I can't speak for this lot,' she said. 'But at Whale Chine we were some way through the actions of alkalines and acids.'

Povl leaned towards Verity and dusted sand from the lapel of her blazer. Verity froze instinctively at the touch of a stranger. He smelled fusty.

'Quite something, to be so scruffy you attract our esteemed teacher's attention,' murmured Miranda. The class sniggered.

'Miss Gallant, I believe,' Povl said, nodding repeatedly. 'You must be thrilled your grandfather has returned.'

Verity looked startled.

'A little of hobby of mine: studying the Gentry past of my family, and others,' he explained.

'Trust the teacher to take a shine to Gallant,' remarked Blake dryly.

The other pupils laughed.

Henry balled up a piece of paper and threw it deftly at Blake's head. Within minutes the class had descended into disarray once more.

'Children, children,' pleaded Brother Povl. But most couldn't hear him, and those who did chose not to.

Verity sighed. Already her happy summer holiday felt very far away.

'Can we go to the library?' asked Martha eagerly as the three friends strode through the park after school.

Verity perked up. The thought of an hour in familiar surroundings sounded comforting.

'How time drags when I'm not surrounded by books,' said Henry sarcastically.

'We can make hot chocolate,' said Verity, to placate him.

'Backgammon gets my vote,' he agreed, cheering up.

'Sounds good,' said Martha. 'I haven't had a chance to beat anyone all summer.'

'Nor will you this afternoon,' Henry replied.

The children strode towards the familiar solid building that stood at the junction of two cliff-top paths. A trail of pale white sand lay patiently in a wind-blown crest on the ground outside. Verity paused to stare at it: more white sand. There seemed to be a lot of it in Wellow recently. But Martha was too excited to wait.

'Come on.' They entered the library. A little cloud of dust swirled around their feet.

It had been several weeks since Verity had last visited the library. Miss Cameron, the librarian, was on a footstool, rearranging one of the higher shelves. She noted the new arrivals with perfect composure.

'There you are,' she murmured. Her sensible heels clicked on the polished wooden floor as she came to greet them. Her face was serene, as ever: her skin smooth and blemish free, with just the faintest of lines at the corners of her eyes.

Verity smiled in reply. Miss Cameron was famously reserved, but she found being in her presence distinctly comforting. And without the librarian's stoical help, Olivia might well not have survived earlier this year. For that alone, Verity's affection ran deep.

Martha was buzzing with excitement at being back in her spiritual home. 'I've got such a lot to tell you,' she said eagerly. 'And I can't wait to hear what I've missed.'

'Not a great deal,' said the librarian. 'Verity and Henry have been quite the absentees this summer.'

Verity felt a pang of guilt. 'How selfish of us.'

Miss Cameron put an end to her teasing. 'My little joke,' she smiled. 'Of course you should be out in the fresh air. Not stuck with your head in a book all the time. Have you enjoyed a much-deserved holiday?'

'It's been idyllic,' said Verity. 'Although it ended abruptly last night.' She told all three about Poppy's brush with the badly covered well. Miss Cameron was silent. A ray of sun lit up her hair. It was shorter, Verity noticed, and curled, but still as neatly styled as ever.

'And your grandfather intends to have it capped?' she asked.

Verity nodded. 'In fact, it was quite a day for things tumbling. We found a cave while we were out sailing. Henry thinks it sits underneath the wishing well. It looked as if it had become unblocked.'

Miss Cameron's face whitened. 'The wishing well is open once more?'

Henry rolled his eyes, as Verity quickly explained to Martha.

'Does it grant wishes?' her friend asked.

'In a manner of speaking,' the librarian said. She pointed to a framed cross-stitch on the wall.

> *So He of the Sky said, 'I will give each element a Keeper, to control them and protect my people.' And he read out a story of their beginning: of four sisters whose duty it was to control the elements. It was a joyous event and as he spoke the words fell from the sky. Each place where they landed around the world became a sacred one of special powers, so when a story was read aloud there it would become true.*

Verity knew it off by heart. It was the story of the four Keepers of the Elements: a tale of Verity's beloved friend Alice who vanished last year, the Mistress, and their two siblings.

'Halfway down the hole known as the wishing well is a very small wellspring – one of the secret locations where a story can be told and become reality,' Miss Cameron admitted.

'*A real one?*' squeaked Martha, her eyes on stalks.

'You must not go there,' said Miss Cameron

quickly. 'It was sealed for good reason. A badly worded story can have terrible consequences. The wishing well is particularly dangerous: there are so many opportunities for the words spoken near it to be distorted.'

'Why don't we just close it up again? I can get my brothers to help,' said Henry.

'That would not be at all safe,' Miss Cameron replied.

Henry bristled. 'I'm a Twogood,' he said. 'I expect it was our family who sealed it up in the first place.'

Martha couldn't resist a wry smile.

Henry shot her a withering look.

'The Twogood brothers are very resourceful,' said Verity.

'I'm afraid it isn't practical,' Miss Cameron said. 'It took several days and twenty grown men to block it last time, with many tons of rubble.'

'Oh.' Verity and Martha both deflated.

Henry looked at them as if they were slightly stupid. 'We won't block up the *whole thing*. But we can create a platform two or three feet in at each end, and then disguise it. The top will be easy: we can just fill it with earth and put some turf on top. The one in the cave, well, we might have to work something out. But I'm sure we can do it.'

'I shouldn't allow you to go anywhere near it,' said the librarian. 'Even a sentence could bring about terrible harm: the well caused many accidents when it was open. It was a tragic incident involving a silly girl who wanted to improve her looks, that finally convinced the people of Wellow to seal it up.'

'What happened?' asked Martha.

'She asked to be pretty,' said Miss Cameron. 'But it seems the wishing well distorted the crucial word to "kitty".'

'*Old Ma Puss,*' said Henry, his eyes wide. 'Do you remember her? She had the hairiest face I've ever seen, with the oddest yellow eyes. And she always wore gloves, even in the summer.'

Miss Cameron looked down at her hands and Martha shuddered.

'We won't talk,' said Henry, after some moments' thought.

Martha snorted. 'That would take some kind of magic.'

Henry scowled at her.

'I shall come with you,' said Miss Cameron at last.

'You're more than welcome, but there won't be any need,' said Henry, scuffing his shoe on the wooden floor.

'No, I'm afraid I insist,' said Miss Cameron. 'When would you like to begin?'

'Bertie and Fred are coming round for supper today,' said Henry, wondering if he was going too quickly for the librarian. 'If we do it this evening I can get them to help as well as Percy and Will.'

'That would be very kind,' said Miss Cameron, walking over to the front desk and picking up a green leather handbag from behind the counter. 'Shall I come with you now?'

Henry shook his head, impressed nonetheless. 'Better wait here. We'll collect you once I've explained what's required . . . and they've eaten.' He looked at Verity and Martha. 'You two can help pack stuff though.'

'There is nothing the Twogood boys enjoy more than a practical problem,' said Verity as they walked to the red double doors, accompanied by Miss Cameron. 'You don't believe for a moment there's really a wellspring.'

'Then it's lucky I like a challenge, isn't it?' said Henry as he stepped into the porch. 'Otherwise, as far as Miss Cameron's concerned, come morning, Wellow would be riddled with people who'd turned themselves to gold, or killed their much-loved wives by accident.'

Verity glanced back with a grin at Miss Cameron. The librarian smiled in reply, then waved a gentle goodbye and closed the doors once more. A late afternoon sea breeze ruffled their hair.

'I didn't say your genius wasn't an impressive thing,' said Verity.

'Don't worry, I'm sure we can find some very menial tasks for you: things on your level,' her friend replied.

## Chapter Three

In the end Henry and his brothers managed to safely disguise the wishing well's opening quite easily. Despite Martha's misgivings, they completed all the work without uttering a single word. Instead they communicated using a complex series of signals, which they had agreed between each other, and the occasional impatient frown. Miss Cameron stood silently with them throughout and seemed impressed: the boys had only needed to break off twice so they could move away from the opening and confer.

Percy had warned that neither end of the wishing well would stand up to much interference but Will had excelled himself in camouflaging both. He took a real pleasure in meeting the challenge. Even though Verity knew perfectly well where the top hole was, she found the patch of grass particularly hard to spot.

'Quite a simple turf job,' he explained, with just a touch of pride.

For the inside of the cave Will had used chicken wire with papier-mâché and paint. It took him several nights to perfect the effect. From then on it was simply a matter of checking occasionally to make sure nothing had been disturbed, which gave Verity an excuse for plenty of long walks. She loved tramping across the downs, staring out to sea, and dreaming of the day when she could travel to faraway places.

Term-time life – both at Priory Bay and home – settled into a comfortable routine for Verity, Henry and Martha. The unfamiliar new timetable became second nature within weeks. Chemistry was still the most chaotic lesson by far: Martha found it quite distressing. The lessons were excruciating for Verity too, although in her case this was because Brother Povl always made at least one enquiry about Rafe, or her family's history. Henry, meanwhile, simply thought their teacher was an idiot.

The glorious weather refused to give in without a fight, which meant the three children could still go out in *Poor Honesty* straight after school. This was fortunate, given that they needed to practise for the renowned Heartsease Cup, which traditionally marked the end of the summer for Wellow. It was the biggest race of the year because any boat or crew could take part: all stood an equal chance of winning, thanks to the handicap system.

The day of the event dawned bright and clear, the sun was still yellow and warm. Verity strode through the streets, enjoying its heat on her face. She always looked forward to a day on the water.

Already, spectators were arriving from other towns: wandering down the hill and towards the harbour in a bid to bag a good spot. Some had even brought rugs or chairs. Entrepreneurial Wellow residents were on hand to sell souvenir pamphlets or themed balloons. Young children chased each other excitedly; oblivious to the tuts and glances of older couples who were intent on marking out their territory with every possession at hand. By the evening, the town would be thrumming with visitors.

Verity threaded her way through the crowd, heading straight for the sailing club. She always thought 'watching' a race was an odd way to spend a day, given that you saw so little. Most of the action was actually out of sight on the water, in other bays. But it was a popular activity, especially for the Heartsease Cup.

There were Henry and Martha: easing *Poor Honesty* off a borrowed trolley and into the water. The slipway was strewn with pale white sand.

'I'm going to hold you back,' said Martha as soon as she saw her friend arrive.

Verity forced herself to smile confidently and cast a look at Henry who glanced innocently back. They'd practised and practised over the last few weeks, but none of it seemed to go into Martha's head. Each time they went sailing, Henry had to explain everything again to her as if it were new. But they'd both agreed that they'd rather have Martha with them and lose.

'Just do as I say, and you'll be fine,' said Henry

with a grin. Martha gave him a friendly shove and got into the dinghy.

The course ran westwards to Tempest Bay: the first boat to sail around the wreck off the point and return to Wellow would be the victor. This was Verity's first year as a contestant too, and to make things even more nerve-wracking, her grandfather had been invited by the Committee to present the coveted glass cup to the winning team.

Verity hopped into the water and held the forestay of the boat while Henry unpacked the mainsail, running it swiftly up the mast and adjusting the sheets. The two of them were so used to crewing with each other now they scarcely needed to say a word. The water around her was cloudy and quite pale: churned by dozens of excited feet. She dug her toes into the seabed. More white sand: but it was much nicer than the usual mud, she thought. The recent tides must have brought it here.

Martha jumped unsteadily onto *Poor Honesty*, grabbing awkwardly onto the boom, which just swung away from her. A couple of nearby contestants smirked.

'Sit here,' said Henry, patting the buoyancy tank.

Verity smiled brightly at Martha, then stared back up at Wellow Sailing Club's viewing platform. There was Jeb's grandfather, Isaac. Rafe had said he'd be joining him. Verity waved. Isaac lifted a hand and smiled warmly in reply. He was drawing on a pipe and Verity could almost smell the fragrant vanilla tobacco.

'Gallant.' A familiar and unwelcome voice pierced Verity's thoughts. Miranda Blake was on the slipway, staring down at her, head tipped to one side. 'I really admire the carefree way you put your ensembles together,' she said lightly. 'It must be so freeing to wear the first thing that comes to hand.'

Verity pulled a face. She'd found Miranda intimidating last year. But a lot had changed since then.

Verity looked around and saw that the Blake family dinghy was right next to *Poor Honesty*. Miranda's brothers, George and Oscar, were both on board, expertly tightening the sails. It hardly seemed possible but both boys were even larger than the last time she'd seen them. Their floppy hair was bleached nearly white from a long summer of sun and their skin looked uncomfortably pink.

*Poor Honesty* was ready now. Verity pulled herself over the gunwale and into the dinghy, sitting at the helm.

'Making up for lost time?' sniggered George. 'Shame your family couldn't be bothered to teach you to sail before.'

'Presumably your parents thought the same about manners,' said Verity tartly, putting a hand on the tiller. Martha glared at the brothers from her seat.

'No need to be like that,' said Miranda, examining her nails. 'You don't have to look down on everyone just because your grandfather's Lord of the Manor.'

'Put a sock in it,' said Henry as he pushed off with an angry shove. Verity steered *Poor Honesty* away, filling the mainsail with wind.

Miranda raised an eyebrow with expert menace. 'May the best team win,' the poisonous little girl lisped sweetly.

'Thanks,' said Henry as he sheeted in the jib. 'We will.'

'Can you believe her cheek?' fumed Martha as they sailed away from the Blakes, and towards the starting line.

'That family has always been rotten to the core,' said Henry.

'Let's just enjoy the race,' said Verity.

'You're right.' Martha looked around. 'It's a lovely day.'

As they left the harbour the wind picked up and *Poor Honesty* began to gather speed. The beauty of sailing in a dinghy was that you were so close to the water. Verity felt as if she were at one with the ocean.

'This is brilliant fun,' shouted Martha, her shiny bob tousled by the breeze. The air out here was fresh. The movement of the ocean was steady, with just a hint of foam.

Verity grinned. 'It's a prevailing wind today,' she explained. 'So winning is mainly about who can go the fastest, and hold their nerve the longest.'

'Just try to bear in mind,' said Henry, 'that we can't win if we don't all get home in one piece.'

The three friends were in a good position when

the starting gun went off, and with Henry and Verity's teamwork they managed to grow their lead along the deserted white cliff coast of Soul Bay. They sped through the ocean, the wind whipping noisily around them.

'Is that the marker?' yelled Martha, pointing to a large floating metal ball that had been painted green.

'Yes, how do you know?' Henry raised his voice to make himself heard over the sound of flapping sheets and rippling sails.

Martha rolled her eyes. 'Obviously I read up on the theory of sailing.'

'One day you'll come across something in life that can't be looked up in an encyclopaedia,' he shouted back, 'and that'll flummox you.'

'I think the fact it has the word 'WRECK' painted on it in large white letters might have helped anyway,' said Martha.

'We're in the lead,' said Verity excitedly. The fresh sea air made her feel alive. 'Only the Blakes are anywhere near us. If we plane to the marker, they'll find it really hard to beat us.'

Henry shook his head furiously. *Poor Honesty* cut, clean and straight, through the water. 'You know this part of the course is tricky,' he argued. 'We have to leave the buoy to port, and the sandbank's between us and the cliff. Why risk a capsize by planing with Martha on board?'

Martha turned around to check out the competition, her cheeks pink. 'Miranda's furious,' she said gleefully.

Verity glanced back. Martha was right. Their diminutive enemy was treating her brothers to the full force of her temper. The wind blew a string of expletives across the waves and they could hear Miranda perfectly.

'If you didn't all pig out so much,' she snarled, 'we'd be halfway back by now.'

Verity, Henry and Martha grinned in delight. The temptation was too much to resist. Without saying a word, Henry slackened the jib and pulled the centreboard up. 'Sit out here alongside me,' he instructed Martha, as Verity took the rudder. 'We've got to keep the boat as flat as possible.'

*Poor Honesty* lifted slightly out of the water and

began to skim across the surface, going faster still. The dinghy began to thrum.

'Move your weight back here,' Henry shouted to Martha, as he sheeted in a little. Verity bore away to keep up their speed. They could hear Miranda's fury turning to incandescent rage. And then a pause – followed by heated debate.

Verity looked back and gasped. 'They're taking a short-cut through the sandbank: cutting off the corner of the course.'

Henry and Martha swivelled round.

'That's cheating and you know it,' Henry bellowed at the top of his voice. George jeered back aggressively.

'We'll have to worry about them in a minute,' said Verity urgently. 'Ready about.'

Henry put a hand on Martha's head to make sure she crouched low enough, then he pushed the centreboard back down fully.

'Lee ho,' came the next warning. The boom snapped across the boat as *Poor Honesty* turned.

Henry smartly un-cleated the jib sheet then re-cleated it on the other side, as he and Martha hopped across the boat. He pulled the centerboard back up a little as Verity prepared to begin planing once more.

She glanced across to the Blakes. It looked as though they were having trouble with their boat, which had slowed visibly.

'They're too close to the cliff,' said Verity. 'Looks like the wind's gone a bit flukey.'

'Happens near cliffs,' Henry explained to Martha, 'because the wind's coming towards them from the sea, it's got nowhere to go but up so you get weird downdrafts, or nothing at all.'

Miranda and her brothers certainly seemed to be regretting their tactic. But worse still, several other competitors had caught up and decided to make the same course alteration.

'The cheating hounds,' said Henry.

The Blakes were snarling now; incensed to see the headway *Poor Honesty* was still making, while they were surrounded by teams who were struggling to control their dinghies. Verity could see a few of the contestants looking panicked. Meanwhile the rest of the boats were approaching fast: all looking in astonishment at the scene playing out before them.

Suddenly a bone-chilling growl rumbled from the cliffs above. Every pair of eyes looked up. A flurry of gulls burst into the air like seeds from a disturbed dandelion, as the land on which they had been resting fell from under their feet.

Verity's jaw dropped. A huge sliver of rock split away from the white chalk cliff with a thunderous crack. It slid towards the water. Time passed with both agonizing sloth and terrifying speed.

The noise was overwhelming. It surged around Verity's head, stripping away all thought; a grinding, splitting bellow that rang out across the water. It was a heaving beast's groan: as if even the cliffs themselves couldn't credit what was happening.

Finally the giant splinter of rock struck the sea with a roaring, ear-splitting blast. As it hit, the ocean boiled and churned. An ominous, fast-moving swell surged towards the competing boats. *Poor Honesty* jerked viciously, throwing the children back and forth. Martha gripped onto the side just in time to stop herself falling overboard.

Stray chunks and boulders rained down. One collided with a dinghy, smashing her mast and ripping her mainsail. Another dropped straight through the floor of a second boat.

Verity could hear screams of alarm ringing out across the water. She blinked, as if coming to. *Poor Honesty* was slightly apart from the other dinghies. But in front of her was a scene of pandemonium. Boats were veering in every direction: smashing into each other as their occupants panicked and lost control of their vessels. One of the contestants had been hit by a small rock and blood was streaming from her head. She looked confused, tears pouring down her cheeks. A boy had been thrown into the water.

It was like a scene from a nightmare.

'We have to help,' shouted Henry.

'Ready about!' Verity pushed the tiller to turn the dinghy around. Henry un-cleated and re-cleated the jib, then jumped to the other side. Martha was sitting completely still. Henry gave her a shove. She started, then moved to join him. All the colour had drained from her face.

'Let's get that boy out of the water first,' she said to him. He nodded.

They passed the Blakes' boat, which was finally picking up some speed as it reached the better air.

'Moor here and we'll ferry people back to you,' Henry yelled to the Blakes.

Miranda looked at him with contempt, then began to fill the sail of the Blake dinghy with wind. George and Oscar sat their weight out: preparing to go as fast as possible. They plainly had no intention of stopping.

'Where d'you think you're going?' Henry barked.

'It's a race, you imbecile,' said Miranda. She seemed oblivious to the turmoil behind her.

'You can't leave,' shouted Martha, her voice catching. 'People are hurt.'

'Don't be naïve,' Miranda sneered, as her dinghy drew further away. 'They'd all do exactly the same.'

A cry of pain rang out. Verity, Henry and Martha swivelled around. The boy who'd fallen overboard had been hit by a dinghy. He was spluttering and coughing, blood streaming down his face. The waves around him were pink.

Martha screamed. 'We've got to help,' she cried, trying to grab hold of the rudder and steer it towards the boy.

'Are you mad? We'll hit him as well,' yelled Henry.

Verity pulled the rudder away from Martha and turned *Poor Honesty* head to wind, bringing the dinghy to a halt right at the edge of the jumble of boats. She grabbed hold of her friend by both arms. Martha's eyes were glassy and strange and she was struggling for air.

'You have to calm down,' Verity said firmly to her. 'We must not panic.'

Verity breathed in encouragingly, nodding at Martha to do the same. A small hint of colour came back to her friend's cheeks.

The scene around them was chaos, but inside Verity felt strangely calm, and purposeful. Henry scrambled for the folding anchor and threw it over the side. Verity swung her legs over the gunwale.

'Henry and I will go and fetch that boy,' she said, turning back to smile confidently at Martha. 'You wait here.'

'She's so sure of what to do,' Martha whispered as Henry dropped into the water.

'The Gallant spirit,' he said with a wry grin. Then he pushed himself off against the hull of *Poor Honesty*.

It took some time to make sure all the competitors and dinghies were in a fit state to head back to Wellow. Mercifully, all the injuries looked worse than they actually were, and there were enough first aid materials to treat everyone. Gradually, as Verity and Henry marshalled people into action, the air of panic and fear diminished.

The three friends were the last to leave. They had agreed to tow the dinghy with the snapped centre plate back to Wellow, and it meant they needed to wait for the water to clear. The crew of the other dinghy helped with paddles, but *Poor Honesty*'s journey along the coast was still slow and difficult.

'We have to make sure the other dinghy has the wind behind her,' Henry explained to Martha. 'Otherwise she'll keep getting blown sideways.'

Verity squashed down a shiver. The air was still,

the waves calm. But the sun was lower in the sky and it was getting colder. She hadn't dried out from swimming around earlier. Both her hands and feet were painfully numb. She tried to wiggle her toes.

'I would have thought someone might come to fetch us,' said Martha, her voice despondent.

Henry shrugged. 'It's a race,' he said. 'Sailing's a tough sport.'

'Is that what Miranda meant earlier? I still can't believe she and her brothers didn't help,' said Martha.

'Don't know why we expected anything else,' said Henry dismissively.

'At least the moral victory is ours,' said Martha. 'It's just so galling to think of them taking the cup.'

'We're nearly home,' said Verity, spotting the familiar sight of Wellow Sailing Club. A large group of spectators were still gathered on the stilted balcony. There were a lot of people, Verity noticed.

'There they are,' shouted a spectator as *Poor Honesty* was sighted. Verity steered Henry's dinghy slowly towards the slipway. She had to be even more careful with the other boat in tow.

Verity's grandfather Rafe was pushing through the crowd with Isaac Tempest.

'Are you all right?' he shouted, cupping his hands. He looked as if he'd been waiting outside for some time.

Verity nodded, with more energy than she felt. She jumped into the freezing water to hold *Poor Honesty* by the gunwale, while Henry furled the sails.

'I can clean the ropes tomorrow,' he said.

Verity's teeth chattered.

'Out. Out of there,' her grandfather insisted when he finally reached the slipway. Pulling her up from the water he took off his wool coat and put it around her shoulders. 'You'll catch your death.'

Isaac grabbed hold of *Poor Honesty*. 'You as well, young Twogood,' he said. 'We'll make sure she's packed up properly.'

Henry beamed, grateful to be allowed into the warm. A group of onlookers patted him on the back as he walked past.

Martha hopped onto the slipway, still buoyed up by the adventure of it all. 'I expect the Blakes have the cup now?' she said to Rafe.

'They were disqualified,' he replied. 'There was a fleet of protests this afternoon.'

Henry's brothers, Percy and Will, burst through the assembled crowd. 'Not bad for a shrimp,' said Percy, knocking him around the head affectionately.

'You're all right I suppose?' said Will.

'Course,' said Henry nonchalantly. 'Another day, another rockfall.'

Percy handed him a paper bag. 'Mum sent some sausage rolls.'

'That's more like it,' said Henry, investigating the bag's contents immediately. 'So the Blakes didn't win?' The three brothers grinned at each other.

Rafe led the children up into the sailing-club hall, which was packed with yet more people. He guided Verity, Henry and Martha to the front and onto a little wooden stage. Verity supposed they must want to know more about the accident. The Blakes were still here. Miranda had her back to the wall. She looked pale. Mrs Blake stood next to her, her sharp face dark with anger.

The sailing club Commodore approached Rafe and handed him a crystal bowl. The room fell quiet. Everyone was watching them, Verity realized.

Verity's grandfather cleared his throat. The noise sounded odd in the silence. 'It was the unanimous decision of the racing committee,' he said, 'that the cup should be awarded to your team.'

The three children stared at him in astonishment.

'But we came last,' said Verity after a few seconds. 'How could we win?'

'According to the other competitors you had a clear lead, which you chose to sacrifice,' said Rafe. 'Many also stepped forward to say that without your quick thinking, and fine seamanship, the entire incident could have been much worse.'

Verity was stunned, her cheeks were hot with embarrassment. Near the back, one of the spectators began to clap loudly, and within seconds the room had exploded into a noisy round of applause. People Verity had never met were cheering. She could see Percy and Will stamping the floor and whooping.

Henry gave a short bow. Martha was pink with excitement, and beaming from ear to ear.

Rafe leaned to whisper in Verity's ear. The scent

of his old-fashioned cologne tickled her nose. 'I am very proud of you.'

Verity felt completely overwhelmed. She brushed the tears from her eyes.

Henry grinned and gave her a hug. 'Personally I think we deserve it,' he said, as if stating an eminently reasonable fact.

Finally the noise died down a little. Rafe passed the crystal bowl to Verity. 'The Heartsease Cup,' he said.

It was an old-fashioned goblet. The bowl was made of a thick lead crystal that sparkled brilliantly in the light. The handle and stand appeared to be wrought silver. They showed three men pulling agonized faces, one holding his hands over his eyes, one over his mouth and one over his ears.

Martha took it eagerly. 'I can't believe we won,' she said delightedly.

'And three bankers' cheques,' added Rafe, handing them out. Henry looked at the amount.

'Wow,' he exclaimed. 'If I'd realized it was this much, I might have been tempted to come back a bit quicker.' Their audience laughed.

'Thank you,' said Verity, and then Martha too, to the crowd.

'Much appreciated,' added Henry, holding up his cheque.

All Verity could see were kindly faces, smiling with approval. This was the best night of her life.

'It would be my honour,' announced Verity's grandfather, 'to stand a round of celebratory drinks.' The crowd cheered enthusiastically, and began immediately to head for the bar. It had been a long day.

The three friends stayed on the stage with Rafe, as the room emptied.

'It's engraved,' said Martha, turning the cup around. She held it up to read. '*Drink from me if you can stomach it*. How fascinating.'

'It belonged to my father,' said Rafe.

'It's a Gentry piece?' Martha squeaked. She raised it to the light. 'It's enchanting,' she said.

Verity pulled a face. It looked slightly creepy to her.

'Who's going to look after it?' asked Percy, jumping up onto the stage in one bound.

'No point putting it in our house,' said Henry. 'Too breakable.'

'Mum gave up on ornaments after Frank was born,' said Will, hopping up to join them. They were the only people left in the hall now.

'It does look fragile,' Verity agreed. She was fairly sure Mother wouldn't welcome it as a knick-knack.

'It belonged to your father?' Martha asked Rafe.

'He donated it to the sailing club.'

'Perhaps it might like to go home?' Martha suggested.

Verity perked up. 'That would be nice,' she said. 'If it's all right, Grandfather?'

'I should be honoured to look after it for you,' said Rafe. 'It will remind me of my father, and my favourite racing team.'

'Sounds good,' said Henry.

'Perhaps we could come to look at it occasionally, in its proper historic setting: just as it would have been in the Gentry heyday,' said Martha hopefully.

Rafe picked up on the hint. 'You would be most

welcome to look at it whenever you choose,' he said. 'In fact, Martha, if Gentry history interests you I could give you a proper tour of the Manor.'

Martha's face lit up. 'I could come tomorrow?' she suggested excitedly. 'After school?'

Rafe laughed. 'Tomorrow would be a pleasure,' he said.

Martha beamed and hugged Verity. 'I think this has categorically been one of the most brilliant, and only a little bit dangerous, days of my life,' she announced.

Verity fell into bed that night, exhausted. Every muscle ached: she was scraped and bruised all over. But her head was still racing. She couldn't sleep yet.

She reached under her bed and pulled out the book she always turned to when seeking comfort: a faded red volume, with a golden globe embossed on the cover. *On the Origin of Stories: A Disquisition*, by Messrs R. Hodge, Heyworth & Helerley.

Verity stroked the worn leather affectionately. Abednego, notorious Captain of the famous smuggling ship the *Storm*, had given this to her last year on Wellow's deserted beach.

Each tale in the book had been spoken by the Mistress in a *wellspring*: those places around the world – such as the wishing well – where stories could be told and become reality. But the Mistress had been greedy, and designed each so it would repeat over and over again.

*Original Stories*, they were known as. Verity always thought of them as wishes that lasted forever.

She turned to the earliest section of the book, savouring the familiar scent of the pages. She yawned. Verity liked these stories best, because they were the happiest. Later, they became darker and more violent: each telling of how the Mistress benefited at the expense of others.

Another yawn. Verity's mind drifted to the day's events. What had caused the earth to move so? A wave of tiredness swept over her. Her head fell back onto the pillow and within seconds she was asleep.

# Book Two

# *Autumn*

# Chapter Four

The next day, Monday morning, was sunny but crisp. There was a tinge in the air that announced autumn's arrival. All the evergreen trees in the park were decorated with bedewed spiders' webs that sparkled and glistened brilliantly.

Verity, Henry and Martha converged at their usual spot in the park, near the standing stone, before completing the final length of their journey to school together. It was quiet, with just the occasional bird breaking the silence.

'I can hardly believe yesterday was real,' said Martha. 'Everything is so calm.'

The path through the parkland was scorched still from the long, hot summer with splintered cracks that ran into the browning grass. Pale white sand was spilling up from them.

'That sand seems to be everywhere,' said Verity.

'This dry spell is creating serious erosion. It's what caused the rockfall, Dad says,' said Henry.

'Is there anything that can be done?' asked Martha.

Henry shrugged. 'Cliff-falls happen around this coast, that's part of life. It's just whether the subsidence starts to affect the town.' He yawned. 'Didn't sleep very well last night,' he explained as they reached Priory Bay's gates. 'Had a bad dream.'

'Probably an effect of yesterday's drama,' said Martha sympathetically. She clutched Verity's arm in excitement. 'Is your grandfather still giving us a tour of the Manor this evening?'

Verity nodded.

'Good job yesterday, well done,' said a tousle-haired boy to her, as he strode past.

Another patted Henry on the back.

'You showed the Blakes, that's for certain.'

Verity and Martha blushed, smiling awkwardly, but Henry grinned, taking it all in his stride.

As they headed to class, it seemed the entire playground was preoccupied with yesterday's events. Their progress was significantly slower than usual, thanks to the number of people who wanted to find out more, or share what they'd heard.

'The club has advised that no one sails too near those cliffs until we know what caused the rock-fall,' said one girl to Martha.

But as the three friends rounded a corner they came to an abrupt halt. Sitting underneath a cedar tree, in the centre of the forecourt, was Miranda Blake. Despite all of yesterday's events, she was still surrounded by a small group of hangers-on.

'What do they see in her?' asked Martha.

'They're just scared,' said Henry. 'Everyone knows you have to be careful with the Blakes: it's a Wellow habit.'

'They *are* frightening,' Verity said.

'They're a nasty collection of bullies and snobs,' said Henry.

Charlotte Chiverton – one of the prettiest and most popular girls at Priory Bay – could be seen currying favour. 'Gallant is very full of herself these days . . . I'm sure she was making eyes at Jeb Tempest last summer.'

'And we all know who Chiverton thinks Tempest should have liked,' muttered Henry.

Miranda silenced Charlotte's chatter and stood up. She had eyes for no one but Verity. But before she could say a word, a door swung open and Povl Usage's tall thin frame appeared on the forecourt path. He seemed lost in a world of academic ponderings.

Miranda sat down with a look of cold fury. Even she knew to wait until the teacher was gone.

Povl headed in the direction of Verity, Henry and Martha, and stopped abruptly in front of them, his reverie apparently broken.

'Miss Gallant,' he said with an anxious smile. 'Always with your friends, quite the triumvirate.'

Verity smiled politely and said nothing.

'And saviour of the day too, I understand.'

'Verity was marvellous,' said Henry in a loud voice, staring pointedly at Miranda, who delicately mimed being sick in the distance.

Povl glanced at Henry. 'Twogood by name, too

good by nature. Isn't that what they used to say? Ah, ha-ha.'

'I know what they used to say about the Usages, but most of it's unrepeatable,' muttered Henry.

The break bell sounded.

'Is that the time?' Henry said. 'What a shame, must be going.'

'Yes, of course.' Povl cleared his throat. He pulled out a pamphlet from his jacket pocket: a tourist guide to Wellow and the Gentry. 'I wondered if your grandfather might be prevailed upon to sign this?' he said to Verity. 'I should be most appreciative.'

Verity took it. 'This is an unusual one,' she said.

Povl flushed with pleasure. 'You collect them too?' he asked eagerly.

Verity smiled awkwardly. 'No, but there's an almanac in the library: I recognized it from that.'

Povl glanced down at the floor. He looked un-characteristically shy for a teacher. 'Of course: quite an unusual preoccupation of mine. I understand.'

Henry was clearly itching to get away, and even Martha looked bored, but Verity felt strangely sorry for the peculiar man. 'I believe it's a popular hobby,' she said kindly. 'And I'm sure Grandfather would be pleased to sign this for you.'

Povl beamed like a child, then took his leave, nodding in thanks.

'He looks sad,' said Verity to her friends, when he was out of hearing. Surely he realized that the pupils' sniggers and whispers as he passed through the playground were all related to him.

'Shouldn't he be bribing us in exchange for signatures and the like?' asked Henry. 'The odd lenient mark wouldn't go amiss.'

'*Henry*,' gasped Martha.

'I'm *joking*,' he replied. 'Honestly. Sometimes I wonder if my comic genius will go unrecognized my entire life.'

The rest of the day passed uneventfully. The most remarkable thing was how Martha managed to contain her excitement at the prospect of Rafe's guided tour. As soon as the end of day bell rang, she practically ran across town with Verity in tow, talking excitedly the whole way.

Rafe was now making them a pot of tea, lifting a kettle from his study fire. His handsome face was lined and brown from years of travel and his blue eyes shone. Today he wore a dark lounge suit and soft cravat. His silver-white hair had grown a little long since the summer.

Verity gazed across the room. The quiet, dusty air was warm, with a tinge of last night's wood smoke. She loved this oak-panelled refuge. Martha was looking around reverently, captivated by the wall of bookshelves to her left. She hovered anxiously near a table covered in maps and charts.

'Please feel free,' said Rafe with a smile.

Martha fell eagerly on the papers.

Rafe had given the Heartsease Cup pride of place on the sideboard. Verity picked it up. The three hideous men grimaced at her.

'It was made by a friend of my father, for storing the Bloodstone originally,' said Rafe. 'But that was lost some time ago.'

'What is the Bloodstone?' asked Martha.

'A Gentry thingamabob,' said Verity.

Rafe smiled. 'I believe the popular term amongst

those with a keen interest in Gentry history is *artefact.*'

'Like the Eye of the Storm, or the Storm Bringer,' Verity explained.

'And what did this one do?' asked Martha. She knew Verity had been in possession of the Eye for several months last year – and it had saved her life. The Storm Bringer was a man-made device commissioned by the Usage family in order to wreck ships.

'It was a blood-red stone that poisoned people. Or rather it poisoned the water it sat in,' said Rafe. 'Sent them quite mad unfortunately. Just as well it's gone.' He paused to pour some tea. 'I touched it once, as a little boy, and it made me very ill. I hold myself accountable for its loss: I had such an aversion to the thing I did not check on it regularly.'

He handed Martha a jewel-coloured cup. 'I thought we'd start with the windows designed by my father for sending signals, then take a look at the family collection of Twogood maritime engineering pieces and finish in the cellar. The tunnels, I'm afraid, are not safe to enter.'

Verity tinkered idly with the mahogany and brass telescope that was positioned by the window. There was a complex network of tunnels underneath Wellow. The oldest ones had been used for hundreds of years, then Rafe had commissioned Henry's family to create more, so the Gentry could carry out their smuggling activities without being caught by the Preventative Men. Verity would have loved to explore them, but they hadn't been maintained for years.

Rafe picked something up from his bureau, and handed it to Martha. 'I found this, and thought you might like to keep it.' It was a sprig of dried herbs pinned to a piece of paper, on which there was a verse:

'*Careful, oh lords. Once they love you no more, who will safeguard us then?*'

Martha beamed.

'My own Gentry blessing,' she said.

She and Verity always looked out for them around Wellow. They were hidden in all sorts of curious places: not just on scraps of paper, but carved into doorways, or on walls.

'It is not, technically, a Gentry blessing. Nor was it made by us,' said Rafe. 'Alice brought it back for me, many years ago, as a warning: a signal that our foolish tales were taking on a life of their own in the wider world. Which reminds me,' he added, tapping his head and beaming at Verity. 'On a happier note, I think Alice anticipated some success for you in yesterday's race. At any rate when she returned briefly in the summer she told me she had left a gift for you in her dining room. *Not to be collected until the day after the Heartsease Race*, she said. She was very particular about that.'

'You saw Alice when she returned to Wellow?' asked Verity, stunned.

Rafe nodded sadly. 'Briefly, yes. She called here before going to the *Storm*. I think she understood she might not be here for very long.'

Verity stared at her grandfather. She felt hurt. Why had Alice taken time to visit Rafe when Verity had seen her only fleetingly? And why had he never mentioned this before?

'Things were very pressured at the time,' Rafe

reminded her gently.

Verity sighed. He was right, of course.

'And it seemed best not to mention your gift. Lest the temptation to retrieve it proved too much.' He smiled mischievously at her, his eyes twinkling.

Verity grinned. 'I may have found it difficult,' she said. Her mind scampered off to thoughts of what Alice might have left behind. She wondered how long Rafe's tour would take.

'Why don't you go now?' said Martha kindly. 'You've seen all of this before, and I'll be going straight home in a bit. Mother's arranged supper with a visiting Professor.'

'Are you sure?' asked Verity.

'Of course,' said Martha.

Verity rummaged through her bag.

'Could you sign this?' she asked Rafe. 'It's for our new Chemistry teacher. He's a Usage actually: Brother Povl. He's one of those people with a keen interest, as you say, in Gentry history.'

'A Usage, eh? Can't say I've heard of him,' said Rafe, scribbling with a practised flourish.

Verity took the signed pamphlet from his hand.

'Thank you,' she beamed, desperate to get to Alice's.

'I'll see you tomorrow at school,' said Martha with a smile.

But Verity was already halfway out the door.

It didn't take long to go back across the top of the town. Verity smiled sadly when she reached Alice's house. She missed her.

Verity quietly pushed open the gate and stepped into the garden. Alice's house had always been in a state of elegant decay, but now it was more ramshackle than ever. The overgrown garden was crammed with different plants, all bearing the last few remnants of flowers and berries or seedpods.

She walked up the path. Suddenly it occurred to her that she didn't have a key. She tried the front door and, in a way, wasn't surprised to see it opened. When you thought about it, if Alice really was a Keeper, what would she fear?

Verity stood quietly in the hallway, breathing the familiar scent of Alice's home. All her old friend's belongings were still there. On the wall to her right hung a large selection of hats – a bowler, a fez, several fascinators, pill-boxes, mounds of knitted items, cloches, a tiara and a diving helmet – all balanced precariously on the over-filled hooks.

By the entrance to the drawing room stood a large Noah's ark, a mannequin and a pair of bellows. Everything was coated in a thin layer of dust. Verity walked silently through. In this room every spare inch of wall was covered in pictures; framed maps, oil paintings and prints. It all looked very much the same as it had the last time Verity was here.

Verity sat on the faded red sofa, next to a battered globe that was propped on a cushion. What had Alice left for her? She glanced across at the dining table. On it was a book.

It was a leather-bound journal: dark with age and terribly tatty. Verity opened it. Inside was a hastily scribbled note, which she read in astonishment:

*Dearest Verity,*

*Please accept this small token of congratulations. I knew I could count on you to do well – and sincerely trust you will look forward to many years more of happy sailing. Especially with two loyal crew members such as Henry and Martha – whose characters seem to me to be as staunch as their ability. The use of* Poor Honesty *over the last year has set the pattern for a friendship that will last a lifetime, I hope.*

*Your loving*
*Alice*

Verity read the note through teary eyes. How very stoic Alice sounded. Verity could tell the implication was that she did not see herself returning to Wellow. She wiped a cheek with her sleeve. There was a final line.

*PS. Use page 120 of your book.*

Verity started in shock. Then she laughed. Dear Alice: extraordinary and slightly batty to the last. What on earth did that mean? She flicked slowly through the diary. A piece of paper dropped out.

She looked at it excitedly, then quelled a pang of disappointment: just a knitting pattern. She stuffed it in her coat pocket.

There were few dates in the book: instead Alice seemed to have used it to record incidents of interest, and paste scraps of paper. On the inside cover she had written:

*'. . . everything must have a Keeper – that is the way of things – and it was the duty of these girls to harness the essential elements of the world: water, fire, earth and wind.*

The words seemed sad to Verity: *the duty of these girls.* It was an imposing task – an eternity spent commanding the elements to shelter the world from harm.

She was bursting to share her discovery and raced across town to Henry's house. It was nearly dark by the time she got there. The Twogood kitchen was deliciously warm, scented with linen airing on the range. There was always washing at Henry's house.

'Hello, dear,' said Mrs Twogood, giving her a big floury kiss on the cheek. She took Verity's hands in hers. 'Chilled to the bone,' she announced. 'You must take more care. A delicate girl like you could catch her death.'

Verity tried not to laugh.

'Better have a jam tart,' said Henry's mum decisively. Verity helped herself willingly to one from the wire rack on the table. Mrs Twogood's pastry was a treat.

Henry's mum tidied Verity's hair into a neater shape. 'So pretty,' she said fondly. 'They're in the sitting room, dear, take a glass of milk with you.'

Verity poked her head round the door to find Henry, Percy and Will toasting crumpets on the fire and arguing vehemently about butter.

'What?' demanded Henry. 'They need a lot to get them right.'

'They don't need half a pat of the stuff,' said Percy, removing the knife and dish from Henry's grasp.

Verity sat down on the floor and began removing her coat. 'Look,' she said triumphantly to Henry, who was now concentrating his efforts on jam.

'Oh good,' he said flatly, 'a book. I'm well known for my fondness of books.'

Verity sighed. 'It's Alice's diary.'

'Even better,' said Percy. 'A purloined book: a heady combination of boredom and imminent punishment.'

'Alice left it in her house for me,' said Verity impatiently. 'So that's not stealing is it?'

'Just breaking and entering,' said Henry. 'How do you know it was for you?'

Verity told them about Rafe's message and read out the letter, emphasizing the PS.

'You're not going to start carrying that red leather book around all the time again, are you?' asked Henry.

Verity stared at him.

'*Obviously* that's what Alice is talking about,' said Percy.

'You never let the flipping thing out of your sight all year,' said Will.

*Use page 120 of your book.*

Of course, the book Abednego had given her. 'Don't you think it's strange, for Alice to leave such a mysterious message?' she said to the three boys.

'Verity, old thing,' said Percy. 'You have a pronounced tendency to label events as unusual.'

'It's the first sign of an overheated imagination,' agreed Will.

'It's the diary of a *Keeper*,' said Verity. 'You can't tell me that's not an astonishing thing.' Henry grabbed the diary from her and read out the page in front of him.

'Flour, meat paste, butter, bicarbonate of soda, ham, eggs . . . that is extraordinary,' he said smugly. 'This could be something of a bestseller.'

Verity huffed, snatching the diary back.

'You know what Alice is like,' she said. 'You've just deliberately chosen to read out a shopping list instead of something more interesting.'

Will pulled out a familiar rectangular wooden box inlaid with different coloured squares. 'It's thrilling,' he agreed innocently. 'Why don't you let us beat you at backgammon and you can get on with reading it.'

Verity raised her eyebrows. 'You haven't won in two weeks,' she said. 'There's no way I'm ruining my record now.'

By the time Verity left, Henry was famished. He wandered into the kitchen. Nothing. His mum was in her habitual position at the ironing board, a gargantuan pile of washing by her side. His dad was at the table, intently scrutinizing a newspaper.

Mrs Twogood smiled affectionately at the sight of her youngest son. 'Hello cherub.'

Henry let the term of endearment pass. He could hear Percy and Will arguing in the sitting room. Mrs Twogood inspected a pair of trousers: still gritty. She shook them at the back door. 'Sand everywhere at the minute, ruining my iron.'

The grains of pale white sand fell to join with others on the ground.

Percy and Will appeared, on the prowl.

'Isn't dinner ready yet?' Percy asked, pulling a pathetic face in a bid to raise some sympathy. 'I am literally *starving*.'

'If I don't eat soon I think my stomach may sub-divide and eat itself,' Will said.

'Henry's managing perfectly well,' their mother pointed out.

'Lovesick,' said Percy. 'Puts you off your food apparently.'

'How many times?' Henry snapped. 'Verity is just a friend.'

'Shortness of temper is another symptom,' said Will sagely.

Henry tried to punch his older brother, who instantly put him in a headlock, while Percy prodded and poked his face.

'You three stop that right now, or I'll get your father on you,' said Mrs Twogood.

Mr Twogood's paper moved not one inch.

'Mum, whatever you're cooking, it smells too good. This is torture,' said Percy as he continued to torment his youngest brother.

'Ngargh,' shouted Henry.

'Daniel,' said Mrs Twogood.

'*Off*,' came a voice from behind the paper.

Percy and Will let go of their brother. '*Henry and Verity sitting in a tree. K.I.S.S.I.N.G.*' they sang in falsetto voices, dancing out of the kitchen together. Henry followed them, determined to put across his own point of view.

Mr Twogood put down his newspaper at last. 'Not sure why he had to pick a Gallant to court.'

Mrs Twogood flicked some ironing water at him affectionately. 'She's a nice girl.'

'Perhaps. But she's from a family that's trouble.'

Upstairs in her room that evening, Verity pulled out her red leather-bound book and flicked eagerly to page 120. It was in the reference section.

*Now the Earth Witch fell in love with a mortal. He knew how to touch her heart and they loved each other dearly. So strong were their feelings, they decided to marry.*

*'I will give my powers back,' she declared, 'and*

*stay with you in this world until I die.'*

*But the Lord of the Sky did not choose to grant such a wish. 'You must spend a year apart from each other,' he said, 'then return to this spot. And if your feelings are the same I will consider your request.'*

*So the lovers separated. The Earth Witch took a lock of her own golden hair, and wove it into a necklace that shone like the sun. Then she gave it to her sweetheart. 'Only my hair can make a charm of this kind,' she said. 'It will keep you safe, and for as long as you wear it, I shall know you love me.'*

*After the year had passed, the Lord of the Sky still would not give his consent. 'Twelve months is no amount of time for a Keeper,' he said. 'Come again next year and I will reconsider.'*

*The Earth Witch wept bitter tears for she had missed her sweetheart sorely: his absence was like a knife in her soul. Only her faithful servant kept her company. But he of the Sky would not be moved, and she could not disobey him.*

*The following year arrived and the Lord of the*

*Sky was still not of a mind to consent. Nor the year after, nor for many following it.*

*'A hundred years have passed,' the Earth Witch said. 'Must I wait a hundred more?'*

*Finally he of the Sky saw her love for this man would not die. 'Wait twelve months,' he replied, 'and I will grant your wish.' The Earth Witch and her lover were overjoyed. Just four more seasons and they would have their hearts' desire.*

The red book was about the Mistress, but Verity knew why this story was here. She flicked through the pages of the main book until she found the tale it related to. She had read it many times.

*The Witch of the Wind had become envious of the love between the Earth Witch and her sweetheart. She could not let it be, and set her mind to possessing him. Nothing would satisfy her but he must be hers.*

*The Earth Witch was beautiful in a tender way, she was enchanting, but none of the Keepers could match the wiles of the Wind Witch. She pursued* her sister's lover, using every trick and device of attraction at her disposal, until eventually he could not resist her.

At the close of the year the Earth Witch returned to the appointed spot to meet with the Lord of the Sky. But her sweetheart was not there.

In his place stood her sister, and in her hand was the Earth Witch's necklace. 'He does not love you,' she crowed.

The Earth Witch was so unhappy she wept tears of blood. But she knew her sister told the truth; it was her own hair.

'Wail all you like,' the Wind Witch laughed. 'He has no need for you.'

At that there was no consoling the Earth Witch and she cried until she was completely white.

How cruel and vindictive the Mistress had been: so pitiless, and yet so enchanting. Verity's eyes fluttered shut, the book still open in front of her.

But Verity didn't sleep well. Her dreams were a cluttered mess of sorrow and pain. She flew around the world, the land a giant curving ball below. In every place was more unhappiness; children stolen from parents, lovers tempted away, cruel husbands, malicious wives, greedy merchants . . .

And all the while, in the background, was a peculiar grating noise. It scoured her mind. It was the hissing, scratching sound of woe: a dogged, unflinching misery.

She opened her eyes. She could tell from the light that it was the early hours of the morning. And the scratching hiss wasn't in her dreams. She could hear it, coming from her old bedroom: the one in the eaves of the roof, which the Mistress had commandeered last year.

Verity slipped out of bed and crept, bare-footed, up the top flight of stairs, holding on to the mahogany banister. A full moon shone through dappled clouds. Its silvery, unearthly light was not enough to scare away the shadows.

She hated walking in the dark. Unspoken fears danced in her stomach. The scratching persisted.

*There's no one here but you.*

Verity paused at the door to her old attic hide-away. She had loved this room when she was

97

younger: so peaceful and quiet, with views straight to the sea. But it would always be tainted by the memory of the Mistress now.

And still the hissing: it was coming from outside.

No, Verity thought to herself. It was similar to the sound in her dreams, but it wasn't the same.

She walked softly into the room. As she came within arms' reach of the window, she saw that the glass was covered with a fine mist of pale, white sand. Small piles of the stuff had collected on the sill outside.

Verity stared wordlessly. The hairs on her arms prickled.

An image flashed through her mind of Povl dusting pale white sand from her blazer lapel. She remembered the pale white sand in the park, in crescents outside the library, between her toes as she stood in the water near the slipway . . .

The story Alice had instructed her to read was about the Earth Witch. What was sand, if not earth?

A gust of wind blew a clump of sand against the glass.

*Thud*.

Verity jumped, and gave a little shriek. She stared out to the sea that surrounded her hometown, her heart thumping. It was pale under the light of the moon.

This was about the Earth Witch. Alice had left her a message about the Earth Witch.

# Chapter Five

Verity's dreams were troubled for the rest of the night. In the morning her head ached, but she dressed quickly and raced through breakfast. Poppy was entertaining the family with a dramatic re-enactment of a chemistry experiment that had gone woefully wrong in Brother Povl's class: darting from one side of the table to the other as she brought to life the parts of teacher and pupils. Mother and Father were trying not to laugh.

'How he manages to keep any hair at all I shall never know,' Poppy said. 'The whole class was in stitches.'

Verity surreptitiously picked up a piece of toast to eat on her way to school, then said goodbye, giving Olivia an affectionate kiss. Her baby sister patted her cheek with a jam-covered hand.

Once out of doors, Verity scurried through the streets. Above her the sun was shining but the sky was a pale translucent grey. The wind buffeted her ears. Finally she reached Priory Bay. She fidgeted anxiously outside the school gates, desperate to share her thoughts.

As soon as the three friends had found a quiet corner of the playground, Henry and Martha listened while Verity told them her suspicions about the pale white sand and the Earth Witch.

Henry stared at her throughout with a look of disquiet, but Martha was more open.

'This white sand *is* new,' she said. 'I don't remember seeing it at all last year, and now I come to think of it, it really does get everywhere. Mother found some in her pen the other day: it clogged up the nib and she was livid.'

'Sand drifts from other places, on the seabed. It can even be blown from country to country by desert winds,' said Henry, taking a bite of a pear.

But Martha wasn't willing to give up so easily.

'Why would Alice leave Verity a letter, telling her to read a story about the Earth Witch?'

'You didn't meet Alice. She was an odd lady.'

'You never want to believe anything like this,' said Verity. '*I* think the story is a warning. And the sand *is* unusual. The beaches near Wellow have never been white. And it's everywhere; in the park, on the streets, outside the library.' She brushed Henry's blazer pointedly. '*Everywhere.*'

'The other two Keepers disappeared a long time ago, didn't they?' said Martha.

Verity nodded. 'That's in the red book.' She put her bag down on the floor to rummage, then flicked expertly to the right page:

. . . *until one day the eldest daughter had to leave for a while. And when she came back only the youngest remained. Where her two sisters were she wouldn't say. Not telling. The youngest she just smiled. Then finally she burst out laughing. And that's when the oldest sister knew she was lost.*

'So the eldest sister was Alice?' said Henry.

'And the youngest the Mistress,' said Martha, 'but no one knows what she did to the two middle sisters.'

'It would be just her style to pretend she made them disappear, even if she didn't,' said Henry.

'If the Earth Witch really is coming back, I wonder what she wants?' Verity murmured.

Martha put a hand on her friend's arm. 'Perhaps just to return to the world?' she said.

Verity smiled, pleased that Martha didn't think there was anything to panic about. She pulled Alice's diary from her bag, presenting it to her friend. 'Alice left me this,' she said. 'It's her diary.'

Martha took it carefully. 'The diary of a Keeper.'

'Henry's not at all impressed,' said Verity.

'That's because it's not a bike, a car or a sausage roll,' said Martha.

'My priorities are exactly as they should be, thank you,' said Henry, wandering off to find a bin for his pear core.

Martha paused, as if something had just occurred to her. 'Henry's already seen it?' she said.

Verity hesitated. Suddenly she felt embarrassed.

Martha would have been closer to Alice's house. 'I showed him last night. You had tea with your mother,' she said awkwardly.

'Of course,' said Martha. She twisted a lock of stray hair.

Verity shrugged ruefully. 'He wasn't interested.'

Martha smiled and only looked a little bit sad. 'What's in it?'

'It's a travel diary,' said Verity. 'I always knew Alice had been to a lot of different places, but this really brings it home.' She turned the pages. 'It feels as if she went everywhere: literally every place in the world.'

'That would explain how she'd managed to hoard so much junk,' said Henry, appearing back at their side.

'I wondered if she might have been looking for her sisters,' said Verity. 'She pasted things in it like this scrap':

*And in a rare moment of despair the Captain of the Storm told me that his mistress's capacity for spite was so great, she had devoted a portion of her power to constantly keeping her sister scattered around the world, and separate, so she could not pull herself back together in one piece.*

'And this drawing . . .' Verity pulled out a sketch of four young women. The girls at either end were obviously the Mistress and Alice. The middle two shared similar features but were very different; one was coloured as if her skin were darker and had a solid, firm beauty, the other was pale – more slight – with a mischievous face and delicate features.

'An actual *picture* of the four Keepers,' whispered Martha. She held the paper as if it were gossamer.

'But also – because it's Alice – there are lots of other things scribbled in there too; shopping lists, errands, recipes . . . that sort of thing,' said Verity.

**Plum and Walnut Jam**
- 1 quantity plums
- 1 quantity oranges
- 1 lemon

- 1 quantity raisins
- 1 quantity sugar
- chopped walnuts

*Cover plum stones with 1 cup water and boil for thirty minutes, then strain liquid and put to one side. Wash fruit, remove pips and chop into medium sized pieces. Mix fruits with reserved liquid and sugar, then soak for one hour, then cook for one hour. Remove from heat and add walnuts. Pour into preserving jars while hot.*

'Sounds good,' said Henry. 'Goes well on toast I expect.'

'It's a very thoughtful gift from her,' said Martha, looking through the diary once more. 'But I think you're going to have to be careful with it. Look, the spine's coming away from the binding, oh, there's something in there: a piece of paper.' Martha's voice had become an octave higher than usual.

She passed the diary back to Verity, who held it up to the light. Martha was right. Verity took hold of the end and pulled out the hidden paper carefully, her fingers trembling. She unfolded it and read aloud:

*She of the Wind was in a mood that day to be quarrelsome. All the other sisters irritated her.*

*The Earth Witch hated her sister now for stealing her one true love. The pain of that loss never left her. Each passing day she felt as if another piece of heart had been sliced off with a jagged blade. But the Wind Witch had begun to find her piteous face irksome.*

*The Keeper of the Wind was boasting about her power and beauty: of how no one could withstand her and none compared to her. 'I can send men mad. I can destroy a ship with just a wave of my little finger,' she said.*

*At this, the Earth Witch very much wished to prove her wrong. 'I am the strongest of us four by far,' she said. 'You know that: stone is stronger than air.'*

*'I'm sure I could beat you,' the Wind Witch replied with angry eyes.*

Then their sister, the Witch of Fire, pleaded with them to make their peace.

'You were not so concerned with your sister's happiness when you helped me steal a lock of her hair,' said the Wind Witch with scorn.

'Why did you do that?' asked the Earth Witch, who was seized by a terrible suspicion.

The Fire Witch was at a loss. 'I do not know what she is talking about,' she said.

But the Wind Witch laughed. 'Of course she would say that now,' she declared.

The Earth Witch was frantic. 'What did you do?' she demanded.

The Fire Witch continued to protest her innocence, which just made the Earth Witch angry.

'You did nothing to help while I was waiting for my love,' she said.

At this, the Fire Witch lost her patience, and let her two sisters continue with their argument.

'Prove your strength and I will tell you the truth,' said the Wind Witch, enjoying herself.

So the Earth Witch changed herself entirely to

*alabaster granite, save for her heart, which stayed blood-red from loving still.*

*Then the Wind Witch seized her chance: she used her power to pick up her sister's stone body, and dashed it down on the earth from a great height, so it broke into many millions of pieces.*

*The Fire Witch was greatly upset. 'What will the Lord of the Sky say when he hears of this?' she asked.*

*'You shall not tell anyone,' the Wind Witch replied.*


'The Mistress broke her sister into a million pieces,' said Verity softly.

'*That's* how she disappeared,' said Martha. 'This is why Alice left the diary for you.'

'*Here comes your friend,*' whispered Henry. Verity glanced around, then quickly stuffed both books and the paper into her bag.

'Miss Gallant,' Brother Povl shouted cheerily as he approached. 'I brought in some journals that might interest your grandfather.'

'Fantastic. Is he going to hound us everywhere we go?' muttered Henry.

'Shh,' hissed Verity. She rummaged in her pocket. 'Grandfather signed your pamphlet,' she said to the teacher. Povl stopped in his tracks. His pale grey eyes glistened.

'That is most kind,' he said quietly. 'It is not often I receive such charity from others.' Verity felt a pang of sympathy for this funny man.

'We'd love to stop and talk,' said Henry firmly. 'But I'd hate to be late for Algebra. Martha doesn't concentrate properly if we don't get a seat at the front.'

Verity glared at Henry.

'We should get on,' Martha agreed. Verity gave up. She took the books from Povl.

'I'm sure Grandfather will be fascinated,' she said to the teacher.

They managed to avoid Brother Povl for the rest of the day. Verity caught a glimpse of him at lunch time in the refectory, straining jerkily over the crowd. But he didn't stand a chance of wading his way through the queues of jostling pupils before Henry and Martha had cajoled her into disappearing. She felt guilty, but he was a grown-up after all. And her mind was brimming.

'I suppose it's the library then?' said Henry as they strode briskly down the hill after school. The weather was bitter. They clutched their coats at the front, heads bowed against the wind.

Verity glanced up. She stopped. Usually the ocean around Wellow was a clear emerald, but today it looked as pale as it had done last night. 'The sea is white,' she said.

'Perhaps the seabed has been churned up?' said Martha.

Verity shook her head. 'I think it's the white sand: the ocean is full of it.' She glanced down at the path. Little crescents of the familiar pale dust lay scattered around, skittering in the wind. From this angle they looked like tears.

'Let's find Miss Cameron and see what she thinks,' said Martha, pushing open the red double doors.

But the librarian was not in her habitual position at the entrance.

The children scouted around the main hall, then the reading room: their former hideaway from the world. Verity looked at the threadbare chairs, the faded rug that covered the heavy wooden parquet near the fireplace. She smiled. She always felt as if nothing bad could happen in this room.

She climbed onto the windowsill and looked out to the headland. White sea. She slid back to the floor, brushing the dark wooden panelling.

*Click.*

'What was that?' asked Henry.

'Nothing,' said Verity uncertainly.

Henry gave her a withering stare. 'Things do not go 'click' for no reason,' he said. He stared intently at the panelling, running his hands along the wood, then pressing and listening carefully.

Verity turned to watch him.

He had pulled back the heavy floor-length curtain and was staring at a panel. 'Virtually undetectable,' he said. 'Didn't even know about this one.' He fished in a pocket for a penknife. From it, he extracted a tiny metal spike with a notch at one end.

'You're not going to scratch the wood are you?'

said Martha. But to her astonishment the metal slid right in.

Henry grinned then jiggled the spike. There it was again: the same click. This time a section of the wall swung forward a few portions of an inch. Martha's mouth fell open.

'My family made a lot of secret doors, to conceal entrances to the tunnel network,' Henry said triumphantly. 'This one was probably Uncle Mick. He was the expert. Jim and Pete relied on mirrors.'

'What do you mean?' asked Martha.

'You mirror a whole wall and it disguises the depth of the room: you can't tell there's a hidden space,' said Henry. 'I think people did the same thing with jewellery. *These* kind, on the other hand, are more difficult to make, and find. I think it must have been on the latch. When Verity leaned on it, she closed the movement. Hence the noise.'

'Henry,' said Verity graciously. 'You are brilliant.'

'I know,' he replied with a grin.

Verity put her head through the door. A stone staircase spiralled downwards. She stared at it in astonishment. Her heart raced. Over the years she must have read hundreds of stories featuring secret passages, and now they'd actually found one.

'Didn't your grandfather commission this library?' asked Henry, extracting a torch from his pocket.

Verity nodded. She peered down into the dark.

'So what are we waiting for?' asked Henry, jumping breezily down the first few steps. 'You can't tell me you're not itching to have a look.'

The two girls followed him, with a hand on the wall for support. The steps were worn and smooth, the turn of the circle tight and steep.

'There's a light on,' said Henry in an excited whisper. At the bottom of the stairs was a curtain. He pulled it back slowly. Verity looked over his shoulder into an underground room. Every wall was covered in shelves of books. Most of the space was filled with oak plan chests, each piled with documents.

At a mahogany desk with drop handles sat Miss Cameron, her back to them. She had a book in front of her. A few seconds passed before she turned around. 'Good afternoon,' she murmured.

Verity cringed with embarrassment. What must Miss Cameron think, to find them prying and poking around?

'We have to talk to you about the Earth Witch,' Martha blurted. Unable to stop herself, she pushed past Verity and Henry into the room. 'Alice left a diary for Verity and we think it's a message of some kind.'

The librarian looked startled.

The floodgates burst. Verity and Henry headed eagerly for the desk and joined in: each of the three friends determined to get their say.

'It's just sand, after all, desert winds are well known to blow it around the world,' said Henry.

'Really is so fascinating, and it has a picture in it,' Martha continued.

'I knew it when I saw the white sand last night,' said Verity. 'It's in the sea and I'm sure it's actually moving . . .'

Miss Cameron stood up. 'I agree the sand does appear to have motion,' she said loudly. The children stopped. For a moment there was utter silence. 'But its purpose is not clear.'

'Does sand need a purpose?' asked Henry glibly.

'Everything has meaning. Even you, Henry Twogood,' said Miss Cameron. Henry flushed.

Verity looked around her. There were hundreds of books, perhaps even more. 'Why are these books kept here, and not in the main library?' she asked.

Miss Cameron looked at her as if the answer should be obvious. 'Every story in them was created in a wellspring,' she said. 'Each one of them became true after the words had been spoken.'

Martha frowned. 'But *Verity*'s book is a collection of all the Original Stories. There are a *lot* more here.'

Miss Cameron stared at the children and sat back down at her desk. Verity was struck by an overwhelming sense that there was a great deal the librarian knew about their world that she chose not to share.

'There are many more Original Stories – that is to say, stories which become true over and over again – than those created by the Mistress,' Miss Cameron said. 'The authors of Verity's book were captivated by the Keeper of the Wind in particular;

they noticed the ones *she* had told. And they were the first to coin the phrase 'Original Story', but in essence there are many others. As you know, any story told in a wellspring is a wish, of kinds. But an Original Story becomes a pattern for the world. So they are kept here for safety. It would be' – here the librarian hesitated – '*undesirable* for anything to happen to them.'

'Some of the Original Stories are terrible,' said Verity. 'It was an Original Story that stole the crew of the *Storm*: they were all drawn to the ship as boys.'

'Not all Original Stories are bad. For each story of lost children there is one of young orphans who travel to far-off cities and make their fortunes. But they are woven together. Unpick one and the whole skein may unravel.' The librarian dusted down her twill skirt and looked at Verity. 'Alice left you her diary?'

Verity put her bag down on the threadbare rug that covered the stone floor, pulled out the book and handed it over.

The librarian read the note with a smile. 'How

very like Alice: she had a lot of faith in you, and quite right too.'

Verity glanced down at the floor, embarrassed. Finally she remembered the most important part of their discovery.

'How stupid of us.' She took out the hidden piece of paper and showed it to Miss Cameron. 'She left it so we would find it, I think.'

The librarian held the paper silently.

'I suppose you must have known this already,' said Verity.

Miss Cameron shook her head. 'On the contrary, I have never seen that before,' she said at last. She sat down, lost in thought.

'I love the wording of the Keeper stories,' Martha sighed. 'It's so romantic.'

'Bit flowery,' Henry said. 'Alabaster and granite are actually two completely different types of stone.'

Verity glanced at the floor. The mysterious white sand had even managed to worm its way in here: it covered the worn flagstones in a thin mist. She stared at it. Her stomach turned. '*Not stone,*' she said urgently. 'Whoever wrote the story meant the colour, alabaster as in *white*. The Earth Witch turned to pure *white* granite, and then the Mistress threw her to the ground. Oh, and it's everywhere.' She shivered, trying to brush it from her. She felt a bit sick.

Martha looked puzzled.

'That's disgusting,' said Henry, realizing what Verity was getting at. He stood up and brushed his clothes, trying not to look too anxious.

Miss Cameron caught her breath.

'A million pieces of granite would look like sand,' Verity explained to Martha. 'This sand isn't just something to do with the Earth Witch, it *is* her: it's her body.'

'*Eurgh*.' Martha frantically tried to brush the pale white dust from her blazer. 'Oh, *eurgh*.' She looked distinctly panicky.

Verity shuddered involuntarily.

'Hey,' said Henry kindly. 'Most sand is ground up shells or the like. Try not to think about it.'

Martha smiled appreciatively, but Verity noticed her toes were still bunched up in her shoes.

'I wonder how she can move, if she's been broken into a million pieces?' said Henry.

'The Keepers were brought to life by a story,' said Martha, obviously talking to take her mind off the sand. 'Legend has it they can't be killed. That's why the Mistress was such a threat. So even though the Earth Witch has been ground into sand, she isn't actually dead.'

'Do you think Verity's right?' asked Henry.

The librarian folded her hands. 'I'm afraid I do,' she said.

'And do you think this is good, or bad?' he asked, characteristically getting to the point.

'I don't know,' Miss Cameron said. 'Alice was a formidable force for good but Aure was not.'

Verity swallowed. Aure was the Mistress of the Storm's real name, but very few people had the confidence to use it.

'We shouldn't assume the Earth Witch is like the Mistress,' said Martha. 'That wouldn't be very fair.'

'You can't tar the whole family with her brush,' Henry agreed.

Miss Cameron stood up from her chair and pulled a book from a shelf above her desk. 'There is very little written about the Earth Witch, but all four sisters were known to be quite different.' She opened the book and showed them a passage at the front:

*She of the Water was a hard-working, practical soul, and the most responsible of the four. She of the Earth had a sympathetic heart: she felt the pain of others as if it were her own. She of the Fire had a mischievous spirit and loved to match-make. And she of the Wind could charm the sun from the sky if she chose, or be as cruel as the sea if she did not.*

'A *sympathetic heart* sounds promising,' said Martha.

Miss Cameron said nothing.

'So what do we do now? We don't know what this means; how do we find out what the Earth Witch wants?' Verity asked, her head crowding with worries.

The librarian stood up and walked towards the

stairs. She smiled at the three children in a bid to lift their spirits. 'We will have to wait,' she said. 'At this precise moment in time, the best thing I can do is make tea and toast for us all.'

'No sense fretting on an empty stomach,' said Henry with approval.

# Chapter Six

Slowly autumn took hold of Wellow and altered it to her palette. From a distance, the town was a tapestry of fading greens, bright yellows, rich browns, dotted with the occasional vibrant red. Up close, the air smelled rich and the ground was a blanket of rustling leaves.

Verity's dreams continued to be troubled. She woke regularly in a state of panic, her head aching and tears running down her cheeks, her breath tight. She awoke convinced that Henry was ignoring her and Martha was nowhere to be found. She dreamed her baby sister Olivia had not survived last year and that the Mistress was still in Wellow, making Verity's life one of daily fear and dread. And in the background, always, was the curious grating sound she'd heard since the first nightmare.

She and her friends set to work immediately trying to discover more about the Earth Witch, but what little there was they already knew.

'She sounded kind enough until the Mistress stole her sweetheart,' said Martha as they walked to Priory Bay one morning.

'At least the Earth Witch is made of stone,' said Henry. 'It'd be pretty gruesome if she were flesh and blood.'

Verity giggled.

'*Henry*,' said Martha, brushing her skirt unconsciously. 'Her powers must be relatively weak. She's just sand after all.'

They arrived at the school gates. There were a few precious minutes to spare before the bell, and all the pupils were making the most of them.

Henry yawned. 'Still not sleeping well,' he said. 'Can't understand it now I've got my own room. I must have got so used to my brothers' snores and grunts I can't rest without them.'

Verity paused. 'Do you have bad dreams?' she

asked. 'With lots of terrible things happening?'

'S'right,' Henry said.

'That's odd,' said Martha. 'I haven't been sleeping well recently either.'

Verity shrieked. Her body jerked awkwardly, as the ground beneath her feet gave way and she dropped a foot or so. Not far, but enough to scare.

In horror, she realized the path had split down its middle. For several yards, one half was lower than the other, like a step.

Even in the middle of her panic, there was a small part of Verity that noticed how odd it was to catch a glimpse of their world's underside. Delicate fingers of dark space crazed the formerly solid surface.

She heard a peal of excited screams and shouts, as news of the hole, and Verity's fall, relayed across the playground.

Martha and Henry sprang to her aid, surrounded by interested onlookers, many offering advice.

*'Are you all right?'*

But her friends' concerns were drowned out by a scornful laugh.

*Miranda Blake.*

Verity's stick-thin enemy was standing on a bench, pointing delightedly. A gleeful smile played on her lips. Some of the children began to giggle.

'Perhaps at last you'll moderate your diet,' Blake crowed. Her audience laughed.

Verity blushed.

Henry swore at them.

Miranda turned up her lips with a knowing look. 'Gallant's little hero,' she sneered with derision. The crowd chortled.

Verity scowled. 'Lucky you're not stuck in here. You might snap in two.' She pulled herself out. Her ankle had twisted painfully.

Martha gave her a hand. Henry offered his too, but Verity turned it down with slightly less grace than was necessary, while he in turn tried not to look hurt.

Several children crept forward to inspect the crack in the earth, while girls like Charlotte Chiverton made great play of being too scared to get close.

The singular silhouette of Povl Usage loomed

into view. 'What has happened here?' he asked in dismay, staring gormlessly at the hole in the ground. 'This terrible dry summer has caused no end of erosion. Miss Gallant, are you injured?'

Verity's heart sank. She nodded imperceptibly. She knew the teacher meant well, but this just gave Blake more ammunition.

Sure enough, Miranda muttered something behind one gracefully cupped hand. A few of the nastier pupils sniggered.

This had gone far enough, Verity decided. 'It's extremely kind of you,' she said, smiling politely at the teacher. 'But I'm fine.'

Over the coming weeks, Wellow's surface began to crack like an egg in a serpent's jaw. No street or path escaped. It was as if the town had only been able to resist the Earth Witch's insistent pressure for so long. Walkways and paths crumbled like soft flour. The town seemed literally to be slipping away under their feet. It was the long hot summer, the council declared: too many weeks of high sun and no rain.

Before long almost every street had some form of repair work ongoing. And everyone was pre-occupied with either helping, attending meetings about repairs, or cleaning up the mess and dirt caused by the disruption.

At Priory Bay, there was an almost daily programme of repair works, with sections of playground cordoned off or declared unsafe.

'Looks like the Earth Witch has more in common with the Mistress than Alice,' said Henry, as he and Martha picked their way through a row of potholes outside the library. Verity was meeting them there.

Martha nodded glumly. 'Presumably that's why Alice warned Verity.' She huffed with frustration as she tried to jump across a particularly large gap.

'Of course, it doesn't help that Verity's grand-father chose to riddle most of Wellow with a network of underground tunnels, in a bid for wealth and fame,' said Henry.

'Tunnels your family helped engineer,' Martha replied. She frowned. 'I think the general air of bad temper is the biggest problem, to be honest.'

Henry nodded glumly. 'Mum hit the roof last night, just because I left a little bit of dirt on the kitchen floor after she'd mopped. You'd have thought she was single-handedly holding back the Sahara desert, not keeping one house clean.'

'I don't think anyone's getting enough sleep,' said Martha. 'I've heard Father going downstairs to fetch a glass of milk every night this week.'

They had navigated their way to the library porch at last. Martha looked at the heaped swirls of white sand on the ground. 'There always seems to be more sand here,' she said.

They pushed through the red double doors. As usual, once inside, the world beyond seemed a very distant place.

Verity turned around to greet them. She was perched on a stool in the reference section, wearing her favourite cream turtleneck jumper and a black velvet skirt that was getting a bit short. 'I'm checking there's nothing more on the Earth Witch,' she said. 'I can't believe how little we've got.'

'I think the Mistress was easier because she

fascinated people. She was interesting to write about,' said Martha.

*Tick.*

'Because she stole, murdered and tortured people,' Henry said disapprovingly.

'Well, yes, but that makes for a better read, doesn't it?'

Verity climbed down from her stool and showed them a book of fairy tales she'd found. 'There's a picture here,' she said. 'Doesn't tell us anything, but it's pretty.'

*Tick, tick.*

It was a pen and ink drawing of the Earth Witch, completely white. The only colour came from her heart, still beating in her chest: a vivid blood red. Her beautiful face looked crushed by grief as though she had been crying for days.

'Bit grisly,' said Henry.

*Tick, tick, tick.*

Verity glanced back up at the shelves. 'I wonder if there are mice,' she said. 'I keep hearing odd little noises: clicks and creaks.'

'Mice don't creak,' said Henry.

'Very funny.'

*Tick, tick, tick, tick.*

'There it is again. Did you hear that?'

Henry looked up. The dark brown shelves – with just a little flourish of golden scroll at the top – were familiar to them all. Each was crammed with a range of faded books in a muted rainbow of shades. They looked as solid as mountains, as immovable as marble.

Henry grabbed Verity's sleeve and jerked her towards him. They stumbled. Verity raised an arm. The towering bookcase toppled forward at terrifying speed. The shelves fell with a resounding crash. The thud of books hitting the wooden tiles continued for what felt like minutes.

'*Martha.*'

Verity looked across to her friend. She lay on the floor, blood trickling down her face. The shelves had caught her head, but mercifully not pinned her underneath them.

Verity felt horribly guilty. Henry had saved her and Martha had been hurt as a consequence. She rushed over. 'Can you move?'

'No broken bones, but I'm going to be black and blue tomorrow,' said Martha, trying to smile bravely and pushing herself up.

Miss Cameron burst through the secret door. 'What is going . . .' She stopped as she took in the scene before her.

Henry was shaking. 'You have got to be more careful,' he shouted at Verity. 'What if we hadn't been here? You'd be under those shelves by now.'

Verity's face filled with confusion. 'I'm fine,' she said. 'It's Martha who's hurt.'

Martha bit her lip. She winced. Her head throbbed.

Miss Cameron helped her up and guided her to a chair. 'I will fetch my first aid kit.' Verity held Martha's hand, glaring at Henry, until the librarian returned. She unpacked a neat box of bandages and medical equipment with comforting efficiency.

Henry examined the cracks in the wall to hide his embarrassment. 'It was subsidence that destabilized the shelves,' he announced. 'Same as the problems in the rest of the town.'

'The Earth Witch seems determined to cause

as much physical disruption as possible,' said Martha while Miss Cameron cleaned her cut.

'Not too bad,' the librarian murmured. 'Do you feel dizzy?'

'I don't think I'm concussed,' said Martha gratefully.

'We will have to keep an eye on you for the rest of the day.'

Verity breathed out. She gave her friend a hug. Martha's pretty green cardigan smelled of lavender. Verity always forgot how slight Martha was, until moments like this. They smiled at each other.

Martha looked around the room. 'The library is the only *building* that's been affected so far,' she said. 'In the rest of Wellow it's just the streets.'

'Perhaps the Earth Witch doesn't like books,' said Henry.

'How do we stop this from happening again?' Verity asked.

'The wall needs underpinning, I think, at the foundation,' said Henry.

Miss Cameron glanced up. 'At the foot of the wall?' she said.

'That's right,' Henry replied.

Miss Cameron pressed a hand to her temple. It was an uncharacteristic gesture. She looked pained.

The children stared at her, worried.

'The vaulted room sits below this wall,' she said. 'It is not a place I would care to reveal to many in Wellow.'

'Someone must have built it originally. There have obviously been repairs,' Henry pointed out.

Miss Cameron paused. 'The Twogood family were responsible for much of the work here,' she said. 'But I do not feel able to ask your father. His views on the Gentry are very clear, and the library was built with their money. I will have to send for assistance.'

What assistance? Verity wondered who Miss Cameron could be talking about. But she knew there was no point asking.

'Percy and Will could help,' said Henry, after a moment's thought. 'We could make a temporary fix.'

'Would they do that?' asked Martha.

'Of course,' said Henry.

'What if your dad found out? And what will you tell them?' Martha persisted.

'That the library's subsiding,' said Henry, looking at her as if she were stupid.

Miss Cameron began to pick up books from the floor.

'It's fine,' said Henry breezily. Sometimes you had to show more confidence than you felt. 'The Earth Witch wants to rip Wellow apart – but my family built it in the first place, so none of us are going to let her.'

Henry's brothers were happy to lend a hand, if only because it gave them a splendid new project that was tinged with an element of the forbidden. Percy and Will were both cock-a-hoop when they first saw the vaulted room.

The underground space was certainly impressive. If anything it was more solidly built than the library above. There were carved stone pillars that looked very old, almost weather-beaten.

'Just like issue two hundred and seventy-two of *The Fearsome Avenger*,' said Percy approvingly.

'I can quite see why you didn't want to let just any Tom, Dick or Harry down here,' added Will.

'It's all right,' said Henry to Miss Cameron. The librarian had said nothing, but there was an unmistakable air of concern. 'They won't say a word.'

The boys soon identified the problem area, and suggested a solution.

'Safest thing we can do is give additional support to the building,' said Will. 'Then when Miss Cameron's friends arrive they can take things from there.'

Over the next few days they began to erect a number of different stout timbers: each propped from below by several opposing wedges. The mess was overwhelming. The entire library was covered in old sheets. Dirt and dust crept into every nook and cranny. Verity managed to help a little. Martha was constantly on hand with cups of tea and biscuits. The cut on her head was much better and had begun to scab over.

'Where did you get all that wood from?' Verity asked the boys.

'What the eye doesn't see the heart can't worry

about,' said Percy with a conspiratorial wink.

'Just wish we had more of these,' said Will sadly. 'But if we take too many, Dad will know something's up for sure.'

Martha inspected the device Will had been holding. It was a telescopic prop.

Percy sighed noisily, obviously tired. 'Wouldn't be so bad if I could get a decent night's sleep,' he grumbled. 'It's the noise that really gets my goat. I've sworn off cheese and everything.'

'You too?' asked Verity. 'I haven't slept well for weeks.'

'*Terrible* nightmares,' announced Will dramatically. 'As if everything in the world was ending badly.'

Verity frowned. Why did that feel important?

'I think everyone's suffering a bit,' said Martha conversationally. 'It must be the worry.'

'But you hear a noise too?' said Verity.

'Yeah,' said Percy, 'a sort of hissing sound. Very odd, might have to get my ears checked out.'

'This is amazing,' said Martha, pointing in astonishment.

'Grandad thought of the idea,' said Will proudly. 'Fred built that one. Slightly better model: it's got a rotating head.'

'We all improve each other's work,' said Percy.

'Your family could be rich if you sold the patents to your ideas,' said Martha, staring incredulously at them. She had seen the Twogoods' house.

'Money brings more problems than it solves,' said Will, as if he had heard that phrase many times before.

'But—'

'Dad says when we're grown-up we can do what we like,' Henry interrupted. 'But in his house he prefers things simple.'

That night in her dreams, Verity soared above the earth once more: the world spinning as she flew. Her body twitched and turned as she fretted in her sleep. She dreamed of orphans who travelled to the big city, only to find, not fame and fortune, but abuse and despair. She watched old women kill and eat the children who were lost in the forest. She saw destined lovers spending their whole lives apart.

'*As if everything in the world was ending badly,*' said Will's voice in her head.

The moon was in the uppermost reaches of the sky when she sat up in bed. Her heart thudded in her chest. It was the noise: an anguished grating. It ached inside her.

She remembered Henry in the library, when the shelves had fallen, '. . . *perhaps the Earth Witch doesn't like books.*'

She got up. Dressing quickly, she crept downstairs and left the house. Silvery, backlit clouds scurried across the night sky. There were no stars to be seen.

It didn't take long to reach her chosen destination: the library. She knocked hesitantly. By her feet the sand waited, still and silent. It shone like pearl in the moonlight. She picked some up and rubbed it between thumb and forefinger: the same unmistakable rasp. She shuddered.

A key turned in the lock. Miss Cameron opened the door in a plaid dressing gown. She had obviously been asleep in her quarters. Her hair was protected in a plain silk scarf.

'Is something the matter?'

Verity opened her mouth, and realized she had no words to explain her presence.

Miss Cameron smiled at her: a typically unusual reaction to the situation. And Verity realized she had nothing to worry about. Regardless of whether the theory was right, her friend would understand.

'I'm worried . . . that I know what the Earth Witch is trying to do,' she said. 'I'm sure I'm wrong,' she added hurriedly. 'I *hope* I'm wrong: it seems so unbelievable but . . .'

She paused, and took a deep breath.

'Might I look at the books in the vaulted room with you?'

'Of course.' Miss Cameron turned, and Verity followed her through the reading room, past the portraits of former Wellow residents, down the stairs . . . Miss Cameron's slippers flapped softly on the stone steps that led to the vaulted space below.

In the room itself they stood opposite each other. There was just one light in the corner.

Their faces were both shrouded with shadow.

Verity felt like a lunatic. *They were just dreams.*

But something inside her wouldn't stop.

'You told us that some of the Original Stories end happily, and some don't?' she said.

'That is correct,' said Miss Cameron.

'Are they categorized according to outcome?'

'They are not.'

'Could we look at the ones that end happily, just those ones?' Verity asked.

Miss Cameron's pupils darkened. Verity knew that the librarian had realized what her theory might be. Together they gathered a number of different volumes. Miss Cameron's breath sounded faster and shallower than usual.

They laid the books open at particular sections – Miss Cameron's knowledge of the stories was such that she knew precisely where to look in each, of course – until all were displayed. The ageing pages were crisp and yellow, with the warm scent of paper and leather.

The underground room was silent, but Verity

could just make out the very lowest of hisses. She looked closely and gasped.

On each story in front of them, a mist of pale white sand was scattered. And, incredibly, it seemed to be moving in tiny, almost imperceptible, whorls. The sand – the Earth Witch – looked as if it was trying to rub out the words on the page.

For once Miss Cameron's emotions showed clearly on her face. She tried to brush the sand off the page: hastily, with fear and anger. But the sand bounced away, as if she and it were magnets, repelling each other.

Verity's breath caught in her throat. 'The town crumbling is just a consequence, I think,' she said. Her voice sounded alien and odd, even to her. 'The Earth Witch's real desire is to erase every tale that ends happily.'

The librarian breathed in. 'How could I have failed to notice?' she muttered, as she flicked through page after page of handwritten text, her fingers trembling. 'The ink is so faded. I knew there was more to the sand's presence.'

Verity felt a steady whirlpool of panic rising

within her. She'd never seen Miss Cameron react like this.

'If these stories are rubbed out, what will happen?' she asked urgently. Perhaps if she kept talking things would go back to normal. Whatever that was.

The librarian sat down on the carver chair that accompanied her desk. She appeared to be regaining her self-control.

'Our world is necessarily a blend of good and bad,' she said slowly. 'Not everything can end well, that is a part of life. But for nothing to end happily would be . . .' She stopped, and looked up at Verity. 'The stories – the happy ones in particular – keep things as we know them to be.'

The librarian's eyes were glassy. She didn't appear able to say any more. Seeing her upset, rather than angry, or anxious, made Verity's skin prickle with fear.

# Chapter Seven

Verity woke early the next morning. She'd had so little sleep that she felt leaden with tiredness, but her head raced with anxiety and wouldn't let her rest. Getting up quickly she raced across town to fetch first Henry, and then Martha.

Wellow was quiet, with just birdsong and the occasional bark from an inquisitive dog in the distance. The air was warm for the time of year. It made everything smell fresher and more fragrant.

Such beautiful weather only seemed to make the situation more worrying, more poignant, thought Verity. How could life carry on as if nothing were under threat?

Both friends stood and listened silently, Henry squinting in the low sun as Verity explained the discovery she had made with Miss Cameron last night.

'What will happen to the stories?' asked Martha quietly.

'I think they disappear from the world. I think that's what the dreams show: a world where everything ends badly,' said Verity.

Martha blanched. 'That's terrible,' she said.

Even Henry looked worried. 'Last night I dreamed the Usage family were in charge of Wellow,' he said soberly. 'Barbarous Usage was still alive. And somehow Mum was married to him. It wasn't good.'

'Could that really happen if the stories are wiped out?' asked Martha.

Henry shrugged. 'Who knows?' he said, starting to walk briskly in the direction of the library. 'But I'm not willing to risk finding out. Let's go and see how we can help.'

The entrance desk in the main hall was unmanned when Verity, Henry and Martha arrived. The three friends strode through the main hall and the reading room, then clattered down to the vaulted room at speed.

Miss Cameron was at her desk. A towering pile of books sat to her left, and a far smaller one to her right: work to do, and work complete. Her hair was noticeably less immaculate than usual.

'You're writing over the stories,' said Verity. 'Re-inking them.'

'The sand works slowly,' Miss Cameron replied. 'This will keep each story alive until assistance arrives.' Her violet-grey eyes looked tired. She must have been up all night.

'We want to help,' said Verity immediately.

'Absolutely,' said Henry.

'Please let us,' said Martha. 'How will you sleep otherwise?'

The silence of the room was rent by a loud hissing of air. The three children jumped, but Miss Cameron merely let slip a disapproving tut. She reached over to lift a wood shutter that was fitted into the wall. Inside was a Bakelite capsule.

Henry craned his neck excitedly over Miss Cameron's shoulder. 'A pneumatic tube messaging system,' he exclaimed. 'I had no idea one had ever been built. I've only seen speculative drawings.'

'Really not as practical as you might think,' Miss Cameron replied. 'Sometimes I think people are more enchanted with the potential of these solutions than their actual efficacy.'

She pulled out a new leaf of paper and placed it in her beloved typewriter, with its ornate copper shield.

> *That is all very well, but in the meantime every story told for good is being erased from record.*
>
> #42

'Number forty-two?' asked Verity.

'There are many of us librarians around the world,' said Miss Cameron. 'We find it easier to refer to ourselves by numeral.'

'A worldwide librarian association?' Martha breathed. 'Is that who you contacted for help? How *exciting*.'

Henry snorted. 'Martha,' he said, patting her on

the back in a worldly manner. 'The words 'librarian' and 'exciting' will never sit comfortably in the same sentence.'

Another message appeared.

> *Help is coming.*
>
> *#1*

'Where is librarian number one?' Verity asked.

Miss Cameron brushed a blouse sleeve. 'We are not encouraged to disclose personal details,' she said.

Martha's eyes nearly popped out of her head. 'Secret locations,' she squeaked. She swivelled round to stare accusingly at Henry. 'You can't tell me *that's* not exciting.'

Verity picked up Miss Cameron's favourite biscuit tin: the lozenge-shaped pastel lemon one. It was empty. 'Biscuits for breakfast?' she said, without thinking.

Miss Cameron glanced down.

Henry whistled.

'That does it,' said Martha. 'You really must accept our help.'

It didn't take long for Miss Cameron and Martha to arrange a rigorously structured rota for the re-inking of Original Stories. The librarian was painstakingly particular about how they were to be preserved.

'That will not be necessary,' she said to Henry, confiscating the battered school pen he had cheerfully extracted from his bag. Instead she gave each of them brand new writing instruments and a bottle of very good ink. Verity held hers in her hand for a moment. It was heavier than she was used to, with a solid gold nib. The barrel was a vivid swirling black. It made her school pens look flimsy by comparison.

She hesitated before drawing the first stroke on the page. Even though she knew she was protecting the story, something about what she was doing felt disrespectful, sacrilegious even. The pen scratched awkwardly, but the black ink flowed, sitting on top of the paper for a moment before it sank in.

'We are fortunate the sand can only move with a certain amount of strength,' said the librarian. 'It takes some time for it to erase any ink.'

'If I was a magical substance,' said Henry, 'I could think of better things to do with my time than rubbing out stories. I'd go on daring missions to seize up the engines of enemy planes, that sort of thing.'

'We can manage the task quite easily between the four of us,' said Martha, ignoring him.

'If you don't mind spending two hours every evening writing,' said Henry as Miss Cameron disappeared out of earshot.

'Would you prefer to let her cope on her own?' Martha asked.

'Of course not,' he replied. 'I'm just saying, that's all.'

Henry was grumbling. But there was no way he would have stopped their task. Practically overnight, their dreams had abated: immediate proof that their actions were keeping the Earth Witch at bay.

'Such a relief not to have those terrible images rattling around my head,' said Martha as they sat in Priory Bay's dining hall one blustery lunch time.

'I know what you mean: some of them really stuck,' said Henry, tucking into his cottage pie with gusto. 'I'm sure my appetite suffered.'

Verity thought of the terrible unhappiness in her visions and shivered with relief: none of those things were going to happen. They were safe. 'It's so lovely to get a good night's sleep,' she said with a big sigh.

'Everyone in town seems more cheerful,' said Martha, nodding in agreement.

'It's worth the time spent in the library, for Mum's temper alone,' Henry admitted.

Verity looked across at his mum in her dinner lady's smock, cheerfully serving lunch behind the counter, then at their fellow pupils busily arguing, gossiping and laughing in equal measure. The room echoed with noise. It was true that everyone in the town seemed more refreshed, and happier too: as if the strain of the dreams had been more than they realized, until they were gone.

Over the next fortnight they became used to the task, completing it with relative ease. They could even talk at the same time without making mistakes. Verity preferred that to silence. In those moments you could hear the faint whisper of the sand.

There had been no further word from the other librarians. Miss Cameron sent off another two message tubes but there was no reply.

'Do you think it's broken?' Martha asked.

'They will think me hasty, pressing them for an answer,' said the librarian.

Verity fought back a smile. Miss Cameron had the patience of a glacier. She got up to stretch her legs and give her hands a break. A leather-bound book – lying open on the librarian's desk – caught her eye. She paused, then bent over in disbelief to peer at the words on the page. 'This story has my name on it,' she said.

The librarian froze. No one spoke. All that could be heard was the movement of the sand.

'That is the Original Story your grandfather made you the subject of,' she said eventually.

'This is it?' Verity knew that Rafe had famously spent years searching the world for one of the secret wellspring locations where an Original Story could be made. 'But you're protecting it from the sand,' she said, with a puzzled frown. 'Which means it ends happily?'

Miss Cameron nodded.

'I thought the point of the Pledge was to create a story which would destroy Verity's grandmother? That's not a *really* happy end,' said Martha.

Miss Cameron looked uncomfortable. 'Rafe changed his mind. Instead, he told a story of how any child who is lonely or out of place will find the friends they need and the love they deserve: and you were to live it first. It was to honour his daughter Ruby's memory without hate.'

'*Any child who is lonely or out of place?*' Verity repeated.

'*The friends they need.* That's us,' said Henry with a grin.

Verity was swept back, instantly, to the dreams she had each night; in which Henry didn't know her and Martha was nowhere to be found. Her face turned ashen. She swallowed. What did this mean? Did her friends actually like her, or had they just been *charmed* into thinking that?

'It doesn't mean anything,' said Martha anxiously. 'Our friendship is real, not fantasy.'

Anger started to burn slowly in Verity. So everything she, her friends and family had endured last year – the Mistress in her family home, her father suffering each day – had been because her grandfather saw that she was lonely and didn't fit in?

'It was my idea,' said Miss Cameron. 'The story was my suggestion.'

Verity's eyes flashed. She stared at the librarian, too furious to speak. But her face said everything.

Miss Cameron glanced at the floor.

With her mouth set in a thin line, Verity picked up her coat and walked towards the door. Throwing one last incensed glance at Miss Cameron, she left.

Verity swept through the Manor door without a knock. Her mind raged with accusations. She scowled at the carved angels hidden in the corners of the porch. Her steps rang out, loud and resentful, across the stone floor of the hall. She headed straight for Rafe's study.

Rafe jumped up to greet her. His desk was covered with plans for fortifications and under-pinnings around the town, which he was helping to fund. But he had obviously become distracted.

'What fortunate timing,' he said happily. 'Just have a look at this. I discovered, quite by accident, that the Heartsease Cup comes apart. And inside there's an inscription.' He showed her the two separate sections: the glass bowl, and the silver stand. Engraved on the hidden inner part of the stand were three words:

*In aqua veritas*

'In water there is the truth: should be *In vino veritas*, of course. A little joke of my father's, I suppose—'

Verity couldn't wait a second longer. 'Miss Cameron told me about the story, *my* story,' she said icily.

Rafe sat down once more, and screwed the cup back together. 'I see,' he said.

The silence howled around them.

'Is that what you thought of me? That I had no chance of finding friends without you?' Verity demanded, standing in the middle of the room. Her face was twisted with anger and hurt.

'I saw you, that morning, in the park,' said Rafe, looking up at her. 'The Blake brothers had been picking on you, the other girls were laughing. Miss Cameron suggested—'

'You both felt *sorry* for me?' Verity interrupted. She wanted to die of shame. What a laughing stock she must have been.

'I didn't think—'

'You never do,' she retorted furiously.

'But look at you now,' he said proudly. 'How happy you are; you love sailing, you have Henry and Martha—'

'Who you *wished* for: now I'll never know if they really like me, or if they just *think* they do . . .' Her throat caught.

'The story tells of each child finding the friends they need and the love they *deserve*,' Rafe insisted firmly. 'They were things you still had to merit yourself. It's an Original Story that has been made by your efforts. It will happen over and over again for thousands of children, because you had the courage to live it first.'

Verity paused. She stared down at the cream rug, with its delicate maroon flowers. 'You should have asked me. Miss Cameron should have asked me, instead of plotting behind my back,' she said, less hotly.

'Would you really choose to undo it?' he asked.

Verity thought of her former life. She remembered the lonely little girl Miss Cameron must have seen coming to her library each day. For a moment she was thrown. She breathed out slowly.

'I regret deeply that you found out so suddenly,' Rafe said, picking up a pair of brass dividers and turning them around in his fingers. 'And I agree, I am often thoughtless.'

Verity stared at him. She could tell her face was sullen, but there were no words in her.

'There are many things I am not proud of,' he said. 'But I cannot accept your story should be one of them.'

'I should get back for supper,' she said quietly, closing the door behind her.

Rafe sat silently in his chair, then watched, through the leaded windows of his study, as Verity walked across the grass, her face crumpled. A first frost was forming. In his mind he saw another little girl on the lawn: his daughter Ruby. She too had once had long brown hair and a temper like a firecracker.

Supper was just being served when Verity arrived home. She didn't hold out much hope of an appetite. Her mood was still damp, and it was their maid Violet's day off. Cooking was not their mother's forte: she had a tendency to under-salt and over-boil.

'At least Olivia's food looks even less appealing,' Poppy whispered to Verity, as she sat down. It was obvious she had been re-arranging the food on her plate for several minutes. Verity tried to smile, but her heart wasn't in it.

Mrs Gallant was spoon-feeding her youngest daughter a thin paste of oatmeal and milk, none of which seemed to be going in. She sighed with frustration. 'Really is the most tiresome thing,' she huffed as the baby girl dribbled another mouthful down her bib, which looked more like a wax-laden candlestick than an item of clothing. It was a sad contrast to the pretty white dress she wore underneath. And it did nothing for their mother's beloved linen tablecloth.

'She must swallow some,' said Poppy, 'otherwise she wouldn't keep growing.'

'Shall I try, and you can eat?' Verity suggested to her mother. She sat next to her baby sister. Olivia scrunched her face into an impish grin. Verity did likewise. It was their private joke.

She took a spoonful of the paste and swooped it towards the baby girl, who opened her mouth obediently. Verity beamed, and leaned forward to gently bump noses. A soft haze of love embraced her. She thought of her dreams, with no Olivia. Of course she didn't regret her story.

After dinner Verity wandered into her father's study, hanging awkwardly on the door. He looked up from reading a leaflet that had been issued by the town council about street and building repairs.

'There's such a lot to be done,' he said to her.

Verity bit her lip. She didn't want to talk about earth works. 'I quarrelled with Grandfather earlier,' she said.

'Oh dear,' said Tom, putting the piece of paper down. 'Might I ask what the cause was?' Normally her parents strongly disapproved of being rude to elders, but her father's reaction was one of concern.

Verity approached his desk, fiddling with an old inkwell. 'I think I felt he had overstepped the mark.'

Tom hid a smile. 'You wouldn't be the first to level that accusation.'

'After we left the *Storm*,' Verity said rapidly, 'just before he returned, you told me you were angry with him for leaving. But now you seem perfectly happy with each other.'

Tom put on his glasses. 'I thought I would be furious,' he said slowly. 'But to see him again . . .' He paused. 'I am just pleased he is here. The last year made me realize there has been enough fighting. I have lost too many of my family.'

Verity squeezed around the side of her father's desk and hugged him. She rested her head on his shoulder. 'I'm worried my friends might not really like me,' she said quietly.

'That's nonsense,' Tom said with a laugh. 'They couldn't possibly spend so much time with someone they didn't like.'

Verity closed her eyes. 'They might be mistaken,' she said. 'Do you ever worry about that?'

He stroked her hair. He smelled of lemon and soap. 'Yes, I find I trouble myself with all sorts of things that are plainly not true.'

## Chapter Eight

The next day Verity felt calmer, but she really didn't want to go to the library. She wasn't sure what was making her prickle with shame more: the thought of Miss Cameron and Grandfather pitying her, or her own hotheaded strop out of the vaulted room yesterday.

But it wouldn't get any easier: she knew that. Better to get it over and done with now. With a heavy heart, and an unpleasant tight feeling in her stomach, she trudged down the hill.

When she entered the main hall, it was silent. She stood awkwardly for a moment, feeling hateful and uncomfortable.

A noise. Martha appeared holding a stack of books. She looked worried. Then she saw Verity and her face lit up. She put down the books and ran over, wrapping her friend up in a hug. Tears stung at the corner of Verity's eyes. Her throat tightened.

'It might have been a story that summoned my parents here, but you chose me, and I am very glad you did,' Martha said firmly.

'My dear.' Miss Cameron must have heard them. She walked calmly towards Verity and Martha. Her face was sanguine, but there was a sadness in her violet-grey eyes.

Verity flushed.

'I spoke to your grandfather last night,' said the librarian. 'The story was made with the best of intentions, but I am sorry. The last thing I would want to do is distress you.'

Verity stared at the polished, dark floor. She still felt hurt, and embarrassed. She wanted to speak: to apologize for her temper. After all Miss Cameron had done for her, in so many other ways, she did not deserve to be ignored. But a little lump of pride was lodged in Verity's throat, and would not let the words out.

Henry bounded in. 'There she is, unable to resist the library's fatal allure.'

Verity giggled. Suddenly things didn't seem so bleak.

'You're not really worried about whether I like you?' he asked.

Verity looked away. He wouldn't understand, but the dreams had shown her what life would be like without him, and Martha.

'As if I'd put up with you otherwise,' he said.

Verity laughed. Henry always knew exactly what to say.

'Why don't we go sailing?' he suggested. 'Get some fresh air?'

'That's a good idea,' said Miss Cameron immediately.

'I'll stay here,' said Martha.

Verity looked out of the library window. A gull wheeled in the sky. A few hours of liberty sounded like heaven.

'Come on,' said Henry, grabbing her coat sleeve. 'We'll be back by lunch time.'

*　*　*

It had turned into a beautiful day. The sun was low: a brilliant haze of white in the sky. It sparkled off the sea. Pebbles crunched underfoot, as they tramped to the fishermen's huts that *Poor Honesty* was kept behind. Then together they pushed the dinghy to the shore. It was a soothing ritual for Verity.

'If telling my story was Miss Cameron's suggestion,' Verity said, once they'd got going on the water, 'then she must know the location of a wellspring.'

Henry sighed. He knew Verity would have been brooding all night. 'I get the impression there are all kinds of things Miss Cameron knows,' he said, glancing up at the mainsail. 'Things she has no intention of telling us.'

'You've changed your tune,' Verity grumbled.

'She did it to help you,' said Henry. 'You're just smarting, that's all.'

Verity pulled a face in reply.

But it was difficult to sulk for long. As they left Wellow, the waves turned from pale white to their usual green once more. The air was briny and fresh, the waves a soothing sheet of emerald silk. Verity always felt more composed on the water, as if in some way the ocean was her home. She let the cool breeze wash over her face, and daydreamed of what it would be like to keep sailing towards the horizon, only stopping to discover new lands.

Then they rounded the point of Tempest Bay, and the air changed.

A chill breeze played lightly around them, making the hairs on Verity's arms stand on end. The temperature dropped. A sea mist was looming in the distance: a dense bank of cloud that billowed over the water and enveloped the cliffs. It surged rapidly across the land. *Like a predator*, she thought to herself.

'Look, there's a ship in trouble,' said Henry urgently. 'I think she's beached on the Shingles.'

Verity glanced up. Just visible through the mist was the distinctive outline of a hull, listing to one side. She must have sailed too close and run aground.

The Shingles was a bank of shifting stones: just visible at low tide on this shore. You could sail over it sometimes, but Verity avoided that. She didn't like the strange, low murmuring of the pebbles as they moved against each other underwater.

'It's high in the water for this time of year,' said Henry. 'No wonder they got caught out.'

'Can you see anyone?' Verity asked.

Henry squinted at the lopsided silhouette. 'No, she looks peculiar,' he said.

Henry loosened the jib and Verity steered *Poor Honesty* in the direction of the stranded boat. The waves were silent in the approaching fog. A powerful smell of rich, dank saltiness surrounded them: the strange and distinct aroma of the ocean.

Verity stared intently. She could see an island, just visible through the waves. But it wasn't made of gravel: it was composed entirely of pure white sand.

'The boat is a wreck,' said Henry. 'Look at the condition of her.'

The outer planking of the hull had been ripped away. The ship's timbers were faded and worn, and she was strewn with seaweed. Her internal layers – the frames – where each deck would have been were clearly visible. Seawater dripped gently, running down her in a percussive melody of tinkling splashes and drops.

'The sand has moved the seabed,' said Henry. 'And pushed her up with it.'

'The Earth Witch,' said Verity. She shivered.

'Hey,' Henry said. ''S'all right.' He held her gaze in his, and grinned. Verity smiled back. She'd never noticed how blue his eyes were before.

The distinctive clang of a ship's bell sounded through the gloom.

Both children swung round.

'Something's approaching,' said Henry incredulously.

Verity's stomach lurched. *This didn't feel right.* A breeze stirred through the fog, rippling and clearing a path.

Verity gasped at the view that appeared before her, and then laughed with an enormous sense of relief.

For a moment she was swept back to a cliff-top, standing with Henry at the top of the downs in the pouring rain. Staring in wonder.

It was the colossal spectacle of the mighty tall-rigged smuggling ship, the *Storm*.

This hulking great vessel had once been the most famous of the Gentry fleet: owned and controlled by the Mistress of the Storm. The ship was still as vivid as Verity remembered. She had a clarity and size that made everything else pale in comparison.

'Why is she here?' asked Henry.

Verity shook her head, smiling in wonder and lost for words. But she was no longer afraid.

The *Storm* was silent in the still green ocean: or as noiseless as a vessel of her kind could be. Only the creaking and straining of timber, the occasional slap and bang of sheet on block gave lie to her presence.

As the ship drew closer, her hull towered above them. Verity and Henry craned their heads back. She was as tall as fifty men: as long as nearly forty of them placed head to toe. Her deck could fit several houses on it.

'The Mistress didn't spare any expense,' said Henry reflectively.

'It took a hundred acres of wood to build her,' Verity said. 'She killed the men after they'd chopped it for her.'

'Nice.'

The *Storm* had once been an intimidating warship. She still kept dozens of guns, which could be seen clearly from this angle.

'They must weigh several tons each,' said Henry, nodding his head at them. Their polished black glinted with just a sparkle of menace.

They were under the ship's famous figurehead now. She stared out defiantly. She was still every bit as fierce, every scrap as wild as the last time Verity had seen her.

With a clatter of rope and wood, a Jacob's ladder was flung over the side of the ship. Both children jumped.

A tall man, black as ebony, leaned over the rail. The warrior captain whose reputation as a pitiless brigand of the seas was known in every land: powerful, muscular and seemingly ageless.

Verity called excitedly, 'Abednego.'

Without saying a word, he beckoned them to climb up and join him.

'And that's it? We're supposed to just do as he says?' asked Henry.

Verity grinned mischievously, her eyes twinkling.

Henry sighed. Leaning out, he grabbed a nearby rope that was hanging from the *Storm* and used it to tie *Poor Honesty* to her. 'I didn't say I wasn't curious,' he admitted.

Verity went first up the shaky rope ladder, her mind racing as she climbed. When she reached the top Verity turned to look back at the ocean. Being up here made her feel as if she could fly. For one terrifying moment she gazed down into the water and had a terrible desire to throw herself in.

Then a strong, ebony hand gripped hers firmly. She swung round to find herself staring into the solemn, almond-shaped eyes of Abednego.

Verity's mouth fell open.

He wore a short red wool coat with gold brocade and a flowing white shirt. On his fingers and thumbs were a number of rings; some gold, some silver and some ivory, or bone.

Abednego helped her over the rail of the *Storm*, then reached for Henry, who had caught her up by now. Once both children were safely on deck, he bowed solemnly. 'Miss Gallant, Master Twogood, it is an honour to see you again.'

Verity half nodded, half bobbed in reply. She had no idea how you were supposed to respond to a bow. Henry stood – eyes wide – completely silent for once.

'Please come this way,' said Abednego. Then he turned and strode across the deck.

Both children stared at him in astonishment.

'You forget how tall he is,' muttered Henry as they followed him. 'And how weird he is: as if he knows what's going to happen before it's even been thought of.'

Verity glanced up at the giant masts as they walked, each hundreds of feet high.

Abednego opened the doors to the cabin suite. These were his quarters now that the Mistress, the woman he had once served with unswerving loyalty, was gone. Verity and Henry stepped inside, and stopped in their tracks, eyes wide. The level of luxury was intimidating. Every wooden panel was finely turned. The hand-built lockers had clearly all been made by craftsmen of the utmost skill. The lamps managed to be both sturdy enough for purpose, but also delicate and beautiful. On the walls were a number of fine paintings. Everything bore the hallmark of the Mistress's taste. Abednego did not appear to have tailored the room to himself in any way; it was as if he were simply camping in it.

'It is fortunate we should find you here,' said the captain. 'We were preparing to leave for the library.'

'You've come all this way for some books?' said Henry.

Abednego opened a desk drawer and pulled an envelope from it. He looked at the thick cream paper. It had been given to him in this very cabin, but in a place far from here.

'There is another, such as you,' the man had said as he passed the letter to Abednego.

'I am aware of all the Keepers' servants,' the captain had replied.

Abednego turned the envelope over and

inspected the seal, then remembered himself: and the expectant children at his side. He tucked it into his inner pocket. *This is a chance to pay back some of what you owe to the world*, he reminded himself.

The door of an inner room opened. Verity and Henry jumped at the sight of a man, dressed in a navy wool jacket with gleaming brass buttons, and a pair of lovingly polished boots. He was carrying an overnight bag.

'*Mr Cutgrass.*'

What was the highly conventional Officer of Customs doing on board this notorious smuggling ship?

'Did you stow away for a *second* time?' asked Henry incredulously.

'We have been sent for by Miss Cameron,' Abednego announced. His voice was rich and melodic.

'She requested help,' Jasper explained.

'Oh,' said Verity. She and Henry stared in astonishment.

Verity concentrated on looking as if it were perfectly natural that a group of mysterious librarians should send a fearsome ship of smugglers, and a Preventative Man, to aid her friend. 'Of course, she's been waiting for you,' she said.

A third person appeared. This time the figure was someone Verity knew much better. A boy: tall, with long brown hair and bright green eyes.

Verity's stomach fluttered. '*Jeb*.'

Henry also recognized the familiar sight of Jeb Tempest. His face dropped. He looked as if he'd just encountered a particularly bad smell.

'Hello,' said Verity, realizing she had better break the silence. Jeb smiled warmly, unable to hide his pleasure at seeing her. She grinned instinctively in reply. Her heart danced. Jeb's shyness was infectious, but she felt ridiculously pleased to see him.

'That was a short set of adventures,' said Henry.

Jeb coloured slightly. 'Met up with Abednego. He asked me to come back.' She'd grown, he thought to himself. She was taller, and slimmer: if anything, even prettier than before.

'I would like to go to Miss Cameron now, the tide will turn again soon,' said Abednego.

Everyone automatically moved towards the door, following the unspoken order without question.

On deck, Abednego began preparing one of the ship's boats. From nowhere, two crewmen materialized to assist.

'Jasper. Go with the children,' said Abednego.

Mr Cutgrass nodded and another crewman came to help Verity and Henry over the side. Jasper followed the two children awkwardly down the ladder to *Poor Honesty*, then dropped clumsily into the dinghy. Henry rolled his eyes, as he gave a practised shove to push off.

Verity silently cursed her luck, as she steered away from the *Storm*. It would be left to her to make polite conversation, she knew. But as they got up speed, it seemed Jasper had better sea legs than his appearance hinted at. The wind was brisk now and the rolling waves were flecked with specks of white.

'Have the effects of the Earth Witch been felt very widely?' Verity asked.

'Around the world,' he replied. 'It is a matter of great concern.'

Verity couldn't stop herself any longer. She knew it wasn't polite to ask, but she had to know. 'Why are you still on board the *Storm*?'

'I asked Abednego to take me with him,' Jasper said.

'And he just agreed?' It seemed odd, to say the least: the crew of the *Storm* was famously wary of strangers.

Jasper gazed happily at the sky. He was enjoying the journey. It reminded him of his childhood. 'Perhaps you recall,' he said, 'that last year I located the Storm Bringer and brought it back to Wellow?'

'Not sure how anyone could forget, after it nearly blew us to pieces,' said Henry.

Jasper nodded earnestly. 'I had been very foolish. I accepted Abednego's invitation to board the *Storm*, believing I would get safe passage to dispose of the device, when in fact he planned to use it against the Mistress.'

'So *that's* what you were doing in a locker,' said Henry.

'But the Storm Bringer was not the only Gentry artefact,' said Jasper. 'There were others. After the

Mistress disappeared, I called on Abednego's honour: we made it our quest to discover the artefacts' whereabouts and make them safe.'

*A quest to uncover dangerous Gentry artefacts around the world?* Verity was thrilled. 'How exciting,' she breathed.

'I owe a great debt to your father,' Jasper said to Henry. 'He started me on the path to enlightenment. He is a man of integrity and wisdom.'

'He has his moments,' Henry snorted. Then he frowned. 'When did you meet him?' he asked.

'Such a noble man: to wait all those years knowing one day the Storm Bringer would certainly return to Wellow, thanks to some fool like me. And to shoulder the responsibility of preventing it causing harm . . .' Jasper stopped. Henry was staring at him, mouth open. The customs man realized, at last, that he had said too much.

'Is that why you are here?' Verity asked.

'No,' said Jasper. 'We are looking for the Bloodstone, but I am certain it is not in Wellow. Our diversion here means we must put our quest on hold. It does not matter: we had reached a dead end.' He looked up at the cliffs. 'For now there are new, and more dangerous, things to battle.'

Verity shivered. She stared at the ocean. The sea was turning white once more, as they drew closer to Wellow. They travelled the rest of the way in silence, all three lost in their own thoughts.

Verity, Henry and Jasper entered the main hall of the library to find Miss Cameron filing books. There was an awkward pause. Verity shifted uncomfortably. She desperately wanted to apologize. Her previous silly bad temper seemed so childish now. But she couldn't do it in front of Jasper.

'I see you have brought a visitor,' Miss Cameron said, looking up.

'Mr Cutgrass has been sent with Abednego, Captain of the *Storm*,' said Verity.

As if summoned, Abednego and Jeb appeared at the entrance.

'By my colleagues?' asked Miss Cameron.

Abednego nodded. 'Jeb has offered to remain in Wellow until further notice. And they suggested that Jasper help with the running of the library.'

Miss Cameron stared at Abednego. Verity got the distinct impression this wasn't what the librarian had been expecting. Who were these mysterious colleagues? They were clearly influential. Abednego had turned his ship around, and sailed back across the world for them.

'I'm sure Jeb and Jasper will be an admirable support,' Miss Cameron said eventually.

'Your colleagues also asked that you come with me. They are waiting for your assistance,' said Abednego.

Miss Cameron smiled with her mouth only. 'Quite out of the question, I'm afraid. I cannot leave the library, I am responsible for it.'

'Not everything—' Jasper started.

'I sent for *help*, I did not seek permission to leave,' Miss Cameron interrupted.

Abednego put a hand on Jasper's arm. He pulled out the envelope. 'They anticipated your concerns,' he said, handing it to her.

Miss Cameron opened it and began to read. Her face was expressionless. She smoothed the front of her hair with her hand.

'Who checked the wellsprings?' she asked.

'It was arranged by your colleagues,' said Abednego.

Miss Cameron scanned the letter once more.

'And that included the original one?' she asked.

Abednego shook his head. 'I do not know.'

'I see,' Miss Cameron said eventually. She stood up. 'Verity, would you help me pack?'

Verity stared at her, completely floored. She felt dizzy. She couldn't imagine life in Wellow without Miss Cameron. She had known the librarian since she was a little girl: her presence was as constant as the sea.

Miss Cameron tilted her head to one side in a silent query. Verity got up and followed her, her heart beating rapidly.

The librarian's sensible shoes rang out as she walked through the main hall. In the storeroom she pulled open a small door in the corner, which Verity had always assumed was a cupboard, but behind it was a tiny set of winding wooden stairs.

Verity stared at them in bewilderment. It had

never occurred to her to wonder precisely *where* in the library Miss Cameron lived. She climbed up after her friend.

Verity emerged into a tiny attic room and looked around in astonishment. It was, of course, clean and very simple. Just a chest of drawers, a walnut wardrobe, a chair and a black iron bedstead with neatly pressed white cotton linen and a quilted throw, folded tidily at the foot.

Miss Cameron sat on her bed. Verity perched next to her.

The light in here was dim. It was harder to see the librarian's face. 'I am not supposed to have grown so attached to Wellow,' she said. Her head dropped. 'I shall miss walking along the coast-line.'

Verity took a breath to calm herself. She was overreacting. 'Why do you need to leave?' she asked.

Miss Cameron picked up her pillow and examined an embroidered flower. 'The association I belong to, the one I spoke of previously . . .' She paused.

Verity held her breath.

'We are known as the *Bibliothecary*,' said Miss Cameron.

Verity remained silent. The name meant nothing to her.

Miss Cameron watched her reaction and continued. 'It is our duty to protect all Original Stories,' she said. 'The re-inking we have been undertaking here in the library is important, but it is merely addressing a symptom, not the root cause. My colleagues have instructed me to leave: every pair of hands is required. And when we find . . .' She stopped. 'When we complete our task,' she continued, 'the sand will stop. The stories will be safe once more.'

'You will come back?' said Verity.

'Of course,' said Miss Cameron, in a tone deliberately intended to reassure.

'Miss Cameron, I . . .' Verity was desperate to apologize. How could she have been so ungrateful yesterday?

'Could I ask that you continue with your duties?' the librarian said softly. 'Mr Cutgrass will not be able to cope alone, and it may take him a while to settle. There will be much you need to show him.'

'Can't *he* go, and you stay here?'

Miss Cameron looked at her sharply.

'We'll help,' said Verity quickly. 'You can rely on us. I promise.'

'Mr Cutgrass is doing his duty, as I must carry out mine,' Miss Cameron said gently.

'*I'm sorry*,' Verity blurted out. This was dreadful. She was going to miss Miss Cameron so much, she realized.

'Hush now,' Miss Cameron said. 'You have nothing to reproach yourself for.'

She obviously didn't want Verity's apology. Verity bit her lip to hold back the tears that were pricking at the corners of her eyes.

Downstairs in the library Abednego took Jasper into the reading room. Martha and Jeb watched them retreat.

'They make an unlikely pair,' she said.

'But they've a bond,' said Jeb.

'Will you be all right?' Abednego asked Jasper, closing the door behind them with a soft click. His hand played unconsciously with a tiny peg doll, covered in scraps of faded material.

'Naturally the librarian must be upset,' said Jasper. 'This is her life's work.'

Abednego gripped his arm reassuringly. 'You see how your ability to understand others improves?' he said.

'I will miss the *Storm*,' Jasper said.

'There will be a berth for you on her for as long as I am captain,' said Abednego.

Jasper shook his hand with feeling. 'That will do for my lifetime,' he said.

'This will be over – one way or another – within the year.'

'That is what concerns me,' Jasper replied.

It did not take long, especially with Verity's help, for Miss Cameron to assemble her few possessions and leave the room in what she considered to be an acceptable state. She stood in the centre of the main hall, dressed in a neatly fitting black travel coat. There was an air about her the children had never seen before. She seemed distracted: dispossessed, almost.

She paused for a moment, gazing at Verity, Henry and Martha, all neatly assembled, as if trying to decide how formal her farewell should be. 'Goodbye my dears,' she said at last.

Verity's throat constricted. First Alice, and now Miss Cameron. She ran over and flung her arms around the librarian. Hot tears streamed down her cheeks. She felt as if she were being punished. 'Please don't leave,' she sobbed.

Miss Cameron's violet-grey eyes shone. She took Verity's hand and held it gently in hers. 'My dear, I do not have a choice.' She looked intently at Verity. 'You do believe that?'

Verity calmed a little, gulping for air. She nodded jerkily.

'It is time for us to leave,' said Abednego regretfully, his handsome face shadowed. 'We cannot wait.'

Verity sniffed as Miss Cameron left, bidding one last farewell. The librarian looked small, and vulnerable, next to the dark giant who carried her worn leather trunk. With one steady push of the doors, he escorted her from the building.

The main hall was silent.

'What time would you like us here in the morning?' asked Martha politely, of Jasper.

Verity wandered over to a display case and sullenly examined its contents.

Jasper stared helplessly at the three children. This is your duty, he reminded himself. 'I believe Miss Cameron had a rota?' he said to Verity.

'That's right,' said Henry, when he realized his friend wasn't going to answer. 'Shall we stick to it for the moment?'

Jasper focused on looking appreciative. 'That would be most considerate.' His words echoed around the main hall. 'You should go home,' he said. 'It is getting late.'

The children didn't wait to be asked twice. Grabbing their coats they bustled out into the cold, dark evening; Martha chatting to Jeb, and Henry grumbling about pretty much everything.

'Isaac will be pleased to see you,' Martha said to Jeb.

Henry pulled a face. 'I suppose someone's got to be,' he muttered.

'I'll be glad to see Isaac,' said Jeb.

'*Ignore him,*' Martha mouthed, nodding her head in Henry's direction. Jeb smiled.

Verity paused for a moment by herself. She closed the red double doors.

They had a hollow ring this evening.

# Book Three

## Winter

# Chapter Nine

The weather turned at last. Winter arrived, and wrapped her thin silver fingers around the town of Wellow. The sand had not relented in its activity, but neither was it any more frantic: keeping its effects under control became a manageable task.

The ground too, seemed to stabilize. There were no more earth movements. The townspeople of Wellow concentrated on mending the damage that had occurred under the assumption that the worst was over.

It was odd to be in the library without Miss Cameron, but Verity and her friends gradually settled into a businesslike order with Jasper Cutgrass. They showed him how the librarian liked the stories to be re-inked, and helped him become familiar with where things were kept. They grew accustomed to his habit of pausing before he spoke, and the fact that the nuances of human emotion were usually lost on him.

It was Verity who found it hardest of all to look him in the eye, or smile in his presence. She tried, but could not remove from her mind the accusation that he had ousted Miss Cameron. And she missed the librarian more than she could say: far more than she would have thought possible.

Each day at least one of them would check the message machine in the vaulted room. And each day there was nothing.

'So we just have to keep writing over the stories?' said Henry to Verity, after the two of them had conducted another fruitless inspection. He closed the wooden shutter. Jasper was sitting at Miss Cameron's desk, making a note of books to be worked on the next day.

Verity pulled a face. They'd talked about this so many times. 'That's all she said: re-inking the text is treating a symptom, not the cause. When the *Bibliothecary* complete their task, the sand will stop, and the stories will be safe again.'

'All a bit cloak and dagger for a library association,' said Henry. 'I suppose they have to do something to make filing sound fun.'

The customs man looked up from his work. 'They are an ancient association – as old as the Keepers – with a noble purpose,' he said.

'To protect every Original Story . . .' said Verity.

'And safeguard the world. They keep their own counsel.' The revenue man dropped his head once more.

Henry twirled a finger near the side of his head.

Verity stifled a giggle. 'We'd better go,' she said to Jasper, who didn't look up.

'He's a queer fish,' said Henry when they were back in the main hall. 'Do you think he realizes how odd he seems?'

'I don't know,' said Verity. He was similar to Miss Cameron, she thought, in that he too was both quiet and reserved, and undoubtedly clever. But his expression – although often unreadable – was more like that of a child than a sage.

\* \* \*

It took a while for Henry to muster the courage to confront his dad, but he could not get the conversation with Jasper out of his mind.

Finally, there came an evening when his home was empty. Percy and Will had disappeared. Their mum had gone for her weekly visit to the assembly hall: today was competitive jam-making. Mr Twogood had taken advantage of her absence to eat a large doorstep of bread in the sitting room, with a book on his lap.

'The revenue man is back,' said Henry, watching his father.

Henry's dad continued reading, but there was something in his demeanour that indicated he was listening.

'He said you helped him realize how dangerous the Storm Bringer was.'

Henry's dad put down his book. The mantel clock ticked.

'You told us there was no such thing as magic,' said Henry. His voice was hurt.

'Magic shouldn't exist, son,' said Mr Twogood.

'But you said it *didn't*.' Henry wasn't sure why

he hadn't asked about this before. How could he have continued to believe his dad didn't know about the Mistress and the Keepers, if he did?

'Magic is the recourse of the greedy, the lazy and the incompetent,' said his father. 'Round these parts, it killed thousands. It ruined your family.'

Henry stared at his father.

'You lads are so clever,' said Mr Twogood. 'You have real talents. Magic taints everything it touches. I wanted a better life for you.' He hung his head. 'I thought I was protecting you. Your mum's never stopped telling me it was a mistake.'

Henry hid a smile. He could imagine.

'I'm sorry,' his dad said. 'I should have told you the truth.'

They sat in silence together.

''S'all right,' said Henry. He gave the fire a poke. 'The revenue man said you had great integrity and wisdom.'

'And what did you reckon to that?'

Henry looked at his dad. His salt and pepper hair was in need of a cut, but his face was that of the honest, intelligent man he loved. 'I think he was right.'

* * *

Verity, meanwhile, was preoccupied by slightly less weighty issues. Her grandfather was planning to host a Christmas Celebration at the Manor. It would be the first in decades. She had never been to a party, of any kind, before and found herself constantly distracted by the thought of it.

She had made her peace with Rafe the morning after Miss Cameron left.

'My dear girl,' Rafe had said after Verity apologized earnestly for her temper. 'Simply the Gallant spirit, rearing its head: I was quite the firebrand in my youth.'

She felt more at ease in her grandfather's company these days, as if arguing with him had, in some contradictory way, brought them closer together. Like the rest of the world, she found his charm difficult to resist.

Verity was not alone in her excitement about the party. Across Wellow, the large embossed invitations, and their accompanying cartridge envelopes, were proudly displayed on mantelpieces and windowsills:

> *You are cordially invited to a Christmas*
> *Celebration at the Manor.*
> *All that is required is your presence.*
> *Attire of your choice.*
> *Christmas Eve: from six in the evening*
> *until midnight.*

It was the main topic of conversation in the town. From the inhabitants of the cliff-top houses, to the denizens of the Spyglass Inn, everyone was consumed with the subject of who was invited, what would be worn and who would talk to whom. Rumours of itineraries, orders and deliveries abounded.

'The theme is *Winter Woodland*,' Poppy told Mother excitedly at the dinner table. 'The Manor is to be decked out with greenery, just like a forest – and all the staff are to have costumes of their own, with animal masks.'

'I'm sure it will look enchanting,' Mrs Gallant replied.

'Do you think there'll be dancing?' asked Poppy.

'And games?' said Verity.

Mrs Gallant smiled. Olivia was balanced on her hip, sucking a wooden spoon.

Mr Gallant quietly buttered a piece of bread. It was a perplexing thing, he reflected, to be a man in a house full of females.

'It says *Attire of your choice* but surely the most appropriate thing is a party dress?' said Poppy, who had already evaluated – and discounted – the entire selection available to her.

Both parents looked at each other. 'I don't think we can stretch to new dresses,' said their father. 'It's only for one evening. You'll have grown out of them in no time.'

'We'll find something from last year that suits,' Mother agreed. 'Hems can always be dropped.'

Poppy's perfect little rosebud mouth fell open. Even Verity couldn't hide her disappointment.

'We'll be the only ones there in old dresses,' said Poppy, her lip trembling visibly.

'That needs to be an end to the matter,' said Mrs Gallant.

'But—'

'Are you questioning your mother?' Mr Gallant asked.

Verity stared at the floor. It felt so unfair. They hadn't even been given a chance to argue their case. She knew, from personal experience, how cruel the other girls in Wellow could be when you didn't look right. 'Of course not,' she replied.

The next day Verity and Poppy spent yet more time looking for something to wear. Outside a fine drizzle was just visible against the steel-grey sky.

Poppy had already tried on all her old dresses and they simply didn't fit. As for her shoes, they were out of the question. No matter how hard she tried, she could not squash all her toes in without hobbling. 'If you followed Mother and Father's reasoning, we shouldn't have any clothes at all until we were fully grown,' she said.

Verity sighed. She completely agreed. 'Perhaps they have to be careful with money now we have Olivia.'

She did up the fastenings on the scarlet silk dress Alice had sent her last winter and stood in front of the mirror borrowed from her mother's room. The dress still fitted around the waist, but was far too short on the knee.

The doorbell rang downstairs. Both girls ignored it.

'You should try it on,' Verity said to Poppy. 'It's a shame to waste it.' Her sister valiantly gave it a go, but it swamped her.

Their mother called up the stairs. Verity and Poppy hurried down the main flight with its red runner and brass rods, their hands trailing lightly over the polished banister.

Grandfather was waiting for them. He had on his best overcoat, and was wearing a hat.

'Are you going somewhere nice?' asked Poppy, giving him a kiss.

'I heard there were two girls in *desperate* need of dresses,' he announced, his mouth twitching with amusement. 'So I thought there was nothing for it but an emergency shopping trip.'

Poppy screamed with excitement, jumping up

and down in a quite unseemly manner. She grabbed hold of Verity and twirled her around in a circle. Verity burst out laughing.

'It's almost as if you had this planned,' said Poppy to her father, who had just appeared in the hallway.

'I don't know what you're talking about,' he replied, affectionately ruffling her hair. 'Now be off with you before your grandfather changes his mind.'

Mrs Gallant's shop of choice when buying clothes for Verity and Poppy was Dereham's: a small and very practical clothes shop. All the other girls at Priory Bay went to Wickham's, which in Verity and Poppy's eyes was the very height of fashion.

But Mrs Gallant did not see the need for any more visits to Wickham's than was absolutely necessary. 'Dereham's have everything in your size. And they are perfectly acceptable,' she would say firmly. 'Just as good and far more economical – sensible well-made clothes that won't fall apart by tomorrow.'

'That's precisely the trouble,' Poppy had once

whispered to Verity. 'They never fall apart quickly enough.'

'Will the well be covered in time for the party?' asked Verity as Rafe drove them to Niton, the nearest large town.

'Can you believe it won't?' Rafe swore. 'There's just a ramshackle fence: absolutely infuriating. Although I suppose they *have* been rather taken up with all the other tasks I gave them. I found my old caravan the other day: completely overgrown. I was so excited, I must show you.'

The two sisters smiled at each other.

'At least the well isn't very deep,' said Verity.

'Shall we go to Wickham's?' asked Rafe as they drove into the main street.

'Really?' said Verity and Poppy excitedly. Then they remembered their manners.

'Somewhere like Dereham's would be just as good,' said Verity politely.

'And far more economical,' agreed Poppy, perhaps just a little flatly.

'Isn't that where you usually go?' said Rafe.

Verity and Poppy looked at him.

'Well, yes,' said Verity, 'it is.'

'Then we should go to Wickham's, shouldn't we?' he concluded.

Verity and Poppy could have stood outside Wickham's for hours, just taking in the window-display. A winter skating scene had been set up. The models were all dressed in pretty little coats with matching hats, taking part in a snowball fight. Both sisters were sure they'd never seen anything so enchanting.

'Shall we go in?' asked Rafe, smiling as he pushed open the door, which tinkled delicately.

The two girls snapped out of their daydream. 'Yes please,' they said, following him.

'Here for the Christmas Celebration?' said Miss Wickham, holding out her hands. 'It seems the whole town can talk of nothing else.'

Verity and Poppy stared around eagerly, their eyes wide with anticipation. On the far side of the shop was a rail of party dresses. They could see different shades of taffeta, skirts of tulle, rich soft velvets, delicate stitching, layers of chiffon, sequins and beads, and a whole rainbow of silk and satin.

'Sit down,' said the shopkeeper with a twinkle, patting a chaise longue, 'and I'll see what we can find to suit.'

Verity placed herself next to Rafe who crossed his legs with composure. 'This is very kind,' she said.

Rafe looked fondly at her. 'The pleasure is entirely mine.'

Poppy ran out of the changing room wearing a cream taffeta dress with matching shoes. It made her look even more slender and delicate.

'You look splendid,' said Rafe heartily as Poppy skipped around, laughing with delight.

Miss Wickham appeared at their side holding a selection of clothes. She held up the first for inspection. Verity was smitten. It was a flame-coloured silk pinafore that seemed to glow with its own light.

'This will go very well against your hair,' said Miss Wickham approvingly. 'And bring out those lovely dark eyes.'

An hour later the shopkeeper was finally wrapping up Verity and Poppy's outfits.

'Beautiful choices,' she said, deftly tucking in a layer of tissue. She looked up conspiratorially. 'I have sold a number of dresses today – I don't think there's a person in Wellow who doesn't plan to attend – but I'm confident you two will be the belles of the ball.' Poppy giggled.

When they finally left the shop, holding their pristine bags carefully, Verity couldn't help smiling excitedly.

'*Miss Gallant,*' a familiar voice shouted feverishly down the street.

Verity's face fell.

'Oh no,' mouthed Poppy silently at her sister.

It was Brother Povl, one arm held out in greeting, the other clutching a small stack of books. He was approaching them with such eagerness he could scarcely walk in a straight line. 'Such an honour,' he gasped. 'Rafe Gallant in the flesh.' He stopped, standing just a little too close to the sisters and their grandfather.

Rafe looked astonished. Verity cringed with embarrassment.

'And the two little stars of Priory Bay, so

205

popular,' Povl added, indicating Verity and Poppy, whose faces froze.

Verity didn't know whether to laugh or cry. 'Brother Povl is a teacher at our school,' she mumbled. 'You signed a pamphlet for him.'

'You're a Gentry enthusiast?' Rafe asked kindly.

Brother Povl nodded shyly. 'I have spent a little time studying the subject,' he said.

By now, Povl was notorious throughout the school for his obsession with all things Gentry. He showed Rafe the collection of books he was carrying; an eclectic assortment that included *Gardens of the Gentry*, *Gentry Artifacts* and *Legends of the Storm*. 'Superb bookshops here,' he said. 'Quite a number of titles I have not seen before. Your garden sounds beautiful. What a thoughtful present to your wife.'

Rafe looked pained. 'Aure made a number of alterations to the house,' he admitted.

Verity looked startled. It had never occurred to her to think of the Mistress actually *living* in Wellow, in the Manor. But of course she must have done.

'It seems she had exquisite taste,' said Povl, flicking open the book to show a number of features: the kitchen garden, a water pump and a particularly fine arched willow and hazel pergola.

Rafe said nothing.

The two men looked so strange, thought Verity, standing opposite each other; Rafe, still handsome, and smartly turned out, was a stark contrast to Povl, who was pale, gawky, and dressed in the same horrible polo neck jumper and corduroy jacket that really ought to have been thrown away. Why did he never wear anything else?

'I should go,' said Brother Povl, apparently detecting an atmosphere at last. 'I shall treasure the memory of this meeting.'

Poppy pulled a face, as their peculiar teacher disappeared down the street.

'Sorry, Grandfather,' said Verity. It was her habit to apologize for things that weren't her fault.

Rafe waved a hand. 'The price of minor recognition,' he said. 'And probably quite necessary as otherwise today might have been too perfect.' He grinned mischievously.

'Thank you so much,' said Poppy, remembering their dresses again. Verity nodded eagerly.

Rafe looked proudly at his two granddaughters. 'It has been my privilege,' he replied.

Christmas Eve, the day of Rafe's Christmas Celebration, arrived at last. Verity awoke, her stomach fizzing with anticipation. Why couldn't the party start *now*? She had no idea how she was going to get through the rest of the day.

Poppy was out visiting a friend and by mid-morning Verity had washed her hair, dusted her new shoes and arranged – then re-arranged – her outfit carefully on her bed. She tried reading, but the words kept skipping away from her on the page.

By early afternoon Verity's room was pristine, with everything in it neatly organized. Felicity huffed as her eldest daughter sidled, once more, into the kitchen looking for something to occupy her. Felicity was cleaning the copper-bottomed pans with vinegar paste, spreading the acidic mixture carefully on the surface and then waiting for it to work its magic: she found the process curiously gratifying. Olivia was upstairs asleep.

Verity sighed. She knew she was irritating her mother, who hated to have her housework interrupted. She was just so restless. An idea popped into her head. She should drop into the library – surely it was only polite to say Merry Christmas to Jasper?

Verity strode down the hill, breathing in the fresh winter air and feeling pleased with her new plan. It had been agreed that the children wouldn't return until after Boxing Day, and although the customs man insisted he would be fine it seemed sad to think of even such a peculiar person spending Christmas alone.

The main hall was empty when Verity got there. Someone had left a cup of cold cocoa and an empty plate of biscuits on a table, together with a pile of books. *Henry*. She picked up the crockery with a frown, and tried to balance the books under her free arm, but merely succeeded in spilling the drink.

Verity groaned. Her woollen stockings were soaked with the sticky cold liquid. She cursed both her friend and her own clumsiness. Her legs were horribly uncomfortable. Glancing around quickly, she decided it would be easier to remove the stockings than waddle any further. She began pulling them down.

With impeccable timing, Verity heard the familiar sound of the red double doors opening. She squeaked in alarm, and dived behind a bookshelf, her stockings around her ankles. Crouched on the floor, and hidden from view, she hastily removed them. Through a gap between the shelves she saw a solid man, with salt and pepper hair. What was Henry's father doing here?

Jasper emerged from the reading room. How embarrassing. She should make herself known.

'What a pleasure to see you, I hope you are well,' said Jasper eagerly, his hand held out to Henry's father.

'Thought I'd better check what other secrets you'd let slip to my son,' Mr Twogood replied gruffly.

Jasper stopped mid-step. He looked dismayed.

Verity shrank back. She'd better stay here, out of sight.

'You mean when we came ashore from the *Storm*? I didn't realize until it was too late. But I told him nothing else. I'm not sure there is anything more.' Jasper looked shamefaced. 'I am very sorry.'

Verity watched as Mr Twogood assessed the look of genuine remorse on Jasper's face, and relented. 'I should have known I couldn't keep secrets from that one,' Henry's father admitted.

'Henry is very bright,' said Jasper.

'Too clever for his own good,' said Mr Twogood, taking off his knitted hat and holding it in both hands. 'You came with the *Storm*?'

'Yes. I asked the captain for board.'

'And he took you? That seems an unusual decision.'

Verity could see Henry's father was looking intently at Jasper. So too could the customs man. 'I was once a crew member of the *Storm*,' Jasper said. Verity stifled a gasp. 'I was stolen by the Mistress as an infant and rescued from her when I was a boy. My adoptive parents were good, responsible people but I have been fascinated by the Gentry ever since.'

'Well I'll be.' Daniel Twogood shook his head in disbelief. '*Storm* crew turned revenue man.' He whistled. 'Couldn't make that up, could you?'

'Are you looking forward to the celebrations?' Jasper asked, seeming unsure of what else to say.

Mr Twogood remembered his manners. 'Always nice to have a day off,' he said. 'There's a place at our table tomorrow if you'll accept it.'

Jasper smiled, a look of genuine appreciation. 'That is kind, but I cannot leave the building empty. Will you have a cup of tea?'

Mr Twogood shook his head. 'I should get on. Presents for seven boys and a wife to wrap.'

Verity peeked through the gap and saw Jasper take Dan Twogood's hand. 'Thank you,' he said sincerely.

The two men bid farewell, wishing each other a Merry Christmas. The red double doors closed behind Mr Twogood.

Verity's mind reeled with excitement. She leaned against the bookshelf, thrilled and intrigued. Suddenly Jasper seemed a great deal more interesting. She wondered if he could remember his time on board the *Storm*. No wonder he and Abednego had such a bond.

With an echoing *thud* a large encyclopaedia fell to the floor. Another reference book followed it swiftly. Verity heard footsteps slowly approaching. She cringed, and forced herself to emerge from her hiding spot. Her cheeks burned. Jasper looked from the puddle of cocoa on the floor near the table, to the woollen stockings in her hand, and back again.

'Henry's habit of leaving things out can be quite frustrating,' he said.

Verity was mortified. 'I'm so sorry,' she said quickly. 'By the time I realized I was eavesdropping it was too late.'

'So now you know,' he said.

She stared at the floor. 'It's easier to understand how you managed on the *Storm*,' she said. 'I should think life could be quite hard.'

'Abednego has very clear rules. I find that makes things easier for me.' Jasper cleared his throat. 'I have never been the kind of person who fits in well.'

Verity felt a pang of sympathy. So he *did* realize. 'Your role within the Preventative Men seems quite unusual,' she said.

'I think my superiors in the Customs Office struggled, at first, to find an appropriate slot,' said Jasper.

Verity smiled. 'And now you are seconded to the *Storm*?'

Jasper paused. 'Not exactly,' he admitted. 'I chose to absent myself from duty, without permission.'

Verity was stunned. 'But won't you be in terrible trouble?' she asked.

'I will be summoned to a court martial, when they find me,' said Jasper. 'But the alternative is to leave you here to defend the stories on your own, while we wait for the *Bibliothecary* to complete their task.'

He seemed to remember something. 'I think I expressed myself poorly the other day,' he said. 'The *Bibliothecary* are famously uncommunicative. I find that frustrating. But we can trust Abednego to contact us at the earliest opportunity.'

'It isn't your job to look after the library,' Verity said.

'Nevertheless, it is my responsibility,' Jasper replied. His lovingly polished buttons glinted in the light. 'I believe you won the Heartsease Cup this year,' he said. 'I did not manage to see it on my previous visit to Wellow. I understand it is most uncommon.'

Verity laughed. 'It certainly is,' she said. 'I should bring it here for you to look at.'

'That would be most kind,' said Jasper appreciatively. He looked up to the dark wood clock on the wall. 'You will be late for the party.'

Verity grabbed her coat, hat and scarf as Jasper walked with her to the red double doors. She paused on the step. The waves crashed gently on the shore below.

'Merry Christmas,' said Jasper. He held out a hand.

Verity smiled. She shook it back. 'Merry Christmas, Jasper,' she said warmly.

The streets were dark and silent as Verity hurried

home, bubbling with seasonal cheer and excitement about the party.

A familiar figure strode across the road. Even in copious layers of winter clothing he was strikingly thin.

'Merry Christmas, Brother Povl,' she shouted cheerily. A stray gust of wind blew a mist of sand in her face as she spoke. She coughed.

Her teacher barely paused, acknowledging her greeting with a cursory wave. Was he preparing for the party? It seemed unlikely. She wasn't sure how Rafe would know to invite him. Verity wondered if Povl and Jasper might like each other. They were both interested in the Gentry.

Home at last, she opened the front door of her house. A warm blast of air hit her. It was scented with pine needles and candle smoke. She could see Poppy dancing around the kitchen, with Olivia in her arms. Both sisters were giggling. Verity eagerly shoved her coat, hat and scarf on a hook and ran to join them.

# Chapter Ten

It was a magical way to spend Christmas Eve, Verity thought as she walked with her parents and Poppy to the Manor. They strode briskly through the streets of the town, their breath in front of them. Cosy cottages threw their happy light onto the streets. Larger houses revealed stockings pinned to mantelpieces, and lush Christmas trees. The sky above was an inky blue. The stars danced their great dance. The air smelled of promise.

Rafe's house, by contrast, was ablaze with light. Giant torches had been placed to mark the way. Even on the stone drive they could hear music and the muffled chatter of an assembled crowd.

They entered the hall. Verity and Poppy gasped at the transformation their grandfather had wrought in his home. Every inch of wooden panelling was sprigged with heavily berried holly and mistletoe. Small decorative bowers had been artfully created to give a woodland feel. A whole row of candelabras was lined up against one wall and towering above everything was a mammoth tree. It dripped with papier-mâché balls depicting winter scenes, and red velvet ribbons.

The heavy oak dining table had been commandeered to hold up a great mound of food and drink; whole hams, roast beef, cheeses, salmon, fresh bread, mince pies, cake, trifle and fruit. On the side a cauldron of mulled wine steamed gently next to a vast array of cordials and spirits.

A line of staff stood in smart dark clothes waiting to help. Each wore the mask of a different woodland animal; owl, stoat, rabbit, hedgehog, badger, fox and even a Muntjac deer. The room thrummed with guests.

'It's enchanting,' Poppy breathed. She slipped off her coat excitedly – anxious for everyone to see her new dress. Verity smoothed the glistening skirt for her.

Rafe came over immediately. 'How are my two favourite girls?' he asked. 'Felicity, you look lovely,' he said, kissing their mother. He shook Tom by the hand.

Isaac Tempest appeared at Rafe's side, with his familiar easy smile. He was wearing a navy wool jacket that may once have been less snug. It smelled faintly of vanilla tobacco. 'A chance to bring all together at a time of peace,' he said.

Verity gazed around. It looked as if half the town were in the house. From what she could hear, most were trading shared memories of the Manor in its heyday – or attempting to trump each other with proof of their connection to Rafe.

There, against a wall, was Miranda Blake with her brothers. George and Oscar looked big, and confident. Their sister was minuscule and dainty by comparison. Even Verity had to admit her ivory gown made her look pretty. She looked less pointed than usual.

Their mother, Mrs Blake, was draped in peacock blue and conversing with a plump elderly lady. As she spoke, her eyes flicked beadily about the room:

constantly on the watch for anyone more worthy of her company. Her husband was wearing a plum coloured cummerbund that did nothing to minimize his girth, and enjoying a particularly large glass of port. He seemed in good spirits.

In the centre of the room was Charlotte Chiverton, giggling and laughing with a group of young men. She looked as if she were having the time of her life. Spotting Verity, she broke up the conversation. 'Such a brilliant party,' she trilled. 'Absolutely everyone's here: all desperate to get some time with your grandfather, and see what's become of the place. Jeb Tempest has turned out to be quite an attraction too.'

Verity looked across the room. Her heart skipped a beat. Jeb was wearing a simple white linen shirt with a pair of soft green trousers; his hair was tied back as usual. He was surrounded by a flock of girls, all vying for his attention. The giggling and shrieking around him was ear splitting, even at this distance.

'You don't think he's going to notice you?' Charlotte teased. She giggled at the notion.

Verity flushed. 'Of course not,' she said defensively.

Miranda Blake appeared at their side. 'Quite the draw, isn't he?' she smirked.

'. . . an absolutely stunning example of classic Wellow architecture,' enthused a familiar voice behind her. 'Have you seen those window gables?' It was Martha, wearing a very simple black silk frock with matching headband.

Verity gave her a relieved hug. 'So glad you're here,' she said.

'Because she's your flunkey?' asked Miranda poisonously.

'My parents,' said Martha to Verity, ignoring Miranda. 'Mother and Father, meet Verity.' They shook hands. No wonder Martha looked so distinctive. Both her parents were tall and dark. Mrs Platt looked fiercely intelligent, with cropped black hair and quite heavy glasses. She wore a black wool dress. Martha's father was slim with longer hair than his wife. He was dressed in a suit that looked as if it were a wardrobe staple. Neither appeared to have made the slightest concession to party wear.

'Your work over the summer sounded fascinating,' Verity said politely.

'I reminded Martha she must write down some of the things you learned last year about the Gentry,' said Mrs Platt. 'It's precisely this kind of groundwork which can prove so useful for future doctorates.'

Charlotte Chiverton snorted.

Verity and Martha swivelled round to glare at her.

'I believe you have a number of those yourself,' said Verity to Mrs Platt. 'I'd love to know more. Why don't we find you a place to hang your coat?'

Once Martha's parents were safely deposited, Martha and Verity went to explore the garden. The lawn was lit with more torches. Hanging paper lanterns adorned every tree. An entire suckling pig was being roasted on a spit, and a few partygoers were gathered around it for warmth as well as sustenance. A gentle debate was taking place as to whether the guests should like to live in such a prominent house, or would find it overwhelming.

Verity and Martha slipped past them and through a gate into the walled kitchen garden. 'Your grandfather's thought of everything,' Martha said, with admiration. 'I didn't realize he employed so many people.'

'I think he recruited a lot for the night,' said Verity. Inside the house the brightly lit kitchen was packed with busy people.

She glanced across the garden, and frowned. A particularly tall, thin servant was standing in a darkened spot near the asparagus beds, facing the garden wall. He appeared to be having difficulty, and was pulling at an iron lever that presumably would not move as he wished it to. She squinted. Was that an old-fashioned pump? He was near the well.

Verity was overcome with curiosity. What was he up to? She grabbed her friend and hurried across.

'What are you doing?' Martha asked.

'Excuse me,' Verity called out. 'Excuse me.' She

knew she must look odd, but she couldn't stop herself.

The man paused and turned to look at them.

'I shouldn't use that,' Verity said breathlessly. 'I think the well it draws from has been abandoned.'

The man said nothing. He held a flask. His fox mask had a fierce look of cunning and ruthlessness about it.

'My grandfather owns the house,' she explained. 'My sister nearly fell down there in the summer. You should be careful. I'm not sure it's safe.'

The man smiled.

'It was very frightening,' she insisted.

He nodded, shaking the flask, which sounded as if it had just the tiniest splash of water in it. 'The well is dry. I shall see the pump is put out of use,' he replied. His voice was commanding and assured.

Verity watched with a puzzled frown as he left. Something about him felt wrong.

'What a peculiar man,' said Martha. She shivered. 'Can we go indoors? I'm freezing.'

Verity pulled herself together. 'Sorry,' she said, looking embarrassed.

''S'all right,' said Martha with a smile. 'Come on, let's go and enjoy the party.' The two friends hurried, arm in arm, to the house.

Back in the warmth of the Manor once more, the evening was really getting going. The sound of conversation was noticeably louder. Verity and Martha wandered over to the dining table to find Rafe pouring wine for guests and encouraging them to try some of the food.

Verity refused the Scotch egg he was trying to press upon her. 'There's a pump in the garden,' she said. 'I don't think the water in it can be fresh.'

Rafe put the bottle of wine down and frowned. 'I thought it was out of action. Hasn't been used since, well, since I was married to Aure. It was a particular favourite of hers: said she found it refreshingly insightful.'

Verity smiled awkwardly. Martha picked up a cheese straw. Neither felt able to comment on the ways of the Mistress.

'She was a peculiar woman,' said Rafe. 'I shall see it is disabled promptly.' He patted Verity reassuringly on the arm then headed for the kitchen, presumably to find a member of staff.

Verity realized someone was at her side.

It was Henry. He was dressed, quite smartly for him, in a pair of dark trousers and a charcoal jumper. He looked slightly put-upon. 'Mum and Dad decided not to come in the end: still too much to do for tomorrow. But wild horses couldn't have kept these two away.'

Percy and Will appeared from behind their youngest brother and bowed with a flourish. Martha choked on her cheese straw. They were wearing the most unlikely combination of clothes.

Percy had dug up a hideous blazer of powder blue, vermillion and brown stripe. His finishing touch was a maroon hat that he'd augmented with a purple feather. 'Easy on the food, Martha,' he said, with a wink. 'You'd better not get carried away either,' he added to Henry. 'We don't want a repeat of Aunty Vi's last year.'

Henry shot him a mutinous look. He was obviously finding their outfits and irrepressible good humour quite mortifying.

Will, meanwhile, was wearing an emerald silk bow-tie and a mustard yellow shirt.

Verity shielded her eyes. 'What original ensembles,' she said.

Will grinned. 'We don't all have access to the Gallant riches,' he said cheekily. 'But you can't thwart natural style.'

Verity laughed.

'I suppose you have to give them credit for trying,' said Martha.

'I see you've scrubbed up tolerably,' noted Will, grabbing a devilled egg. 'Don't you think, Henry?'

His younger brother looked at Verity in her flame-coloured dress. 'Oh, of course,' he said uncomfortably. 'Very nice.'

'You could say it with a bit more conviction,' said Verity. Martha smiled wryly to herself.

'Can't believe Ma and Pa missed this,' said Percy, jumping up and down to get a better view across the room.

Verity glanced at Jeb in the distance. He was talking to a girl in a peony dress. Did he look just a little bit bored? She saw him excuse himself with an apologetic smile, and leave the room.

A second, livelier, group of musicians began playing in the dining room and, with a number of cheers, various partygoers selected their partners.

An hour later Verity, Martha, Poppy, Henry, Percy and Will were having a splendid time, taking it in turns to dance with each other.

'Did you learn this from a book too?' Will grinned as he spun around with Martha, who poked her tongue out at him.

Mr Gallant whirled around the floor with his wife. 'It's been such a long time since we went to anything like this,' she said. He smiled fondly at her.

Even Miranda Blake had a colour to her cheeks.

Grandfather really did have a knack with parties, Verity thought to herself. He knew just how to blend the right combination of generosity and excitement with an ability to put each guest perfectly at ease.

Jeb Tempest watched unhappily as Verity laughed and danced with Henry Twogood.

'Ask her,' his grandfather Isaac insisted, yet again. Jeb ignored him.

'Never thought I'd see the day when you lacked courage,' Isaac mused.

That did it. Steeling himself to the task, Jeb forced himself across the room. He stood awkwardly in front of Verity, who stopped in surprise. At precisely the same time the music came to an unexpected halt.

Jeb flushed as if he wished the floor would swallow him up. 'Could I cut in?' he asked.

Henry looked as if he'd just bitten on a lemon. Even Percy and Will were shocked.

A dozen pairs of eyes fixed on Verity. Every girl that had been gathered adoringly around Jeb earlier was now staring at her with outrage. She smiled awkwardly. 'Of course.'

'Not even very pretty,' the girl in the peony dress complained in a shrill tone. Henry shot the offending onlooker a foul stare and walked to the side of the room. The servant in the fox mask poured him a consolatory drink which Henry took and downed in one gulp.

The music started once more. Jeb grinned as he took Verity's hand. Together they began to dance, and Verity couldn't stop herself smiling back.

'I didn't realize asking for a turn would cause such an upset,' he said. His vivid green eyes locked with hers.

Verity tried desperately to stop her cheeks going pink.

'That dress suits you very well,' he said admiringly.

'Thank you.' She felt dizzily happy. As the music played on, people grew bored of watching them, and turned back to their own merrymaking.

'You looked busy earlier,' she couldn't resist commenting.

'Bored out of my mind,' said Jeb. 'Every one of 'em talked of nothing but clothes and shopping.'

Verity giggled. She looked up at him. He was so handsome. Was it very silly to wonder if he liked her? Her mind scampered away to imagine what that would be like. Perhaps if they were grown up they could travel the world together, sail to far-off places . . .

Suddenly a terrible noise rang out across the dance floor, followed shortly by a chorus of screams and disgusted groans. Verity looked across the room. Someone had been horribly, violently sick on the floor. It was Henry. He was bent over double, clutching his head, surrounded by a circle of horrified and fascinated onlookers.

Verity ran over, closely followed by Jeb. Henry stood up: his eyes watering and his breath ragged.

'Are you all right?' she asked.

Henry looked at Verity as if she'd slapped him. 'Fine,' he said.

She tried to touch his arm, but he pulled away.

'Of course it smells bad, I've just been sick,' he snapped at a nearby girl.

'I didn't say anything,' she protested, stepping back.

Like a small, bony vulture, Miranda Blake elbowed her way into their midst. 'This is what happens when you eat like someone's going to take it away from you,' she said with no little satisfaction.

Henry glared at her.

A sizeable crowd had gathered to see what was going on. With a number of shoves and 'Excuse-me's Percy and Will pushed their way through it, ignoring the disgruntled stares and complaints of onlookers.

'Move away, please. Nothing to see here,' said Percy authoritatively.

'I told you to leave the buffet alone,' said Will.

'I *didn't* eat too much,' said Henry.

'No, of course not: I'm sick on a quite regular basis for no reason whatsoever. Come on, let's get you some fresh air.'

'I don't think he did, there was a—' said Verity, but Percy was having none of it.

'It's kind of you to defend him,' he said, 'but I think we know our little brother by now.'

Verity watched, anxious and deflated, as Percy and Will led Henry to the main hall. He kept his eyes glued to the floor throughout. A group of servants moved swiftly to the spot where he had been and began clearing up the mess with minimum fuss. Tentatively the musicians began to play once more. The crowd burst back into conversation and speculation. The noise level rose again.

Jeb took her hand. 'Would you like to sit this one out?' he asked.

Verity smiled apologetically. She felt like a drip, but it didn't seem quite right to carry on as if nothing had happened. 'Do you mind?' she said.

# Chapter Eleven

The next morning Verity woke early and sat quietly at her window, a lone witness as the sun crept into the world. It spread a glow of pink through the marbled grey sky. The leafless trees drew crisp, clear patterns against the clouds.

She thought of their plans for celebrating this first Christmas with Grandfather and her stomach tingled. It had been arranged that they would spend the whole day at the Manor and she was really looking forward to it. Several months ago she had decided to use her share of the prize money from the Heartsease Cup to buy presents for all her family. She had spent weeks choosing each.

Leaving her room, she walked softly down the stairs to find her father enjoying a quiet pot of tea on his own. He too was boyishly excited.

'I can't remember spending Christmas with my father,' he said, 'so I have been really looking forward to today.'

'Do you remember him at all?' Verity asked.

'I recall playing with my sister Ruby on the lawn.' He smiled benevolently. 'You look just like her when you laugh.'

Verity didn't know what to say; the Mistress had murdered Ruby – drowned her in her dinghy – when Verity's father was a toddler.

'I like to be reminded of her,' he said, guessing at Verity's thoughts. Verity gave him a hug and began to slice some bread for toast.

By the time Mother, Poppy and Olivia were also up, and everyone was ready to stroll to the Manor, the sun had cleared every cloud from the sky. It was a perfect walk. The cold air tingled in Verity's nose. It was tinged with fragrant wood smoke from the chimneys above. She looked down over the silent roofs and houses to the sea beyond and hugged herself with happiness.

'Merry Christmas,' Rafe declared, as he opened

the front door of the Manor. The carved angels beamed as Tom, Felicity, Verity, Poppy and Olivia greeted him.

The hall was back to its usual cool, dark self after the party. All traces of the previous night's merriment had been removed. The steady tick of the walnut long-case clock was the loudest noise once more.

'Can I have another look?' asked Poppy, sprinting across the stone tiles to the sitting room.

'At what?' Verity followed her sister at a more leisurely pace, closely accompanied by Felicity, Olivia, Tom and Rafe. She stopped in surprise: in the middle of the front room was a brand new grand piano. Poppy was perched on the accompanying stool, looking up with shining eyes.

'You don't seem very *surprised*,' said Verity with a laugh.

Poppy waved a pretty hand in the air. 'Grandfather wanted to make sure I got just the right one. Isn't it delightful? And listen to the tone.' She rattled off an arpeggio.

Verity smiled. The Gallant's sturdy upright

piano needed to be tuned with increasing frequency. This polished black beauty was sleek and sonorous. Tom approached to admire it.

'Grandfather says I can keep it here where there's room for it,' said Poppy.

Rafe beamed indulgently.

'It is beautiful,' said Felicity, moving Olivia from one hip to the other.

'Is there something for you?' Verity asked her youngest sister, stroking her cheek.

'I found it quite taxing, choosing presents for someone who is not yet one,' said Rafe with a frown. 'In the end I settled for this.' He pointed to a gift that was nearly as tall as the mantelpiece.

Felicity put Olivia down on the floor. Verity helped her tear the cream and gold wrapping paper. Her sister laughed and cooed. Verity couldn't stop herself giving another cuddle. She looked like a cherub, with her soft, pink cheeks and wispy platinum curls.

Finally the gift was unwrapped. It was a magnificent hand-carved dapple-grey horse on a bow rocker. The leather tack glinted proudly. The tiny stirrups were elegantly styled. Verity stroked the flowing mane. On the corner of the bridle was a crimson rosette.

'Da, da, da,' said Olivia enthusiastically. She smacked the lush red saddle repeatedly.

Verity picked her up and held her on the horse, while everyone crowded round appreciatively. Olivia accepted their praise with the casual confidence of one who knows she is at the centre of her universe.

'Aren't you lucky?' said Verity. She kissed her sister's scrumptious face.

'And now for Verity,' Rafe announced, clapping his hands. 'I thought we might go to the kitchen garden.' Verity was puzzled. What could he have bought? Some plants?

'Just for today, of course, I've arranged for you to have your own, well, you'll see . . .' Rafe was clearly having trouble containing his excitement. He beckoned for them to follow.

Poppy giggled.

'Why don't you make sure Verity doesn't peek?' said Rafe, pausing.

'Good idea.' Poppy made Verity stop, so she could put her hands over her eyes.

The two girls continued walking with difficulty. They kept tripping, which just made Poppy more excitable.

'You can look now,' Poppy announced at last. They were at the kitchen door. Verity stepped through it into the garden. The air was crisp. She gasped.

Poppy laughed with delight.

It was a brand new dinghy on a trailer. She was so different to *Poor Honesty*. Her mainsail was a vivid blood red. The freshly varnished wood of her hull had a golden lustre that sparkled in the winter sun. The webbing toe straps were dark black, rather than faded grey.

'She is beautiful,' Verity gasped, completely overwhelmed. She didn't know what to say. Softly, she touched the gunwale.

'I asked your father, of course,' said Rafe. 'After what happened all those years ago to Ruby . . .' He stopped.

'But I worried you might never forgive me if I forbade your very own dinghy,' said Tom.

Verity turned round and hugged her father, burying her head in his shirt. 'It's too much – *she's* too much.'

'It is a little indulgent,' Rafe said. He played with the silver-blue silk tie he had chosen that morning. It went very well with his smoking jacket. 'But you would be denying me a considerable pleasure if you turned it down.'

Verity realized she was being rude. 'I didn't mean—'

'Come on, silly,' said Poppy. 'Aren't you supposed to be thinking of names?'

Verity gazed, love-struck, at her new boat. 'I think I should call her . . .' She paused, and thought of her conversation with Father that morning. 'I'd like to name her *Ruby*,' she said. 'After my aunt.'

Rafe and Tom said nothing. Tom's eyes glistened.

'I think that is a marvellous idea,' her father said at last. 'A touching memorial to my sister.' He pushed the hair back from Verity's forehead.

Rafe cleared his throat. 'If she were alive, I know she would have been delighted,' he said.

*  *  *

The next hour passed in a whirl of present opening. Mother and Father had bought a spare set of sails for Verity, a wealth of sheet music for Poppy and a variety of wooden puzzles and toys for Olivia. Better still, Rafe had persuaded Felicity to accompany him on a much-needed trip to Wickham's. Poppy screamed with delight as she and Verity opened two large boxes of clothes, delicately wrapped in tissue. There were new skirts, jumpers, stockings, blouses and tops. All in just the right sizes for two growing girls.

Verity grinned. No more tugging on her clothes, to make their length less embarrassing. She lifted out a red cotton sundress from her selection. It came with a delicate crocheted cardigan. Poppy had a beautiful pale blue velvet dress that flowed like water and set off her eyes perfectly.

Poppy deftly helped Verity on with a new red coat, then artfully arranged a fluffy charcoal scarf with matching hat. 'Stunning,' she said. She in turn was already wearing a navy smock coat that was extremely flattering. She twirled delicately around the room, leading Verity by the hand. 'We'll have the best clothes in school,' she said. Her eyes sparkled.

'Your mother chose well,' said Rafe.

Verity and Poppy took the hint and ran to thank her.

'They're all beautiful,' they both said together, hugging her.

'It wasn't quite as frivolous as I expected,' Felicity said. 'I think their stock-keeping policy may have changed.' Verity bit her bottom lip. She felt sure her mother's change of heart had significantly more to do with Rafe's considerable charm than any new range of clothes. She glanced at her grandfather who winked in reply.

Finally, only the presents from Verity remained unopened. She was worried they would look a bit small now.

Poppy opened hers first. It was a book on acting that Verity had spotted Poppy looking at each time they went into the local bookshop. 'You noticed,' said Poppy, hugging Verity tightly.

For Olivia there was a tiny toy dinghy for the

boating lake. 'Perhaps she'll have your sailing skill one day,' said Poppy.

For Mother she had bought an ornament from her favourite pottery. And to her father and grandfather she gave the same gift - a picture of Rafe, with Tom as a baby. 'Miss Cameron found it in the library. I had it copied and framed,' she said. Rafe and Tom looked at them proudly.

'Do you need any help with preparations for lunch?' asked Felicity, looking at the clock.

Rafe glanced up in surprise. '*Lunch*,' he said.

Poppy's face fell. Verity tried not to look too disappointed. Had Grandfather forgotten?

They needn't have worried. Rafe had given his staff the day off, but the goose – stuffed with apricots – was already cooking in the lower oven. The rest of the meal was not quite as far on as it might have been, so for the rest of the morning the family prepared the remainder. Cook had left copious supplies in the larder; chicken liver pâté to start, chestnut stuffing, bread sauce, a suet pudding covered with a cloth and a big jug of thick yellow cream.

Verity and Felicity peeled and chopped vegetables, which Poppy cooked to perfection, with just the right quantity of salt. Rafe set the table, aired the wine and even made the gravy. Together they chatted and laughed while Tom played with Olivia. It seemed, to Verity, to be the happiest Christmas Day ever.

'Merry Christmas,' they toasted, once lunch was finally prepared. If anything, working together had made the food even more delicious.

'Isn't it time we pulled the crackers?' said Rafe.

Poppy began handing them out. 'Try to remember that if you win two prizes it isn't nice to keep both,' she said.

They all crossed hands.

'Rubbish,' said Rafe grinning wickedly as he leaned across the table. 'If *I* get two, I shall take great pleasure in flaunting them.'

With lunch over, Verity and Poppy sat together playing rummy while Olivia napped upstairs. Tom and Rafe were both asleep in their armchairs. The front doorbell rang.

'I'll answer it,' said Poppy, slipping down from the table. She returned a minute later, brimming with excitement. 'It's Jeb Tempest,' she said, her eyes sparkling mischievously.

Verity's stomach flipped. 'Really?' she asked.

'Really,' Poppy replied, unable to resist a knowing smile.

'Don't be silly,' said Verity, a little more primly than she'd intended.

Jeb looked different, Verity realized when she reached the door. She glanced down at his boots. They were polished. Though the act of polishing hadn't made them much smarter.

'Merry Christmas,' he said shyly. He handed her a present.

Verity's chest fluttered. She stood at the door and opened the wrapping paper. It was a small wooden charm in the shape of a boat.

'Carved it while I were travelling,' he said.

'It's beautiful,' Verity said, smiling. And it was: tiny but perfectly formed. It had a comforting weight to it. Just looking at its fluid lines reminded her of being at sea. There was a little hoop at the stern for threading on a chain or bracelet. 'I'll put it in my pocket until I find something to wear it on,' she said.

Jeb looked crestfallen. 'I should've thought.'

'Don't be silly. It's really lovely,' she insisted. 'I haven't bought you anything.'

But Jeb wouldn't be persuaded. 'How are you supposed to wear it otherwise?' He reached into his pocket and pulled out a golden chain. 'Use this for now,' he said.

Verity looked at the necklace. It was a thin woven plait of bright yellow. It didn't look very substantial but in the dim light of the porch, it shone. There was a liquid grace to the way it draped across his palm.

'I can't take that,' she said, 'even to borrow. What if it's valuable?'

Jeb shook his head. ''S pretty, but it ain't got no value. My godfather gave it to me this morning and he never had no money at all. He would have sold it, I'm sure, if it were worth something.'

'I can't keep it,' said Verity, sensing she wasn't going to win this argument.

''S'all right,' Jeb replied. 'I'll fetch you one after the holidays.'

He took the boat charm from Verity's hand and threaded it on the chain, then fastened it around her neck. Verity thanked the fates her hair was covering her face.

He took a step back to admire his work. 'Very pretty,' he said with satisfaction. 'Now will you come for a walk?'

'I'd love to.' Verity beamed. 'Do you mind coming in while I fetch a coat?'

The sun was shining but the air was ice cold: just right for walking briskly through the top of the town and towards the downs. Verity could feel the little wooden charm against her skin. She smiled.

Jeb chose a path she had never noticed before. 'Leads to Burnt Wood,' he said.

'That's a mysterious sounding name,' said Verity.

'Not really: used to be Wheeler's Wood, but then old man Wheeler fell out with the Usages. Barbarous Usage wrecked a package ship carrying a hold of rum. He had his men bring every last barrel up here. Poured all of it, save one, on the wood and set light to it. Went up like a firecracker. That last keg Barbarous drank, while he watched.'

Verity shivered.

To their right, a long stretch of trees reached down to the sea. As she peered into it, the spaces between the ashes, beeches and oaks became smaller and darker.

'A lot of new stock,' explained Jeb. 'Rafe sent word it should be re-planted at his expense. He were appalled that Barbarous could lay claim to the name Gentry and commit such acts of vandalism.'

Verity felt a quiet spark of pride for her grandfather.

The path they were on ran through fields that lay beside the wood. A herd of cows grazed nearby. Verity smiled at them; they chewed thoughtfully in reply. The track had become increasingly boggy. Her shoes were filthy.

Jeb looked embarrassed. 'I shouldn't've suggested this,' he said. 'What will your mother think?' She'd never be allowed out with him again he thought to himself.

'It's fine,' Verity said. She pushed aside all notion of the pained looks she would receive at home.

They reached a crumbling stile. As she stepped over it, the whole thing swayed in the direction of the ground. She shrieked and clung on for dear life.

The constant bouts of rain had made the ground very soft: at this boundary every scrap of earth had been churned up by the cows. Suddenly it dawned on Verity that she was balancing on a rickety piece of wood in a sea of mud.

She had a fit of the giggles. 'I don't think I came prepared for this,' she said.

The cows ambled towards them, their curiosity aroused.

Jeb burst out laughing. He offered his hand. Verity took it and jumped, still laughing. She sank in the mud up to her ankles. Now they were both in hysterics.

'No point turning back,' she said. 'I can't get any dirtier.' She lifted her feet out with some difficulty.

In one swift movement, Jeb picked her up. 'Put your arms around me,' he said.

'I'm fine,' Verity protested. She was far too heavy, she knew.

'Rafe would kill me if he heard I'd brought you down here then let you wade through an acre of mud,' he said firmly.

Verity gave in. She put her arms around his neck as instructed. Her weight didn't seem to bother him in the slightest. She fixed her gaze on the cows. She could feel the heat of his body through her coat. 'It was good of you to come back,' she said, anxious to fill the silence. 'It must be frustrating that nothing much is happening in Wellow at the moment.'

'I were happy to stay,' he said. They had reached the drier end of the field now. He set Verity down on the ground. His green eyes looked directly into hers. 'I missed the people here.'

'Yes, it must have been strange without Isaac,' said Verity, wiping her shoes on a clump of grass.

Jeb said nothing. That wasn't what he had

meant. He watched her pensively. He felt as though he was making a fool of himself.

It was beautiful up here. Inland, the rolling downs stretched for miles in a blanket of green. Out at sea, the sun shone brightly. The ocean, at this distance from Wellow, was emerald and the sky an intense blue. Verity breathed in. The air was fresh and earthy. She watched her feet as she strode along the springy grass, hands deep in her coat pockets.

In the distance they saw two figures approaching. They weren't hard to recognize.

'*Henry and Martha.*'

'We called at the Manor,' said Martha, once they were within talking distance, 'but you'd already left. Henry's got a new bike.'

'Five speed rear hub,' he said. 'Bertie and Fred helped Dad fix it up for me.'

Verity beamed. 'That's brilliant: you've wanted a bigger bike for months.'

'Yeah,' said Henry noncommittally. There was an awkward pause. Verity felt a tightness in her chest. Jeb looked embarrassed too.

'Are you feeling better now?' she asked sympathetically. Henry glowered.

'I *didn't* eat too much,' he said, in the tone of one who has had this conversation many times in recent hours.

Verity tried not to look hurt. 'I didn't think you had actually—'

'Look,' said Martha frowning. She pointed to the cliff edge. There was a man.

Henry swivelled round. 'He's near the wishing well,' he said tersely.

The figure was crouched low. Verity squinted. He was unusually thin, and tall, with short white hair. His jacket was bottle green.

'It's Povl Usage.'

Their teacher was scrabbling at the ground, his head bowed and his shoulders heaving. Verity's heart squeezed in sympathy: he was crying, she was sure of it. She remembered from last year how lonely Christmas Day could be.

'He's digging,' said Martha anxiously. 'I wonder if he knows the wishing well is there?'

'He probably wants to wish for a resurrection of

the Gentry or something like that,' said Henry to Verity. 'Brilliant. And now he's unblocked the hole we're going to have to fix it: just what we need on Christmas Day.'

'He's obviously upset,' said Verity.

She sprinted towards Brother Povl. 'Please stop,' she shouted.

'Don't get too close, it's dangerous,' said Martha.

The teacher glanced up for a moment then continued with his task.

Verity reached him. She could hear Henry, Martha and Jeb behind her. Povl had lifted out the turf and was digging up earth and stones. There was a hollow sucking of water, somewhere far below.

'Please don't,' said Verity kindly. 'However bad life might seem, wishing isn't going to make it better. It must be tempting, but you're just going to hurt yourself, or others.'

Their teacher looked up. His face was even paler than usual, his cheeks hollow and gaunt. His spiky hair was matted and his full small lips were unpleasantly dark. His shadowed grey eyes were cold.

'We will hurt a lot of people before we are done,' he said quietly.

Verity stared at her teacher. An icy trickle of fear traced its way through her stomach. This man looked very different to the bumbling, slightly incompetent loner who had appeared at school each day of term. He had a glint of knife-like cunning in his eye.

'What?' Henry demanded. He looked fed up.

'Just come away from the hole,' said Jeb, 'before you hurt yourself.'

Povl snorted. In one darting movement he sprang up and ran towards the cliff top. Soundlessly he plunged from view. Martha screamed. They raced to the edge. Miraculously the teacher had chosen an area of cliff that wasn't a vertical drop. Here it stepped in banks, each covered in grass. He was like a wild animal: howling, scrabbling and rolling in his descent.

'*I serve my mistress the Earth Witch*,' he screamed defiantly at the children. 'She needs strength to re-form and I shall secure it for her.'

The children stared down the cliff.

'A servant of the Earth Witch,' Verity whispered.

'We've got to stop him,' said Martha.

Henry watched the disappearing teacher and thought of the conversation he'd had with his dad; the greedy, the lazy and the incompetent. He tugged his hair. 'For crying out loud.' He lowered himself over the edge.

Verity immediately followed, not really thinking about her decision. The tufts of grass were sparser here: mostly she was grappling with bare earth.

Jeb looked up at the sky. 'Stay here,' he said to Martha, preparing to go after Henry and Verity.

Martha shook her head stubbornly at Jeb. 'I'm coming too,' she insisted.

Several feet below them, Verity continued to manoeuvre nervously down the steep slope. Her heart thumped in her chest. The wind cut through her coat like a blade. Her hands were numb. This was insanity. She steeled herself to focus only on the clump of grass, or patch of chalk, underneath. She mustn't look down.

'Don't slide on your bum,' Henry called up. 'You won't be able to stop.'

Povl had reached the bottom. He stood triumphantly on the beach, legs apart, arms flung out in victory. 'The Mistress of the Storm is gone, she cannot keep my beloved mistress scattered any longer.' The wind blew his words up to them. He disappeared into the entrance of the cave that housed the wishing well.

Verity stared in horror. 'How stupid. Why didn't we think of that before?' she shouted.

'What now?' asked Henry impatiently. They were nearing the foot of the cliff.

'The Mistress was *keeping* the Earth Witch apart, that's what Povl just said. That's why the Earth Witch is coming back. Think of what the Mistress did to my father last year. She tormented him for months. She could easily keep her sister's body strewn around the world.'

'So now the Earth Witch can pull herself back into one piece.' Henry cursed.

Verity felt sick. 'She wants to be whole again: *strength to re-form*, that's what he said.'

Henry scrambled down the last few feet of mud and sandstone on all fours. He stood on the beach and held out a hand for Verity, who took it and jumped down to join him.

Povl emerged from the cave. 'It is done,' he said with satisfaction. 'You are too late.'

Verity stared at him, aghast. 'She's trying to end all happy stories and you're bringing her *back*?' she screamed. 'Don't you see what will happen?'

'It will be no more than she suffered: her heart was broken, and so was she. But when she is whole we will rule over the doom and perdition of our making.' He span around the flat wet sand, his voice ragged.

Verity grabbed at him angrily. But instead of drawing away he pulled her close, his face a breath from hers. With a dirt-smeared finger he gently lifted up her boat charm. She gagged at his touch. The smell of decaying earth was overpowering.

'I have reserved a special torment for you,' he whispered.

Verity let go in shock. Sneering, the teacher sprinted off at inhuman speed. Instinctively, Verity began to chase.

'Leave him,' said Henry, grabbing her.

'He's dangerous,' Jeb agreed.

'Exactly,' said Verity, wriggling to escape Henry's grasp. 'How can we let him run loose?'

'We can't kidnap him, can we?' said Henry.

Verity calmed down. She caught her breath. Henry was right.

'Thank you,' she said, standing opposite him. 'For chasing down the cliff.'

''S'all right,' said Henry. She gave him a hug. He looked sad. 'Come on. We'd better get to the library.'

# Chapter Twelve

The sun dropped with wintry speed over the horizon. Povl had disappeared, but his wish had crackled into the world, like the tiniest of sparks. Now it would slowly blaze its determined trail. Daylight retreated and withdrew, like a flicker of hope.

The children half-sprinted, half-ran along the shore below the cliffs to the library: too scared to lose precious minutes. Verity's throat stung from gasping the ice-cold air.

In the twilight, the rock face was still but they could hear land beginning to move and slip. An ominous hiss of sliding earth grew ever louder. It was as if the Earth Witch's body was creeping into every crack and gap: leveraging each weakness in a determined bid to make her presence known.

Small clouds of dust billowed into the air. Little rocks clattered and scattered down.

'It doesn't *sound* too bad,' said Martha as they raced along the beach.

'Yes, but if this carries on, the whole cliff is going to start collapsing,' said Henry, panting. 'Once even a small piece of earth erodes, it can destabilize a much bigger area of land.'

Like a gathering storm, Povl's wish accelerated from the southern shore to the town. They were nearing the western shore of Wellow harbour. In a moment they would reach the fishermen's huts.

The beach was narrower here: drawing them closer to the steep wall of rock. Verity looked up anxiously. If the cliffs started to fall, they would all be crushed. A boulder broke loose from the sandstone and bounced, helter-skelter, down the rockface, gathering debris as it fell. Then came a lower, growling, rumble. It filtered up, through the earth, from deep below. Verity could feel it trembling through her feet as she ran. Her stomach shrank.

Martha's face was ashen, her pace slowed. The boys, too, were ghostly white.

'Faster,' urged Jeb.

'One last sprint and we'll be in the bay,' said Henry, grabbing Martha's arm in encouragement. 'The town's built on more stable land than this.'

A stomach-chilling groan echoed from above. The children stopped and turned round. A tranche of cliff – several feet wide and many feet deep – had wrenched itself free.

Verity felt pure, physical fear coursing through her like ice water. Without uttering a word the children turned and fled again. They ran faster than they'd run in their lives. Verity didn't feel the ache of her legs, or the burning in her lungs. Her mind was quiet and still: her body took over. Like the cogs of a clock that is winding down, time slowed. They scrambled over the seaweed-strewn rocks that littered the headland: unable to stop themselves glancing up every few seconds, as if this might offer some form of protection.

Then just behind them the descending cliff hit the beach. The noise ripped the air like the sound of thunder. Debris flew out in every direction: several tons of rubble smashed to the ground by the silken, persistent white sand.

From a safe distance they paused to watch, panting and gasping for breath, clammy with sweat and fear. And still, in the background, the delicate hiss.

A cold, scentless wind blew in from the sea. It cut Verity's hot cheeks like a blade. It lifted her hair from her shoulders. She felt sick with dread. This was just the start: she could feel it. Beside her, her friends stood silently, each as frightened and worried as her.

Without a word, they turned and staggered as fast as they could across the harbour beach, reaching the quay at last and then pulling themselves up the steps that led to the library. Verity paused at the top. The ground in front of her was a devastated shadow of its former self: a crazed and buckled mosaic. Verity's stomach ran cold. How could the library itself possibly stand up to the power of the Earth Witch? 'This is very bad,' she whispered.

'It's not even that good,' said Henry from right behind her.

Martha and Jeb climbed the last few steps and stood next to them, turning to survey the damage.

'The library seems to be the focus,' said Martha. Her eyes were dark.

Jeb nodded. 'Reckon the Earth Witch plans to finish them stories – one way or another.'

Verity ran across the street and pushed on the red double doors. 'The library is locked.' It had never been closed before. She shook the handles violently. Why was it shut?

Henry and Martha darted to either side of her and banged on the windows. The glass shook in the frames. Jeb ran up the side of the building to check for signs of life.

*The sound of a key turning.* They stopped.

Martha shrieked.

A figure in overalls loomed out of the doors. On its head was a canvas bag, with goggles for vision.

It pulled off the mask: *Jasper.* His hair was astray

and there was a smudge of dirt on his nose. 'Thank goodness you're here,' he gasped. 'I locked the door to stop anyone from wandering in and getting hurt.'

They followed him inside. He pulled off the workman's suit. His normally smart navy uniform was covered with sand. The gleaming buttons no longer shone.

'The sand has gone berserk. It's a lot stronger, and it's wiping out the stories faster than ever,' he said.

'Why are you wearing those clothes?' Verity asked.

'The sand was attacking me as I tried to re-ink the pages: so I pulled this makeshift protection together.'

'*Attacking* you?' said Henry. 'This just gets better and better.'

Verity shuddered. Oh, it was disgusting: the Earth Witch's remains, swarming everywhere.

Martha ran a hand through her hair.

'I think we should see for ourselves,' said Verity. 'We'll be all right for a few minutes, won't we?'

Jasper opened the secret door. 'You'll be fine as

long as you don't try to touch the books,' he said.

They followed him down the stairs to the vaulted room, the dark stone walls cold to the touch, then fell into one another at the bottom as each came to a dead stop. All four children stared in shock.

The thing that hit Verity first was the noise. It was a writhing, rasping, hiss of unhappiness. It filled her ears and flooded her head. The room was dim, as usual. But as Verity's eyes grew accustomed to the light she realized every scrap of paper was alive with sand: squirming and swirling like a terrible white infestation. It didn't cloud in the air, like the pictures she'd seen in encyclopaedias of desert storms. Instead it scurried and swarmed through each book, searching determinedly for any Original Story that was happy. In these places only, it scoured furiously.

'It can sense your thoughts,' Jasper shouted above the noise. 'I believe that's how it knew I was trying to protect the stories.'

'*Sympathy*, in the old fashioned sense of the word,' said Martha, her eyes wide, 'as in the capacity to share others' feelings. I bet Miss Cameron suspected all along.'

'*She of the Earth had a sympathetic heart: she felt the pain of others as if it were her own,*' said Verity, realizing what Martha meant. Her breath was fast and light. The sand – the Earth Witch – was more powerful now, and she could read their minds. 'This is Povl. He told us she needed more strength. He's used the wishing well to do this.'

Jasper looked confused. The children explained where they had been.

'Brother Povl, of the Usages,' said Jasper. 'I have read about him. He did not fit in with the rest of his family, so the Earth Witch offered to take him with her. I wish I had known he was teaching at your school.'

'Do you think he was the Earth Witch's sweetheart: the man she loved?' asked Martha.

'No,' said Jasper, 'in fact I have read several stories which mention that they did not get on.'

'I can see the sweetheart's point of view,' said Henry.

Above them, one of the supporting timber

266

struts that Henry, Percy and Will had put up earlier in the year creaked loudly. A sprinkle of sand hissed from ceiling to floor and a crack appeared in the plaster of the far wall. It splintered rapidly.

'Upstairs *now*,' said Verity. They ran quickly to the steps, and up to the main hall. They stood together in the middle of the space: a small, confused huddle of friends.

'This isn't safe,' said Martha. Her voice wobbled.

Verity took a deep breath. It was time to take charge. She stepped into the centre of their circle, and turned to look at each of them. 'First we've got to close off the wishing well again,' she said, with more authority than she felt. 'Henry, could you ask Percy and Will if they'll help?'

'We'll go tonight: get it over and done with,' he said.

'Once that's complete we need to keep the library from collapsing around us.' Verity looked to Henry once more. 'Is that possible?'

'I think so,' he said. 'This is an old, sturdy building. We can make it as secure as anywhere in Wellow at the minute.'

'Jasper, will you help protect the stories? I think, if we can, we should keep them in the vaulted room.'

'Absolutely,' said the customs man. 'We cannot let them be erased.'

'And me too,' added Martha anxiously.

Verity squeezed her friend's hand. 'Are you sure?' she asked.

Martha nodded insistently. 'You can rely on me.'

'Do you need Jeb's help?' Verity asked Henry.

'No, Percy and Will can muck in,' he said hurriedly.

'That should leave you free to find Povl?' She turned to face Jeb.

'I'll be happy to,' he said.

'A good task for you,' said Henry, 'out in the fresh air.'

Jeb stared thoughtfully at him.

'And I think we should use Miss Cameron's message machine to try and contact the *Bibliothecary*,' Verity added. 'Do you think you could work out how to do that?'

'I'll try,' said Henry.

'What about the town? You saw what's happening out there. The streets are devastated,' said Martha.

'We'll have to leave that to the grown-ups,' said Verity. 'The town council was tackling the subsidence before; I saw the plans at Grandfather's. They'll start again now. We have to protect the stories until the librarians complete their task.'

The rest of the Christmas holiday offered no relaxation for the children now the Earth Witch had the strength to increase her assault; each day the sand scoured the stories in the library and the town crumbled a little more.

The prophetic dreams returned with a renewed ferocity throughout the town. Within days the children could see – just walking through the streets – that everyone in Wellow was suffering from a lack of sleep.

Henry brought a range of overalls for the children to wear while they were inking over the stories. All were far more bulky and stuffy than any clothes either Verity or Martha were used to.

But they were essential for protection against the scouring action of the sand.

The vaulted room was cramped if all of them were squeezed in at once and heated up quickly with so much activity. The sand got everywhere. Each day was a relentless slog of hot, gritty hard work.

Verity was relieved to find that Percy and Will were brilliant about the whole thing. They helped Henry plug up the wishing well on Christmas evening without a murmur of complaint, then turned up each day, relentlessly full of good humour. Their ingenuity in shoring up the library knew no bounds.

'Thank you,' said Henry to his brothers one morning after they'd finished testing the security of the wooden struts in the vaulted room. The three boys were alone with Martha.

''S'all right,' said Percy, putting a drill back in its box.

'Got to help you keep an eye on that Tempest ruffian,' said Will. 'Can't have him running off with your girl.'

'She's not my girl,' said Henry automatically.

Percy ruffled his hair. 'Not having much luck tracking down that Povl blighter, is he?'

Henry shook his head. 'Him and Isaac have scoured every last inch of the town. Nothing's been seen of Povl since Christmas Day.'

'And *Tempest*'s family must know every disreputable hiding place in Wellow,' said Percy.

'Plus several more,' Will agreed.

'Don't be mean,' said Martha, looking up from her work. 'It's as if Povl's evaporated,' she said.

'Perhaps he drowned,' said Henry darkly.

No one protested at the thought.

'I'd like to wring his neck,' said Percy.

Day and night, the Earth Witch was wearing them down, removing all light and compassion. The children didn't talk about their dreams with each other any more. None of them wanted to share their innermost fears. Secretly Verity worried that even saying the words out loud might make them more likely to come true.

Eventually Jeb stopped searching for Povl.

Instead he helped re-ink the stories, like everyone else. Together they waited for the librarians, and worked.

All the adults in the town had been called upon to help defend Wellow against the sudden onslaught of earth movement. Martha's parents had been drafted in to help research possible causes, or remedies. With the dreams, and so much extra work to do, many of the grown-ups were getting just a few hours sleep each night. In every area of life tempers were frayed, and patience in short supply.

'Are there any trousers ironed?' Mr Twogood demanded one morning, as Verity sat in Henry's kitchen waiting for him to come downstairs.

Mrs Twogood had been standing over her, refusing to move until she saw Verity had finished all the jam and bread she'd put in front of her. 'Practically skin and bone,' she muttered disapprovingly.

Normally Verity would have giggled at this but this morning she was happy just to eat, and delay any thoughts about their task. Mrs Twogood's bread was delicious too, especially at the crust, and she always slathered it with a thick layer of butter under the vivid black red preserve.

Mrs Twogood stared at her husband crossly. 'You're already wearing some,' she said tetchily.

'I'll need more for tonight. Got to go straight to the earthworks at Pepperpot Point, you know that.'

'I ironed *three* pairs last night,' Mrs Twogood said. 'I press several pairs *most* nights,' she added pointedly.

Mr Twogood frowned. 'I've gone through 'em,' he said. 'The pair I left in were soaked with mud by midnight, so I came back and fetched the others.'

Mrs Twogood tutted. 'How was I supposed to know?' she demanded. 'Four of you, still, I've to wash and iron for. And you're going through trousers at that rate?'

'So there's none clean?' Mr Twogood asked.

Mrs Twogood walked over to the overwhelming pile of washing she had only just brought in from the line, and pulled out a pair of trousers. 'Give me five minutes and I'll have them ready,' she said frostily.

Her husband took them from her hands, picked

up his lunch pack and opened the kitchen door. 'I don't have time,' he said curtly.

As the door shut, and her husband disappeared from view, Mrs Twogood's face flickered between fury and hurt.

Verity jumped up anxiously, feeling terrible. 'It's a trying time,' she said sympathetically, putting an arm around Henry's mother. 'Why don't I make you a cup of tea?'

Mrs Twogood sat on a chair. She looked washed out.

The sound of Henry thundering down the stairs whistling tunelessly signalled his approach. He walked into the kitchen, and came to an abrupt halt. 'Dad being Dad again?' he said.

'I know he's doing important work for the town . . .' Mrs Twogood said, and then trailed off.

'But sometimes he's an absolute stinker,' said Henry, giving her an unsolicited hug.

Mrs Twogood sniffed. 'My little cherub,' she said, smiling fondly.

'Mu-um,' said Henry, and Verity laughed.

But he gave her another hug anyway.

The only positive side to their situation, for Verity and her friends, was that their parents were too distracted by the crumbling town, and the crippling lack of sleep, to wonder what their children were up to.

The whole of Wellow was suffering: too often, Verity would wake in the middle of the night, tears streaming down her cheeks, convinced she had lost Olivia, that Henry was dead or Martha missing. And as she staggered out of bed, gasping in panic, she would throw open the window of her room to see dozens of lights quietly burning: each keeping the silent vigil of fellow insomniacs.

Eventually Henry, Percy and Will worked out how to send a message to the first librarian. But its reply was short and to the point. Everyone but Martha was in the vaulted room when it arrived. The Twogood brothers read it first.

> *Miss Cameron will return when matters are resolved. Please protect the Stories.*
> #1

'That's it?' demanded Henry, who had slept particularly badly the previous night. He kicked a table leg.

'Perhaps they are busy,' said Jasper doubtfully, after he'd examined it himself.

Martha came running down the stairs, slightly out of breath. 'Sorry I'm late. My parents kept loitering around the house, and I had to wait until they'd left for the council office. Mother was in a *foul* mood, all because Father had left a spoon in the marmalade pot. They won't be back until well after dinner though, thank goodness.' She looked at her friends' faces: variously desolate, frustrated and just plain angry. 'What's wrong?'

Verity handed her the message, and Martha read it silently. She opened her mouth, then closed it again, too furious to speak. She put the piece of paper down. Taking off her coat, she grabbed a pen and began working.

Will read the message once more and dabbed an imaginary hanky to his eye. 'A polite enquiry about our health wouldn't have gone amiss,' he said.

'Not even a thank you,' said Percy, miming a face that had taken grievous offence.

Verity tried to smile, but the corners of her mouth wouldn't turn up. How much longer would they have to keep going?

Unconsciously she flexed and stretched her hands – to pull them out of the claw that was now their habitual shape. Even sleep didn't stop the ache. She was constantly tired, sticky and grubby. There was a permanent indent on her finger from pushing her pen. And still no end in sight.

A wave of dull panic washed over her. Would this ever be over? She turned her wooden boat charm anxiously in her fingers, then shoved the fear back down. There was no time for that. They had to keep going.

'You really must stop pushing yourself like this,' said Poppy one evening, as she helped fasten Verity's nightgown in her bedroom. 'Mother's vague, and Father's working all hours with Grandfather to help the town council, but they're going to notice *something's* wrong. You look like the walking dead.'

Verity pulled a face. 'It's only for a while,' she said, trying to sound braver than she felt.

'You're worrying me,' said Poppy. 'Oh, *just look* at your hair.' She picked up Verity's bristle brush, and began gently pulling it through her sister's tangled locks.

Verity sat down on her bed. It was lovely to have someone looking after her, for a moment.

'It's something to do with the subsidence, isn't it?' Poppy insisted. 'Why don't you tell me? I could help.'

Verity shook her head. 'It's nothing.' She didn't want Poppy to be involved; Poppy suffered enough last year, and besides, the *Bibliothecary* wasn't Verity's secret to share.

'I'm capable of a lot more than you give me credit for,' said Poppy crossly.

Now Verity felt guilty. 'I'd tell you if I could,' she said anxiously.

Poppy sighed, as she finished the final section of Verity's hair. 'I suppose I'll have to content myself with keeping an eye on Olivia.'

Verity's face cleared. 'That would be wonderful. I don't know why, but I worry about her terribly.'

'She's a heart-stealer, isn't she? Don't worry, I'll keep her safe: not particularly sure Mother's tactic of screaming hysterically will help in a genuine emergency.'

Verity smiled. The thought of Poppy watching over Olivia comforted her.

Poppy kissed her good night. 'Sweet dreams. *Try* to get some rest.'

Verity hugged Poppy in reply. But she didn't hold out any hope. Sleep brought no comfort. The visions of what the world would be like, if the Earth Witch succeeded in erasing all happy stories, never let her rest.

All too quickly the last day of the school holidays came around. Verity, Henry and Martha were numb with dread at the prospect of returning to Priory Bay.

'We can't keep this up, and go back to school,' said Henry as the three of them packed up their things to go home. 'We'll run ourselves into the ground.'

'We have to,' said Martha. She looked a bit desperate.

'I will do more,' said Jasper valiantly. He was taking over for the evening on his own, as he so often did. 'You mustn't let your studies suffer.'

Verity shook her head. 'You do too much already.'

Henry and Martha nodded in agreement.

'No one works harder than you,' said Martha.

'You're like an automaton,' said Henry.

Secretly, Verity had no idea how she and her friends would cope when they had schoolwork to do as well. The sand was unceasing. Its insistent motion never let up. Every day was a weary struggle of rising before the sun, then working relentlessly. There was no break for lunch, no time for walks, no possibility of evenings off. Each night she fell into bed, praying for rest, knowing it wouldn't come. It felt hopeless.

'We will just have to get through this,' she said, stacking a pile of books on the table for emphasis. 'People deal with worse. We will be fine.' She smiled bravely at her friends.

'We'll be fine,' Martha repeated uncertainly as they walked up the stairs to go home.

The next morning Verity, Henry and Martha trudged through the town, like world-weary spectres. The day was as bleak as their mood. A sunless sky hung over them.

The road directly outside the school had been closed off for repairs. Consequently, all pupils were required to funnel down a single narrow pathway to get in: every child shuffling slowly, and craning to inspect the progress of the men carrying out works. All the pushing and shoving did nothing to improve anyone's temper.

When they finally got through the school gates, the playground was a throng of tired and grumpy children. It seemed the dreams were making everyone suffer. Nobody looked as if they'd benefited from a holiday at all.

The only topic of conversation this morning was gossip about the missing chemistry teacher. The three friends stood together, listening dispiritedly.

'Have you heard?' said Charlotte Chiverton.

There were slight shadows under her eyes, but nothing perked her up like rumour and speculation. 'Povl Usage joined the Foreign Legion. I wonder what it is that sends the teachers here mad?'

'I was told he blew himself to pieces,' said another girl. 'Experimenting with explosives; the school is trying to hush it up.'

Charlotte nodded sagely.

Verity, Henry and Martha exchanged looks; all this talk of the missing teacher made Verity go hot and cold with fear.

As if to add to her woes, Miranda Blake approached. 'Sad to lose your little admirer?' she asked. Lack of sleep seemed to have made her thinner than ever.

'Devastated,' said Verity tersely. She stared blankly at Blake.

Miranda smiled approvingly. 'There's the spirit I admire so,' she murmured. She turned her attention to Martha. 'Here for another turn in the Verity show?' she asked, with acid sweetness.

'Back off, Blake,' muttered Martha.

'Oh dear,' smirked Miranda. 'Looks like none of us have had a good Christmas.'

Verity and her friends struggled through. It was the heat that Verity really loathed. There were days at the library when she longed to stop wearing her workman's outfit. But that would have exposed her to the sand still more, and she already had a number of nasty grazes on her neck, hands and face.

'We could try not to think about the story we're re-inking,' Martha suggested one day after school, as they worked.

'How is that possible?' Henry scoffed.

'There are mystics who learn to keep their minds blank,' she said. 'In other countries: I've read about them.'

'We could give it a go,' said Verity doubtfully. There had to be something.

But Martha was right: when they managed to clear their minds it seemed to have an effect. Jasper was best at it, of course. His stoic presence had been a comfort to them all. He never complained, hardly slept. His loyalty to their task was unflinching.

It was an odd state of being, Verity thought one Sunday afternoon in the vaulted room, as the children all scribbled on the books in their care: concentrating on the mechanics of the task, not its purpose. She found it helped to focus on other things, like walks on the downs, or dancing at Rafe's party. She glanced at Jeb, who was sitting at the same bench. Those times seemed very far away now.

Verity wiped a dusty hand through gritty hair, and winced as her work clothes chafed against one of the nastier injuries on her neck.

Jeb looked up with concern. 'Your clothes should be done up tighter,' he said, walking over to help her. 'Here, like this.' He adjusted the overalls at the back. His fingers brushed the nape of her neck.

Verity's cheeks burned.

Jeb turned her around to assess his work. 'That should help.'

Verity felt the weight of the boat charm against her throat, hanging on Jeb's chain. She pulled it out, and held it up. 'I should have given this back by now,' she said, grateful for something to say.

Jeb looked at the necklace and then directly at Verity. 'No,' he said. 'My godfather told me I should give it to someone I—' He paused.

Verity looked confused.

'He said it were a charm,' said Jeb. 'Said it were made to be so, because it were the original, not the copy. I'd like you to have it.' He hesitated. 'I think you're the right person for it.'

Verity was acutely aware of how unflattering this outfit must be. But something about the way Jeb looked at her told her he didn't care at all. She grinned instinctively.

Henry watched from the other side of the room. '*Blast.*' He picked up the pot of ink he'd just spilled on one of the stories.

'Henry,' scolded Martha, frantically dabbing at the dripping black liquid with a hankie. 'Really, of all the stupid—'

'All right,' he snapped. 'There's no need to go on about it.'

'You're supposed to rescue the stories, not obliterate them,' said Martha.

'It was an accident,' Henry bit back. Throwing

down his pen, he stormed out of the room and up the stairs.

Martha looked at Jeb and Verity standing next to each other. She bit her lip guiltily and sighed.

Jasper pulled off his mask. 'Did I miss something?' he asked.

'It's fine,' said Verity. 'I'll see if he's all right.'

'*No*,' Martha interrupted. 'That won't help.'

'But—' Verity looked confused.

Martha looked as if she were struggling for words. Which was incredibly unusual. 'Let me talk to him,' she said after a moment. 'Really: it'll be better.'

Verity opened her mouth to argue then stopped. Her head ached, she realized. 'Fine,' she said tightly. 'Whatever you think.'

Martha walked quietly along the cliff-top. Henry was sitting, hunched forward, on a pile of boulders that were waiting to be used for sea defences. The sky was a slanting flurry of grey cloud, lit up from behind by a distant sun. Its light shone silver on the water.

'You could tell her how you feel,' said Martha softly. She climbed up the rocks and sat down next to him. The wind blew her hair in all directions but underneath her face was worried. 'You might regret it one day if you don't.'

Henry buried his hands deeper in his pockets. His blue eyes were focused intently on the sea. He was growing taller by the day: his open round face increasingly angular. 'I'd regret it more if I did,' he said.

Martha sighed heavily. A momentary flicker of irritation darted across her face. 'I wouldn't mind but she's not that—'

'Don't,' said Henry, swivelling round. 'Just don't.'

# Chapter Thirteen

Despite their crippling exhaustion, Martha couldn't let go of her determination to learn more about the Earth Witch, and to discover the hidden meaning of Alice's letter.

'Lunacy,' said Henry one day. He had just caught Martha in the reading room, re-examining page 120 of the red leather-bound book. She was supposed to be having a break with Verity, but instead she was curled up in an armchair reading. Jasper was putting more wood on the fire.

She'd searched in dozens of ways for different interpretations of the words, or hidden meanings, but still there was nothing.

Verity looked up with a start from the other wing-back chair. She must have pretty much fallen asleep.

'Do you think we're supposed to find the necklace?' Martha asked. 'The Mistress used it to prove the Earth Witch's sweetheart didn't love her, but I wonder what happened to it after that?'

'You should be taking it easy,' said Henry, trying to take the book away from her.

Martha resisted with a grumpy shove. 'I'm tired of waiting for Miss Cameron,' she muttered. She picked up Alice's diary, which Verity had let her borrow. 'There *must* be another clue,' she fumed.

'Abednego will return with Miss Cameron, when the *Bibliothecary* have a solution,' said Jasper. His face spoke of absolute conviction. 'He will not let us down.'

Verity too couldn't believe Miss Cameron would desert them. But she had thought that once of Alice. It felt as if they had been abandoned to this task.

In another part of the world entirely, Miss Cameron was also trying to read, and her thoughts were equally bleak. Eventually she put the volume down: tired of looking at the same sentence over and over again.

She had woken early as usual and washed quickly. But by mid-morning the heat was overwhelming.

Abednego entered the tent. He had accompanied Miss Cameron from the port where the *Storm* was moored, and remained with her since they arrived. It was an astonishing sacrifice on his part, but she had not heard one word of complaint.

He was wearing a robe of dull gold cotton, with embroidered blue and white stripes. It had a short, stiff collar. Around his neck he wore a coral necklace. Miss Cameron had taken to wearing a shirt-dress, and a large brimmed hat.

'Are you ready?' he asked.

Despite the constant sun, Miss Cameron's face was pale. The bruised shadows under her eyes grew more pronounced each day.

'They will not let you send word,' he said. Abednego knew what troubled her mind. He could see it: preying on her, gnawing at her composure. It was as if the weather was cracking her veneer.

'The children will feel we have abandoned them,' she said, her voice laced with self-reproach.

Abednego shook his head. 'Jasper knows I will return. And he will look after them.'

He crouched down, his face level with hers. 'You love Verity, I know,' he said. 'But for now we must work here.'

Miss Cameron's head dropped. A single tear traced a path down her cheek. Abednego opened his mouth to speak.

The librarian stood up. 'We should report for duty,' she said.

He held open the canvas door of the tent for her.

Miss Cameron grimaced as she emerged. She could not grow accustomed to the heat. Sometimes she was so overcome by it, she could scarcely move. Around them, hundreds of people were also appearing from identical makeshift shelters.

It was a short walk to the building. They, and the others, poured towards the immense structure: it towered over them. But it was a speck in comparison to its location: a lone geometric shape, surrounded by a flutter of white canvas, in an eternity of rippling sand.

Slowly they shuffled through the small door.

Once inside, the vast interior of the hangar was filled with row after row of desks: each manned by busy, intelligent-looking people. Every workspace was covered with piles of paper. Lining one wall was a row of message machines: bigger and more efficient relatives to the one in the vaulted room at Wellow. Around the clock they spewed out reports; sightings, new research, further information. The job of the staff was to piece together the clues.

They were searching for the place in which the Earth Witch would re-form: for a wellspring in particular. In one of those she could tell any story she wished, and make it a reality.

They had systematically scoured the globe. New sites were discovered daily. Most were small, all were under observation: not a trace of the Keeper was to be found in any of them.

'Surely the sand in Wellow library must be getting stronger now?' Miss Cameron said to Abednego.

'Your leaders believe all hands are required here. You cannot deny the task is immense.'

Miss Cameron's scalp prickled with sweat.

A man with a clipboard approached. He wore a white robe over linen trousers. He was very senior for this task, but everyone in the *Bibliothecary* was on call at present. And it suited him to emphasize that in their organization no one was above the mission.

He looked as cool and collected as if it were a spring day by the sea. 'You have been allocated to messages from the polar regions, desk 4b, section A,' he said.

Abednego nodded and began to walk to the designated area.

Miss Cameron did not move. 'Has my request to contact the children been considered?' she asked.

'Yes, and permission is denied. Please concentrate on your work.'

'I am concerned for their welfare.'

'You do not need to trouble yourself. The Preventative Man is helping to guard the library. If we do not find the wellspring, no one will be safe.' He scribbled something down, not bothering to look at her.

Miss Cameron opened her mouth.

'The records show clearly that Wellow is the one place she will not choose,' he said.

'I think you are wrong: Wellow is special,' she replied.

A look of irritation flashed across the man's face. This loss of control, in turn, angered him further. 'I will not have this conversation every day. How dare you question the efficacy of our research methods?'

'You did not give me the chance to check before I left,' she said. 'I know the town best. Why won't you say whether you searched the original wellspring?'

Her colleague stared at her as if she had just ripped off all her clothes and danced around in a circle. This woman – this lone irritation – needed to be stopped. 'Perhaps we should tell a new story and see if that will resolve matters?' he said. His voice could have frozen fire.

Miss Cameron forgot to breathe.

The man, whose name was Simeon, permitted himself a cold stare. 'Your time there has tainted your judgement. It was a mistake to leave you in isolation for so long. Try to do as you are instructed.'

Miss Cameron walked to join Abednego. She

felt dizzy. But she knew now that her position in the *Bibliothecary* was in jeopardy. There would be no way to contact Verity, or anyone in Wellow, until this was over.

'Seriously Martha, you have to rest,' said Henry the next day. It was lunch time. School had finished early, thanks to an unexpected movement of the gym building. The children had gone straight to the library and Martha was becoming increasingly unapologetic about her desire to interpret Alice's message. She was supposed to be taking a break, but Henry and his brothers had just wandered into the main hall, in search of a picnic spot, to discover she had arranged all her work so far on a table.

Jasper was sitting next to her, helping to catalogue findings. He looked torn between guilt and his desire to help.

Percy and Will pulled up a bench and began to eat the sandwiches that had been packed by their mum, who thought they were on a fishing trip.

'Who knows whether the *Bibliothecary* are doing

anything at all?' said Martha crossly. 'Do you feel we can rely on them?'

Percy sighed. 'They're a brusque lot,' he admitted, 'but we don't have much choice. If you keep up this pace you're going to collapse.'

Verity walked in with several cups of tea and began handing them out.

Martha's intelligent round face was pale and wan. Her freckles had all but disappeared. 'There are a lot of glued pieces of paper,' she said, changing the subject. 'Perhaps something fell out.'

Verity put a cup of tea in front of Martha and felt a chill of shame wash over her. *How could she have forgotten all this time?* 'Um.' She looked up. 'Now you come to mention it, there was one piece of paper, with a knitting pattern on it.'

Martha stared at her in horror.

Jasper coughed anxiously.

Verity felt a bit sick. She ran to fetch her coat from the hooks, then sighed with relief. It was still there. 'It's just a knitting pattern,' she said quickly. 'Nothing important.'

Martha took the piece of paper and slowly inspected it.

---

**Striped winter mittens**

1 ball Aran
1 ball worsted

Use double pointed needles. Cast on 30 sts and divide evenly between 3 needles
    round one CC
        needle 1 - k to 2 sts from end, m1, k2
        needle 2 - k1, m1, k to end
        needle 3 - k across
    round two CC
    k across all needles
    round three MC
        needle 1 - k to 2 sts from end, m1, k2
        needle 2 - k2, m1, k to end
        needle 3 - k across
    round four MC
    k across all needles

---

**hcwillodrhsethidetrenciseknirvuhtyip
sauptpttunnetrehsrhncrs**

    round five CC

        needle 1 - k to 2 sts from end, m1, k2

        needle 2 - k3, m1, k to end

        needle 3 - k across

    round six CC

        k across all needles

    round seven MC

        needle 1 - k to 2 sts from end, m1, k2

        needle 2 - k4, m1, k to end

        needle 3 - k across

    round eight CC

Martha looked up and glared at Verity.

'There's nothing there,' said Verity, in reply to the silent accusation.

Martha held it up and jabbed her finger at a line of incomprehensible text hidden in the middle of the pattern. Her face was thunderous.

    round four MC

        k across all needles

```
hcwillodrhsethidetrenciseknirvuhtyip
sauptpttunnetrehsrhncrs
```

Verity's stomach lurched and her cheeks burned with shame as she studied the text.

'I'm so sorry. All that time you've spent, I feel awful. It looks like a code of some kind,' she said anxiously.

'*Obviously* it's an encrypted message,' said Martha, moving the pattern away as Verity tried to take it for a closer look.

'It's not the Gentry cipher,' said Jasper, peering over her shoulder.

'It's in one string,' said Martha casting a resentful glance at Verity, 'which will be really difficult to decode. To think of all the time we've lost—'

Something in Verity broke. Did Martha think she was the only one who hadn't slept for weeks? That only she was exhausted and scared? 'I didn't do it on purpose. And I *said* I'm sorry,' she snapped.

Martha stared at her coldly. 'Oh. I do apologize: I should get back in line. I mustn't overshadow the main character in the Verity show.'

'You could take charge of something for once,' Verity said, her eyes flashing. 'Have your own show if you like.' She'd had enough. Her mind raging, she stormed out of the library, slamming the red double doors behind her.

# Chapter Fourteen

Verity stormed down the cliff steps to Wellow harbour. Her wet cheeks stung in the icy air. She stumbled down the crumbling path, swiping furiously at her eyes. It was easy for Martha to criticize. She didn't know what it was like being the one everybody looked to for an answer. She'd hardly slept, didn't eat properly, barely saw her family . . .

The tears wouldn't stop. All the pressure, worry and fear flooded out in great, heaving sobs. She spent every day surrounded by people, but had never felt so alone. And now Martha hated her.

She stopped at the water's edge. Her hair blew back in the wind. The scent of salt air was tantalizing. She breathed in and her heart pined.

She wished she could be out there, amongst the waves. Everything felt better at sea.

The idea sang in her head. And now she'd thought of it, why shouldn't she go sailing? *Ruby* was right here in the harbour. Rafe had arranged her mooring, but Verity had scarcely had time to check her new dinghy. She scanned the rows of neatly packed boats, lined up like bobbing ducks. There *Ruby* was: her smart wooden hull sparkled.

Verity jumped down to the jetty. Despite all her cares she couldn't help smiling at the sight of *Ruby*. She was a beauty. Rafe had arranged for her name to be painted in a neat black script on the side of the hull.

Just a quick spin couldn't hurt. The water was choppy, but she could sail to the channel marker and back. She didn't have the right clothes. Her oilskin smock, navy cotton trousers and battered old deck shoes were all at home.

*It didn't matter.*

With a leap she jumped nimbly onto the dinghy in front of her, across the next and then to *Ruby*.

She investigated the locker. All the sails were

stowed tidily: fresh and new. Verity ran them up the mast, tightening and adjusting as she went. What a joy *Ruby* was. Everything on her ran smoothly. Verity's spirits lifted. She untied the painter to free the boat from her mooring. This was just what she needed.

The dinghy rocked. Verity lurched forward, grabbing the gunwale.

'I have had enough of you,' muttered a low, chill voice.

She froze as a painfully thin arm circled around her, its grip like a vice. She felt something cold and metal at her neck.

*Brother Povl.*

'If you do anything I have not told you to, I will hurt you.' His voice was rasping and hateful.

Verity's skin prickled. She felt sick. She couldn't see Povl's face, but she could smell his fusty aroma: a scent of mould and rot. She coughed. He must have been waiting for her.

Povl held a pasty white cheek to hers, and breathed in noisily. 'A pretty little neck,' he said, stroking her skin. Verity shuddered.

'Unclip the tiller and move off,' he instructed.

Verity did as she was told, filling the mainsail with wind and steering away from the quay. Her hands shook, and her fingers were numb.

'Don't pretend you can't sail,' he said, pressing his knife a little harder.

She swallowed and pulled herself together. Her mind was a storm of activity. How could she escape before they got too far? She glanced at the waves. They were white: she was surrounded by the Earth Witch, in all her millions of pieces.

Povl put a hand over Verity's on the tiller to control their direction, gripping it tight and pushing the dinghy for speed. Verity winced. He was strong for someone so thin.

Verity could see him clearly now. His short, white hair was dirtier still. His cadaverous skin was flaky, and his pale eyes glowed. He held Verity tightly, pulling her back so they could go as fast as possible. The sky was grey and turning darker. The wind whipped at her hair, strands of it sticking in her eyes. Normally she loved to sail fast, but this was petrifying.

'You are an interference,' he said. 'But there is

more than one way to rub out a happy story: by killing you, for example.'

Verity's heart skittered. Her mouth was dry. She craned her eyes, to look back at the harbour, and the town above.

'I am not minded to accept your bustling ways any more,' Povl shouted above the wind. 'A short trip along the coast will put everything right. A second tragic mishap involving *Ruby Gallant*.' He sniggered with pleasure at the thought. 'Your grandfather will never forgive himself, which is an enjoyable consequence.'

Verity tried to control her shallow breathing. He wanted to make it look like an accident. He wasn't planning to kill her straight away. She should keep him talking.

'We have nothing against the Earth Witch. We just want to protect the stories,' she said.

'That is your insolence. The stories must end. All shall suffer as she did. When my Queen re-forms she will punish the world.'

'How do you know this is what she wants?' asked Verity. 'After all these years?'

'She and I speak to each other,' said Povl. 'We are one.'

Verity felt a shiver of disquiet. There was nothing left of the Earth Witch now but millions of grains of sand. Povl really was completely unhinged. But she still had to keep him talking. 'Why are you so loyal to her?' she asked hesitantly.

Her sinister captor loosened visibly and his eyes glistened. 'Mistress Terre rescued me from Wellow. My family was addled with sloth and greed. She took me as her servant and we travelled the world together.' His face clouded over. 'But then she fell in love. He was not worthy of her. She gave up everything to protect this world and was rewarded with misery and pain.' He pinched Verity's skin nastily. His knife glinted in the corner of her eye. 'As will you be, shortly.'

They were barrelling through the water. The little red-sailed dinghy thrummed. Povl was steering very close to the wind, sailing as fast as possible. It was a risky policy that made them more likely to capsize. Verity glanced up at the burgee, the little flag at the top of the mast, which was pointing away from the mainsail. The wind had changed direction, but Povl obviously hadn't noticed. An idea flitted through Verity's mind: a dangerous idea. Her stomach shrank.

*He's going to kill you anyway*, said a cool voice in her head.

With a grunt of effort, Verity pushed down her fear and pulled the tiller swiftly towards her.

The wind caught the sail and the boom snapped across the dinghy. The boat turned violently. Verity flew through the air: plunging into the freezing white sea. She pushed herself back up to the surface, choking and spluttering for breath, then trod water. The intense cold gripped her chest.

She glanced around. In the nick of time she saw the crewless *Ruby* speeding towards her. She took a lungful of air and dived under the water to avoid her boat. Too late, the wooden hull glanced against her head. A flare of pain glowed in her skull. She came up again. The icy water squeezed her ribs.

*Ruby* had turned turtle. Povl was nowhere to be seen. Verity stared at the dinghy in shock, her head racing. Then a grim survival instinct kicked in; if she stayed in the water for even a few minutes she would freeze and drown. She swam urgently towards the upturned boat, her mind consumed by one purpose: to right *Ruby* before Povl appeared again, and get back to shore. She couldn't think any further ahead than that.

There was a loose sheet. She reached to throw it over the hull.

She screamed, a gurgling shriek of terror – half water, half air – as she felt herself dragged under the surface by her legs. Povl had her by the ankles and was pulling her down. Verity struggled angrily underneath the waves, holding her breath, but his grip was strong and pitiless.

She looked up through the murky sea, her lungs straining. They were underneath the capsized *Ruby* now. Fighting and kicking, she wriggled free and darted up to pull herself into the over-turned hull. There was just the dimmest light, and barely space for her head. She gasped noisily for air, thrashing her legs as hard as she could. Her foot hit his body. She hoped it hurt.

*She was going to die*. The thought flashed

through her head, but just as quickly she knew it couldn't end here. She hadn't said sorry to Martha, she hadn't cuddled Olivia or laughed with Henry. In a heartbeat the little wooden boat charm bobbed against her chin. *She hadn't kissed Jeb.*

Then Povl hauled her back down into the sea again. He pulled her hard by the legs, gripping her calves with his wiry hands till her muscles burned. Verity's mouth pressed to a thin, angry line. If she were going to drown here, she would make it a battle.

Completely submersed, she grabbed hold of his bony arms and began to punch and kick with all her might. She could hardly see through the cloudy white water, but it didn't matter. She hit at his bony chest, his loathsome pasty white head and stick-like arms. He raged back, punching and pummelling her under the water.

Then Verity thought she heard a muffled thud through the water and Povl's body fell limp and lifeless. She let go in shock.

Suddenly Povl's face loomed past her in the gloom. It looked as if the sea around him was clear.

He was grinning: a maniacal leer of delight. Then he sped away from her, his silhouette fading as he disappeared from view, like a ghost.

Verity shot up to the surface and gasped for air, breathing it in greedy, heaving gulps. Her lungs were on fire. Her throat was raw. She scrabbled onto the upturned hull, fear pushing her to grab a hold on the wet, slippery wood. Then she clung to *Ruby*, and stared wild-eyed at the water. But there was nothing. Povl was gone. She retched, and cried, and retched once more. The waves were calm around her.

Verity hardly knew how she righted *Ruby*. She stood on the centreboard – her body wracked with sobs – and pulled up the sopping wet sails. Then she climbed in the dinghy and sculled slowly back to harbour.

She felt numb. Her body was shuddering with cold. The sky was a sooty swirl of charcoal, as dark as her thoughts. But the waves were noticeably less pale.

'Are you all right?' a familiar voice shouted. It

was Jeb, running along the jetty. He looked white with fear; his long hair loose for once. Verity stared blankly. She didn't know how to respond.

He pulled *Ruby* towards him and lifted Verity out. Pulling off his coat, he wrapped it around her, and held her tight. She put her head on his shoulder and let the tears fall.

'I saw you,' he said, his voice catching. 'Out there, with *him*, but I was at the top of the cliff. I was terrified. I don't know what I'd do, Verity, if anything happened to you.' He stroked her hair.

Martha came sprinting across the harbour. She raced down the jetty. 'I'm so sorry,' she sobbed. Her round face was pink and blotchy. 'Are you all right? I'm such a terrible friend.' She threw her arms around Verity.

'You're the best friend I could wish for,' Verity replied, holding her tight.

Henry approached, slowly for him. 'You shouldn't make a habit of this,' he said quietly.

'I'm sorry,' Verity blurted out. 'I shouldn't have disappeared like that. It was selfish. I'll stay longer tonight to help.'

Martha shook her head. 'You won't believe it but the sand has stopped,' she said, her eyes sparkling.

Verity blinked. 'What do you mean?'

'Jeb ran into the library, to tell us you were in trouble. *And the sand stopped*,' said Martha. She grinned. 'It's quite eerie: it's so quiet in there now.'

Verity felt lightheaded with disbelief. 'But how—?'

Martha shrugged. 'We don't know,' she said blithely. 'But it's not moving.'

Verity laughed out loud with relief. She and Martha skipped an exhausted dance of joy. She sat down again quickly: dizzy with tiredness. Thoughts were darting around her head.

'Povl disappeared,' she said. 'He shot off: it was really strange. I think I might have knocked his head, but I'm not sure that's why he vanished. He looked *happy*.'

'Perhaps something's happened to make the Earth Witch change her mind?' said Martha.

'But what?' asked Henry.

'Maybe Miss Cameron and the librarians have finished their task?' said Jeb.

Verity chewed her lip. She felt burned out and confused: she wasn't sure of anything any more. Her teeth began to chatter.

'Let's get you back to the library,' said Henry, pressing her hands to check them. 'I think you'll be fine, once you've warmed up.'

'It *must* be the librarians,' said Martha, helping Verity up the cliff steps. 'They'll probably send a message in the next few days.'

Verity nodded. If Martha thought so, then perhaps it was true. At any rate, it was the first good news they'd had in months. 'We can stop working for a bit,' she said.

'We can get some rest,' said Henry.

Verity turned back to look at the ocean. It was returning to its former green, almost before their eyes. The Earth Witch was disappearing from sight. Verity could see a small chink of light on the horizon. A tiny patch of blue lit the cloud around it, like a jewel.

The four children clattered into the library. They stopped dead.

Jasper was in a corner sweeping up. Slowly they

took in the scene before them. Life had been so fraught over the last few months they'd become used to the building's deteriorating state. But now they saw it afresh. It was a scene of devastation.

'I hadn't realized quite what a mess things were,' said Martha. They all stared in dismay. Stacks of paper littered the room. Dust, mud and sand covered everything.

'We can tidy up tomorrow,' said Jasper, dropping the broom.

'I think the least we deserve is an afternoon off,' Henry agreed. Jeb nodded.

'Why don't I run to the bakery and fetch some cakes?' said Martha.

The children escaped to the reading room. Henry lit a fire while Jeb fetched more wood. Verity changed her clothes and sat in one of the thread-bare chairs, wrapped in a blanket. She could feel life creeping back into her fingers and toes. Jasper put on the kettle and made tea. Then Martha returned with Percy and Will, both carrying two very large white card boxes.

'I tried to get rid of these two, but they wouldn't stop following me,' said Martha with a grin.

'It's your peculiar charisma,' said Percy.

'I find myself compelled to trail you at every opportunity,' said Will, putting down his carton on the table and beginning to unpack an astonishing array of cakes and buns.

Verity gasped.

'We caught this one trying to skimp on the order,' said Percy.

Will tutted. 'No one likes to go hungry at a celebration,' he said, shaking his head.

'I'm not sure they sell enough cakes to satisfy you two,' said Martha dryly.

'Shut up and pass me some plates,' said Will.

Jeb walked around the room and drew the thick red curtains. They were covered in dust and dirt, but somehow it still felt comforting.

Jasper began to pass around tea in a variety of receptacles that had been to hand.

'Here's to us,' said Henry, raising his cream jug. 'I think we deserve a break.' The children and Jasper gathered in a relieved circle by Verity, who stood up from her chair, and they toasted in return.

'To us.'

Martha, who was standing next to Verity, grabbed hold of her friend and hugged her once more, beaming ecstatically. Verity closed her eyes and grinned.

They spent the rest of the afternoon playing backgammon, and the Twogood family-favourite, Okey: a Turkish game with chips of different colours and numbers. Verity looked gratefully around the dark burgundy room that was her home from home, and at her friends.

Martha was sitting on the floor, legs tucked under her, playing backgammon with Will, and trouncing him every time.

Henry and Percy were absorbed in a fierce match of Okey with Jasper and Jeb. The Preventative Man was a natural for the game of strategy and competitive feeling was obviously running high.

The warmth of the fire lit her cheeks. The air was filled with happy chat and banter. Verity felt a soft glow of happiness inside.

* * *

A few short hours later it was time to go home.

'It's Olivia's first birthday tomorrow,' Verity said, putting on her coat and scarf.

'Lovely. You'll be able to relax and enjoy it,' said Martha, as she got rid of her final two backgammon counters.

Will groaned. 'Can't someone else play this one?' he grumbled, laying out the board again.

Verity smiled. 'We're having a party for her, at lunch time.'

Martha got up and walked with Verity to the main hall. She picked up Alice's diary from the table where she'd been working. 'You should put this somewhere safe,' she said, handing it to Verity.

'I suppose we'll never know what the message was,' said Verity ruefully. 'Odd that Alice didn't leave the cipher where we could find it. She was usually a bit more straightforward than that.'

Martha looked at the diary. 'On second thoughts,' she said, 'do you mind if I keep it for another day?'

For a moment, Verity was prey to a flicker of curiosity, but it went out like a damp match. She didn't want to know; she needed to go home and sleep.

'Of course,' she said.

*In her dreams that night Verity was at Soul Bay, on the beach collecting shells. She'd found a beauty. Ridged with pale orange and brown, its delicate white underside glistened like pearl. She sat happily in the sun, digging her toes through the hot sand to the cooler grains beneath.*

*In the distance she saw Jeb. The tide was out. He was heading straight for her, across the seaweed-strewn flats. She jumped up to greet him.*

*He stopped opposite her. They were close: within an inch of each other. His green eyes looked into hers.*

*'I don't know what I'd do, Verity, if anything happened to you,' he said.*

*Then he kissed her.*

## Chapter Fifteen

Verity drew open her curtains the next morning and beamed with delight. It was light, but in her home everyone slept: presumably making up for weeks of poor sleep. What a birthday surprise for Olivia; Verity's view was a kaleidoscope of snow. She pressed her nose to the glass, and watched her breath steam the window.

The house was silent as her family rested. Verity pulled on her warmest clothes, and stole down the red-carpeted stairs. She flung open the front door and ran into the garden.

The air was silent, the street still undisturbed. Every sound was muffled. The only noise came from the snow creaking underfoot. It was another world.

She looked up. Plump snowflakes sped towards her. She felt protected by the delicate swirl of descending white. It was beautiful, and humbling. She twirled round and around, her arms flung out, laughing with relief and joy.

Fleetingly she wondered about Povl. Then she threw the worry out of her mind. Her dreams last night had been happy. No grating hiss of sand, no terrifying visions. Surely that, more than anything, meant they didn't need to worry? And she'd *slept*. She felt better rested than she had in months.

She looked up. At the corner of the road was Jeb, swaddled against the cold in a short dark coat and large boots. He looked nervous. Verity flushed.

'Would you like to go for a walk?' he asked. ''S beautiful before everyone's up.'

All thoughts of Povl, the Earth Witch and danger evaporated.

'I'd love to,' she said with a smile.

They set off in the direction of the downs. The snow had stopped, but it coated and softened everything in a glistening blanket. Verity strolled happily, gazing at the leafless trees, their ebony fingers iced with a trim of white. Her mitten-clad hands swung at her side. She felt the boat charm under her scarf and smiled at its protecting touch. She couldn't remember the last time she had been so happy.

They walked for hours, talking and laughing. The thick white clouds dispersed and the sun emerged. It lit up the swirling sky. The snow shone. Jeb kept glancing at her as if to check she were still there.

Finally they reached the cliffs. Verity climbed onto a stile that marked the gateway to the downs. She turned to look at him.

Silently, Jeb adjusted her scarf and pulled her hat over her ears, to cover her escaping curls.

Verity gazed into his vivid green eyes. Her lips parted.

'Nipper,' a voice shouted across the downs. They looked up.

It was Isaac. Jeb cursed under his breath.

His grandfather strolled towards them, smiling, a pipe of vanilla tobacco in his hand. 'Beautiful day for it,' he beamed, waving at the fantasy of white. 'Late for the time of year.'

Jeb grunted.

'Martha's looking for you both,' said Isaac. 'Something about it being urgent.'

Verity and Jeb glanced at each other. Neither moved.

'Best get going then,' said Isaac with a twinkle. 'Lucky I found you here.'

'Very fortunate,' said Jeb.

Verity couldn't stop herself smiling. 'It's nearly time for Olivia's lunch,' she said. 'But I can stop for a minute.'

'Is the library all right?' Jeb asked.

'Looked fine to me,' said Isaac.

'Better safe than sorry I suppose,' said Jeb. He took hold of Verity's hand, as if it were the most natural thing in the world. She glanced up, and he smiled. Isaac appeared not to notice.

The three of them tramped back to the town, chatting and joking. Verity gazed at the marbled sky, her fingers linked with Jeb's.

*   *   *

'Where were you?' asked Henry, when they got to the library. He was standing, bristling with frustration, by a window, in the main hall. 'Martha dragged us here first thing, and we've been searching everywhere.'

Martha and Jasper were both sitting at a table, surrounded by books and papers. The Preventative Man's neat handwriting was scribbled methodically on various notes.

'We went for a walk. Is something wrong?' she asked.

'Nothing a long stroll off a short cliff wouldn't sort out,' said Henry, glaring at Jeb.

'Can we get on please?' asked Martha, tapping her pen on the desk. She'd had a bagful of Twogood this morning.

'I can't stay. It's nearly time for Olivia's birthday party,' said Verity.

'Martha's decrypted Alice's message,' said Henry.

Verity's mouth fell open. 'I thought it would be difficult to crack?'

Martha shook her head. 'Alice *did* make it

straightforward. She left the instructions in the letter to you.' She showed Verity Alice's letter, at the front of her diary, and pointed to the first word of each line with a finger as she spoke:

*Dearest Verity,*

<u>*Please*</u> *accept this small token of congratulations. I knew I could* <u>*count*</u> *on you to do well – and sincerely trust you will look* <u>*forward*</u> *to many years more of happy sailing. Especially with* <u>*two*</u> *loyal crew members such as Henry and Martha – whose* <u>*characters*</u> *seem to me to be as staunch as their ability. The* <u>*use*</u> *of Poor Honesty over the last year has set the* <u>*pattern*</u> *for a friendship that will last a lifetime, I hope.*

*Your loving*
*Alice*

*PS. Use page 120 of your book.*

'Please count forward two characters, use pattern,' Martha said. 'Page one hundred and twenty is for decoding the message. It's a standard encryption method. You go to an instance of the letter then use the character two spaces in front.' She underlined the corresponding letters. 'There's some guesswork involved, but that's how it works.'

*Now the Earth Witch fell in love with a mortal. He knew how to touch her heart and they loved each other dearly. So strong were their feelings that they decided to marry. 'I will give my powers back,' she declared, 'and stay with you in this world until I die.'*

'What does it say?' asked Jeb.
Martha showed the translated sentence:

---

**hcwillodrhsethidetrencisekniruhtyip**
**sauptpttunnetrehsrhncrs**

*Ifthesandstopsterreisnearlycomplete.butshe*
*needsthebloodstone*

If the sand stops Terre is nearly complete.
But she needs the Bloodstone.

---

Verity felt blindly for a chair, and sat down. 'Mistress *Terre*, that's what Povl called the Earth Witch.' She paused. 'So we're not safe. We're not safe at all.'

The room felt darker, as if everything was closing in on her. Her mind was heavy with fear. It wasn't over: it was just beginning.

'The Bloodstone has been missing for years,' said Jeb.

Martha pushed her glasses up her nose. 'As a matter of fact it was the artefact Jasper was looking for last year. Luckily he brought his research with him.' She indicated a pile of books and papers on the other side of the table.

Verity's heart leapt. 'You mean you already know where it might be?' she said eagerly.

But the customs man shook his head. He looked miserable. 'The trail was dead.'

Verity tried not to look as disappointed as she felt. 'Well, I'm sure you've discovered more about it today,' she said hopefully. 'You worked out the location of the Storm Bringer from old records.'

Jasper opened his mouth to continue, but Henry

interrupted. 'Not really,' he said curtly. 'We spent most of our time looking for you.'

'I was fine.' Verity tugged her hair, confused and frustrated.

'You nearly drowned yesterday,' said Henry. 'So we were slightly concerned.'

Martha suppressed a wave of irritation. Henry had refused to let any of them get on with learning more about the Bloodstone until they found Verity. He'd been totally obstinate. Jasper had found the whole situation inexplicable. 'Water tainted by the Bloodstone was used to poison people, so clearly she wants it for that reason,' she said, rearranging some of the books in front of her to hide her bad temper.

'I suppose it would be easier than destroying all the happy stories,' said Jeb.

Verity took one of the titles from Martha. It was open at a colour illustration of the Bloodstone.

'It looks like a heart,' said Henry.

'No it doesn't,' said Martha.

'I mean an anatomical heart, dimwit.'

Verity stared at the drawing. She wrestled a terrible sinking feeling.

In the same pile of books was the selection of fairy tales from the reference section. Verity searched for the picture of the Earth Witch.

'*Save for her heart which stayed blood-red from loving still,*' it said underneath.

The scratchy lines of the monochrome illustration contrasted vividly with the gruesome red heart.

'It *is* her heart,' said Verity.

Jasper, Henry, Martha and Jeb stared at her blankly.

'The Earth Witch turned to granite, but her heart stayed red. As Henry says, it would look just like the Bloodstone. Presumably, when she was smashed to pieces, it didn't shatter and, somehow, the Mistress kept it.'

Martha looked a little nauseous.

'How could it have ended up in the hands of the Gentry?' asked Jasper.

'I've no idea,' said Verity. 'But it feels like the right explanation. That was the Mistress's level of cruelty.'

She glanced up at the clock. She was finding it hard to think straight, her head was buzzing. *It hadn't finished.* She wasn't sure she could keep fighting. The others were talking excitedly to each other, already convinced by her theory. Verity could hear them, but it was as if she wasn't in the same room.

'She doesn't want it to poison people. Povl wished for strength so the Earth Witch could re-form. But in order to be whole presumably she needs her heart too,' said Martha.

'The Bloodstone is the missing piece of her jigsaw puzzle,' said Jasper.

'So we've got to find it before she does,' said Martha. She picked up the book and stared at the illustration.

Henry pressed his temples with the fingers of one hand. For a moment he looked much older than his years.

Verity shook her head. She couldn't cope any more. 'I have to go,' she said shakily. 'I can't miss Olivia's birthday party. I'll be back later.'

She stood up, scraping her chair, and lurched

towards the door. She couldn't breathe. She felt as if time had ground to a halt. She glanced back at Jeb, standing near Martha, and her face softened. He winked just slightly in reply.

Henry watched with narrowed eyes, his jaw line set as Verity disappeared from the library.

Martha stood up too. She'd really had enough.

'I think I should—' Jasper began.

'If you don't mind, I'm going to work on my own for a while,' Martha said firmly, exiting the main hall and heading for the reading room.

'Could you give us a minute?' said Henry to the customs man.

Jasper looked completely nonplussed. 'Perhaps I should go to my quarters,' he said, in a disappointed tone.

'Great,' said Henry.

Jasper walked slowly to the back of the main hall, wondering if perhaps he had upset the children. But Henry and Jeb were oblivious to his worries.

As soon as the room was empty, the youngest Twogood turned to more pressing matters.

'What do you think you're playing at?' he demanded.

'How do you mean?' said Jeb.

'Everyone's familiar with the Tempest reputation,' said Henry. 'Verity deserves better.'

Jeb stared silently at the ground. 'I suppose you would think that,' he said. He looked hurt.

'Yes I do. You've got your pick of girls in Wellow. Leave her alone.'

'Right,' said Jeb. He pulled on his coat and left.


Verity didn't know how she got through Olivia's birthday tea. She wouldn't have missed her sister's celebration for the world, but her mind wandered constantly, and her vision kept blurring.

She sat with the baby girl on her lap, as her family sang together in the dining room, a mouth-watering display of sandwiches, cakes and scones laid out in front of them.

What would happen to the world if the Earth Witch found her heart? They had to get the Bloodstone before she did. Verity stroked her sister's plump arms, and closed her eyes. But her worries crowded in more insistently.

She tried to eat, but ended up hiding her food in the sideboard when no one was looking. She'd throw it away later. Olivia pulled Verity towards her and gave her a funny little flat-mouthed kiss, and her eldest sister closed her eyes to hide her tears, smiling with brittle determination.

But once the birthday candles had been blown out, and Olivia taken upstairs to bed, Verity put on her coat and scarf and headed to the library once more.

As she walked down her street, a fleeting image of Jeb flashed through her mind. She smiled briefly. He, at least, was a glimmer of sunshine amongst the clouds.

She turned the corner and jumped, nearly walking straight into Miranda Blake who was wrapped against the cold in a soft woollen coat with fur hat and matching muff. Every item of clothing was pristine.

Her gaze trailed down to Verity's shoes, which were scuffed, then up once more to her hat, which had a snag in it. 'Pleasant walk on the downs?' she murmured.

Verity was silent: she needed an encounter with Blake like a hole in the head.

Miranda's poise was unassailable. 'I was saying to Twogood only this morning, you really should stop throwing yourself at Tempest,' she said. 'He must find it embarrassing.'

Verity closed her eyes. No wonder Henry had been in such a vile mood if he'd been cornered by Blake.

'I do hope Jeb didn't get carried away in the moment,' Miranda whispered softly. 'That happened to poor Louisa Green. Then he realized it was all a terrible mistake. She was devastated.'

Verity said nothing. Don't listen, she told herself. She's poison.

'I'm sure he is *fond* of you,' Miranda persisted. 'But you can't think you're the kind of girl he'd want to be seen with? I mean, look at you.'

Verity stopped in her tracks. It was true that she had no idea what Jeb saw in her.

Miranda studied her with pity. 'Penny dropped,

has it?' she said. 'He's got to be nice to you. Isaac Tempest is your grandfather's best friend. Did he seem uncomfortable with you at first?'

Verity's cheeks burned. 'Jeb is just a family friend,' she replied.

'I know,' said Miranda smugly as she walked away.

Verity was nearly at the library when she spotted Jeb. She wasn't sure whether to be pleased or dismayed. She was consumed with misgivings: she had analyzed every minute of her walk with him. Jeb, in turn, had been running an errand for Isaac and was lost in self-reproach. Verity was too good for him.

They spotted each other at the same moment. Both flushed.

Verity felt sick with nerves. Would Jeb prove Miranda wrong, and be happy to see her?

Jeb stared silently at Verity. What had he been thinking? Twogood was right. She deserved better.

'Hello,' she said.

Jeb shifted awkwardly. She looked uncomfortable. He said nothing.

*It was true*, Verity thought to herself, he *was* embarrassed by her. A little piece of her died inside. How could she have thought a boy like him would look at her?

'I should get on,' he said. She'd probably realized he was a dead loss.

Verity nodded ever so slightly. She stared at the ground when he passed. Neither saw the other's glance.

She walked into the main hall, blinking back tears, only to be met instantly by Henry.

'Is Tempest going to be a permanent fixture?' he asked.

'I shouldn't think so,' she replied, in a flat tone.

'Because I have better things to do with my time than mix with that family, and so do Percy and Will,' Henry continued.

Verity's lip wobbled. 'Do you mind if we talk about this later?' she said, trying not to let her voice break. 'I'm not feeling great at the minute.'

'It looked like you were on top of the world this morning,' said Henry.

Verity walked over to a table where Martha had

left a huge pile of books, some open, some waiting to be worked through. She breathed out slowly. 'I doubt you'll have to put up with Jeb any more.'

'Oh really? You two seem quite cosy; nice little walks, the occasional dance.'

'It's not like that,' she said.

'Don't lie to me,' he snapped. 'I heard you at the Christmas Party, tripping the light fantastic. *Perhaps if we were grown up we could travel the world together, sail to far-off places . . .*'

Verity was astounded. 'I'm sure I didn't say anything like that.' A terrible suspicion crept upon her. She remembered *thinking* something of the kind. Had she really said it out loud? Her whole body flushed with embarrassment.

She paused. 'Is there some other reason why you don't like him?' she asked.

Henry's cheeks turned puce. 'I'm going home,' he said, slamming the doors on his way out.

Verity sat down with a bump at the table. She stared hopelessly at the work in front of her. It was a passage from the red leather-bound book, about the Earth Witch. The words swam into view:

*In his place stood her sister, and in her hand was
the Earth Witch's necklace. 'He does not love you,'
she crowed.*

Verity's face crumpled. Folding her arms on the
table, she dropped her head and dissolved into
tears.

Jasper walked into the room, then immediately
backed out.

'It's all right,' said Verity, hastily wiping her eyes.

'I'll fetch Martha,' said Jasper, disappearing.

Her friend appeared seconds later, looking
concerned, which just made Verity cry all the more.
'It's not important,' she said, between sniffs.

'Why don't you tell me, and we'll see?' Martha
said, taking her hand.

Verity stared helplessly at her friend. She looked
so composed. As if nothing this trivial would ever
trouble her. 'I went for a walk with Jeb,' she said.

'Yes, you told us,' said Martha.

Verity gulped. 'We held hands,' she said.

'How exciting. Jeb's always liked you, of course.'

Verity felt baffled. How could Martha say that

as if it were perfectly obvious? 'I think he's changed his mind,' she replied quietly.

'Oh dear.' Martha gave her a hug. Her sleek hair smelled fresh and clean.

Verity closed her eyes. 'This is really the last thing I should be worrying about, and now Henry's in a mood with me too,' she admitted.

The two friends held each other silently, and eventually Verity stopped crying.

Martha dried her tears with a neatly pressed handkerchief. 'Henry will snap out of it,' she said firmly, pinning Verity's unruly brown hair back in its clasp. 'He's just tired. And Jebediah Tempest is the twit, not you. Honestly, he'd be lucky to have you.'

Verity giggled, with a sniff. 'Can we go for a walk?' she asked.

# Chapter Sixteen

The next day Verity woke early. She lay in bed, staring dully at the wall and listening to the sounds of a day starting outside. Light was creeping in around the edges of the curtains. But the promise of a new morning couldn't cheer her: the events of yesterday filled her head, blocking out all happy thoughts. Finally, she made herself roll heavily out of bed, and dress. There was work to be done. But first she had an errand to run.

An hour later, when Verity got to the library, she found Jasper sitting alone in the corner of the main hall. In front of him, on a large pine table, were piles of paper, opened books and boxes of documents.

'I decided I should start work,' he said, looking

up. 'There is a small chance I may have missed a clue to the Bloodstone's location.'

'I'm sorry I was so upset yesterday,' said Verity. 'We were all wrapped up in our own problems. It wasn't fair.' She felt terrible: Jasper of all people didn't deserve such treatment after the way he'd supported them.

She put her bag down on the table. 'I stopped at the Manor to fetch this for you. It's been a while since you told me you'd like to see it, but perhaps you'll feel it's better late than never?'

She pulled out the Heartsease Cup. Grandfather had helped her wrap it in a blanket.

'We have had a number of things to contend with since that conversation,' said Jasper, standing up. 'How kind of you to remember.' His eyes shone. He took the old-fashioned goblet from Verity and turned it around in his hands. The lead crystal sparkled vividly. 'It is just as curious as the illustrations imply,' he said.

'I wondered if it might hold a clue,' said Verity.

'It might,' said Jasper. 'Although the Bloodstone

has proved to be an elusive artefact: it was the one on which I gathered the least documentation. We were duped into following a false trail.'

'Could someone have broken it, perhaps?' asked Verity. 'And kept it a secret?'

Jasper shook his head. 'It was famously indestructible. Not even diamond could cut it.'

Still standing, Jasper pointed to the men depicted in the wrought silver handle. 'The three victims: not wishing to hear, speak or see the truth.'

Verity came and stood next to him. She stared at their agonized faces.

*In water there is the truth.* She remembered her argument with Rafe. 'It comes apart,' she said. 'Grandfather showed me.'

'I believe it detaches like so,' said Jasper. He expertly unscrewed the two halves, then looked at the hidden inscription – *in aqua veritas* – and smiled like a little boy.

'Is there anything about the Gentry you don't know?' asked Verity.

'There are many things I would like to

understand.' Jasper looked down at the table. 'That is why I was particularly keen to recover the Bloodstone: there was a part of me that wanted to use it.'

Verity jolted, aghast. 'To poison someone?'

Jasper looked shocked. 'Certainly not,' he said. He looked a bit hurt.

'To poison yourself?' she asked, confused.

'The Bloodstone was not always fatal,' said Jasper. 'Nor was that the intention of its use: it depended how much water you ingested. No, I wanted to understand how other people *feel*. It has always been such a weakness of mine.'

Verity stared wordlessly at him.

'I thought you knew,' said Jasper. 'Drinking water that had been touched by the Bloodstone showed you what was in other people's minds.'

'The only thing I've read was that the water poisoned people,' said Verity.

'*Legends and Myths of the Gentry, Pamphlet Nineteen?*' he said.

Verity nodded.

Jasper shook his head crossly, putting the cup

down on the table. 'That publishing house has a lot to answer for: quite scurrilous.'

'It showed you what other people *thought*,' said Verity slowly.

'I believe the whole experience was traumatic for many,' he said. 'The engraving was a play on words. *Drink from me* if you can stomach the sickness, but also if you are able to bear knowing what others think of you.'

Verity's mind raced. 'And you came to a dead end?'

'I have often wondered if the false trail was left by the Mistress,' said Jasper. 'It bore her hallmarks and led to the Indies – where I found the Storm Bringer. But when we investigated, it became clear the Bloodstone could never have been there.'

'What about Wellow? That's where it was last seen?'

'I have records describing the searches of a meticulous investigator,' said Jasper, leaning forward to pick up a folder of documents. 'He scoured every inch of the town and found nothing.'

'Does Martha know all of this?' Verity asked.

'I tried to tell her, but Henry kept interrupting. He was in a very bad mood,' said Jasper.

The strange argument with Henry shot through Verity's mind. *'Perhaps if we were grown up we could travel the world together, sail to far-off places . . .'*

An image of Henry at the Christmas party flashed through her head: eyes watering and breath ragged.

A terrible suspicion struck her. She pulled up a chair and sat down, her head racing. 'That would be just like the Mistress,' she said, 'to make people believe the Bloodstone definitely wasn't in Wellow if it *was.'*

She thought of what it meant and shivered with embarrassment. There she had been, prancing about with Jeb on the dance floor while all the time . . .

'Henry was sick,' she said to Jasper urgently, 'and I think, somehow, he read my thoughts: I think he drank water that was contaminated by the Bloodstone.'

Jasper's mouth fell open.

A fleeting vision shot through Verity's mind. A tall thin man dressed in a dark suit standing by a pump in her grandfather's garden: and a fox mask with a look of ruthless cunning. She stood up. 'We have to go to the Manor,' she said, grabbing at Jasper.

'What about the others?' he asked. 'Shouldn't we wait?'

Verity shook her head. 'I think I know where it is, or at least where it was on Christmas Eve. But it could be gone by now.'

'We mustn't waste any more time,' said Jasper earnestly. He scribbled a hasty note and they ran out of the library together.

Jasper didn't press Verity for more answers as they sprinted through the town: he seemed happy to follow. And in truth, Verity couldn't have explained right now. Her mind was racing.

Jasper's eyes widened as they walked up the drive so familiar to him from countless illustrations. 'Wellow Manor,' he said breathlessly. 'What a shame I cannot be here in happier circumstances.'

Verity led Jasper through the wooden front door, shattering the heavy silence of the stone-floored hall with her calls for Rafe. But there was no reply to her echoing voice.

She looked around, her hands twitching with frustration. The hallway clock solemnly marked the passing seconds. Would Grandfather mind her searching his house? Well, it couldn't wait: this was important.

'Where are we going?' asked Jasper, as she ushered him to the kitchen, and the back door.

Verity's thoughts were quite clear now, to her at least. Everything she suspected came out in a rush as she led him across the kitchen garden. She could see the asparagus beds from here. 'I should have realized at the Christmas Celebration,' she gabbled, 'when Grandfather explained the pump hadn't been used since he was married to the Mistress. He said, you see, that she found the water from it *refreshingly insightful*. Which was just her kind of peculiar joke.'

'Povl must have known, somehow, that she hid it at the Manor. Then presumably he came to the party, in the fox mask. I *thought* he seemed familiar.

But his voice was different . . . and I didn't know what he was really like then.'

Jasper stopped in mid-step, his forehead furrowed. Verity realized she wasn't making any sense.

'I think the Mistress stole the Bloodstone from Grandfather when they were first married,' she explained, 'and hid it at the bottom of the well in this garden. It's a brilliant spot: amongst a collection of other stones. And I think it's been there ever since, all these years.'

Jasper's mouth formed a perfect circle of astonishment.

Verity stopped. They were at the old pump. 'I think it draws from here.' She pointed to the well. It was still fenced off.

'It's dry now. But I wonder if Povl gave Henry a tiny splash of water from it. He had some in a flask at the party: *if* he was the man in the fox mask. I suppose he would have thought it amusing to check the effects on someone else. Then I'm sure Henry heard what I was thinking. I *can't* have said it out loud.'

Jasper was standing perfectly still, and staring at

the pump. 'I will try it,' he said at last. 'There is no need for you to drink stale water.'

Verity started to protest, and then realized Jasper would never give in on this point. 'Only the tiniest amount then,' she said. 'It made Henry very sick.'

Jasper put a finger to the pump. A single drop appeared at the rim of the tap. He tasted it. They stared at each other silently. Seconds passed.

'I don't think it took long to have an effect on Henry,' said Verity.

The customs man's eyes widened and he dropped to the ground. His pupils were disturbingly large. 'I don't intend to be so aloof,' he said quietly. 'Is that really how I am?'

Verity felt terribly guilty. These were her thoughts he was reading.

Now Jasper looked puzzled. 'Jeb Tempest?' he said. 'But what about Henry?'

Instantly Verity tried to clear her head, which of course was impossible.

Jasper's complexion turned pale, and then distinctly green. He closed his eyes, then opened them again: that had obviously made things worse.

'This should be over soon,' said Verity. She reached out to reassure Jasper. And in an instant saw he was himself once more.

Jasper leapt to his feet. 'The Bloodstone really is here,' he said. He and Verity grinned at each other.

'I can't believe we found it,' beamed Verity.

'And Povl hasn't had a chance to move it,' said Jasper.

Verity came back to earth. 'We've got to get it now,' she said anxiously. 'It's not safe to leave it.'

'Does your grandfather have any rope?' asked Jasper. 'I could jump down, but I'll need a way to climb back up.'

'I'm sure there's some in the stables,' said Verity.

'Excellent.' Jasper began to run towards the Manor. The stables were on the other side.

Verity turned to follow.

'No,' Jasper shouted back excitedly. 'You stay there. We don't want to lose it now.'

Verity frowned, but he was right: they should

keep the Bloodstone's hiding place in sight now they knew where it was.

'I won't be long,' Jasper called over his shoulder, as he disappeared around the corner of the house. 'We'll have the Bloodstone in no time.'

# Chapter Seventeen

Verity paced the kitchen garden path as Jasper hurried off. She whiled away a few minutes inspecting the various bushes near the wall, and then sat on a border, her stomach tight. The earth smelt fresh and wet. She could see the individual blades of grass, the clover and other small green plants; each stalk spotted with an occasional drop of dew. An ant was making its way laboriously from one leaf to another.

Verity froze. She could hear a scrabbling of stones from the well and a strange, keening singing.

She crawled nervously towards the dark pit and peered hesitantly over the edge. She could see the light of a torch, searching in the darkness. It illuminated a streak of pure white hair, dappled with dirt and mud. A round, white face looked up.

It was Povl.

Verity felt every last scrap of blood drain from her face.

'Hello Verity,' he said, evidently enjoying her shock.

'You're back,' she whispered. Of course he was. They would never be rid of him.

'Now my mistress is nearly whole I have returned for her heart,' said Povl. He smiled: a curved blade of a grin.

Verity jumped up in horror, glancing around anxiously for someone, anyone. She felt sick with panic. This lunatic was going to trip them at the final hurdle.

'Shall I come up?' he asked nastily. She took a step back, even though she knew his threat was empty. The well wasn't terribly deep, perhaps fifteen feet, but he was still too far below her to climb up the slippery stones. There must be a tunnel entrance down there.

'*Jasper*,' she screamed at the top of her voice.

She stared about her, straining her ears. No

reply. The stables were on the other side of the Manor. She could run to fetch him, but by that time Povl could have found the Bloodstone and disappeared.

'I shall be long gone by the time your friend arrives, girly. Then my mistress and I will begin our revenge on the world,' Povl crowed.

Verity's chest clenched, her hands tensed to claws. She threw a stone angrily down the well. Another came spinning back up, slicing past her head with mystifying accuracy. She flinched.

'*Jasper,*' she screeched.

Nothing.

Verity stared at the well opening. With a sense of complete and utter terror, she realized she had to go down there to stop him.

'Come here, do,' sneered Povl, as if reading her mind. 'I have a friend who wishes to meet you, and he likes the darkness. It makes him shine prettily.'

If she tried to fight Povl, in the well, he would kill her. But if she stayed here, he would take the Bloodstone and use it to bring the Earth Witch back to life.

'*Death and destruction, no hope, no joy . . .*' Povl sang tunelessly.

A vision of the nightmarish dreams reeled through Verity's head. They were what would happen to the world if the Earth Witch was whole once more.

Perhaps she could drop something on him? Verity wished Henry were here. She saw Povl crouching on the floor, lit by his torch and feeling with one skinny hand for the Bloodstone. Suddenly his face contorted. 'Mistress, I will have it for you in a moment.'

Verity's heart lurched. Everyone would suffer if she didn't act now. She dropped to the ground and began to lower herself, feet first, over the edge and into the well. Was the structure even safe? But she had to delay this deranged man for as long as she could.

Povl stopped his search and looked up at her with interest. He grinned viciously. 'What a treat: to kill you first will be sweeter still. I have formed a particular hatred of your solemn little face.' He stood up and clawed eagerly at her legs, pulling her the final few feet to the bottom of the well.

Verity landed clumsily, then scrabbled to stand, her back against the wall.

Povl was opposite her, his head tilted. His torch was still on the floor but as Verity's eyes grew accustomed to the dark she could see he wore the same filthy polo neck jumper and corduroy jacket. His face was a mottled, chalky white: his eyes paler than ever.

'You mustn't put the Earth Witch's heart back,' she said quickly. 'She wants to make the world a kind of hell. Surely you can see that?'

'It is only what this ungrateful realm deserves,' said Povl.

'But why?' asked Verity. She had to keep him talking.

'If she had been released from her duty to the world I would have her now,' Povl spat. 'She was everything. I loved her. The world must hurt as she did.'

His liverish lips glistened in the dark. 'I suppose you think you can stop me,' he said. 'Insolent fool: the heart belongs to my mistress. You will help me find it.' He grabbed Verity, putting his knife to her neck. With his other hand he pushed her to the ground: forcing her onto all fours in a vile-smelling pool of water, mud and sand.

'Search for it,' he snapped.

'What does it look like?' she asked, her arms shaking.

'You will know it when you touch it,' he sneered.

On her hands and knees, Verity sifted through the slippery dirt with her fingers, hands grazing over the stones. Her skin crawled. She reached out further. Suddenly she was horribly and violently sick. She blinked in the darkness, her mouth rancid. The smell was disgusting. But it was the noise that really threw her: it felt as if a thousand people had shouted in her head at once.

Povl smiled. 'Again,' he commanded. She brushed her hand over the same area, the stones wet with her own vomit. She gagged. Her stomach heaved again. The voices were louder still.

Povl crouched down next to her. With the knife still casually pointed at her throat, he highlighted one particular spot on the ground.

Verity stared in astonishment. There it was: a polished, vivid red stone shaped like a real heart. The Bloodstone. It shone in the wet and dark.

Povl pulled a simple cloth bag from his pocket and handed it to her. 'In this,' he said.

Verity steeled herself to reach for the Earth Witch's heart. She picked it up. The babble flew around her head. She retched. The voices were relentless. Her vision turned a scrambled black and white. With one last gut-wrenching heave of her stomach, she dropped it in Povl's bag then sat, exhausted, against the wall of the well, her head tipped back, retching and gasping for breath, oblivious to the smell and filth.

Povl kissed the cloth bag slowly then put it in his jacket pocket. He swivelled to face Verity; his mouth a rictus grin. As her stomach calmed, Verity wondered what she could possibly do to delay him now.

But Povl was in no hurry. He continued to squat: playing lovingly with his knife, turning it in his hand. 'I will kill you slowly,' he said.

Verity's mind raced. 'You must have loved her

very much,' she blurted out, her body trembling. She could feel the chill of the stones through her clothes.

Povl paused. A flicker of raw emotion darted across his face. 'No one will ever know the depth of my feelings for her,' he said quietly.

'And she loved you in return?' Verity asked.

Povl cast his eyes to the ground. 'As her servant,' he said.

'I read that she was beautiful,' said Verity.

'She lit up the world,' said Povl. 'Her skin was caramel, her locks pure gold.' He leant across and stroked Verity's cheek with his knife; trailed the flat of the blade over her hair.

Verity froze. Not one part of her moved. But she had to keep him talking. 'How have you lived so long?' she asked, the words spilling from her mouth.

'The Keepers have their ways, for those of us who serve them.' Povl gently traced a path with his knife down Verity's coat until the point was resting at her heart.

Verity stared wordlessly; her chest pounding.

Every minute Povl spent talking was sixty seconds of hope. But she couldn't see any way to escape this.

She glanced up. The circle of daylight at the top of the well was so close, and yet completely beyond reach. She would never climb out of here now.

A silhouette appeared. Jeb. Verity's heart soared.

Jeb jumped down into the well, a look of fury on his face, and landed confidently on his feet. He held a piece of wood. With one swift blow, he hit Povl and knocked the strange, thin man to the ground. Povl's head hit the stones with a crunch.

'The Bloodstone: it's in his jacket,' said Verity urgently.

Jeb turned Povl over roughly and ferreted through his clothes until he found the cloth bag. He checked it and put it in his own pocket.

Verity felt dizzy. She closed her eyes.

Jeb knelt over her. His face crumpled with fear. 'What were you thinking?' he said.

A sound. They turned to see Povl conscious once

more. Her emaciated enemy had already pulled himself up.

'*No!*' Jeb shouted.

Povl had already disappeared. So there *was* a tunnel entrance down here, thought Verity. She heard his laughter echoing as he ran. Jeb looked torn. But she knew Povl now. He would melt into the darkness like a wraith . . . and return for the Bloodstone when it suited him.

She heard voices above them: Henry, Martha and Jasper too. 'Is Verity there?' Henry shouted. She could hear the fear in his voice. There was jostling and commotion, a few brief instructions.

A rope dropped into the well. Jeb took hold of it. 'I don't think she's hurt,' he yelled.

Henry scrambled down. He crouched on the floor, oblivious to the water and mud, and began checking her. 'Can you move your fingers here? And this, your arm?'

'I'm fine,' she insisted, embarrassed: she was filthy and must stink. But her voice was croaky.

Henry's face did a dance of anger and relief. '*Of all the idiotic things to do.*' He swore. 'Are you planning to pull a stunt like this every year?'

'We've got the Bloodstone,' she said with a deliberately winning smile.

Henry burst out laughing. 'I wouldn't expect any less, Verity Gallant,' he said.

Jeb coughed. The well was extremely cramped with three of them in it.

Henry started organizing briskly. 'You go first,' he said to Jeb, 'and I'll follow Verity.'

Jeb looked as if he was about to argue, but then he nodded and took hold of the rope. He climbed up it in a few short pulls.

Verity watched him disappear.

'I'm sorry,' said Henry, as soon as Jeb was gone. 'I was in a foul mood, and took it out on you.'

Verity smiled at him. 'It's fine,' she said. 'Usually it's me being unreasonable.' She pushed down a shudder of embarrassment at the thought of their argument: *he had heard her thoughts*. But it wasn't his fault.

'Jeb isn't as bad as you think he is,' she said tentatively. 'He's always been there to help . . . and he was first here just now.'

Henry reflected that this was typical Tempest luck but Verity pursued her advantage. 'I would really like it if you could try to give him the benefit of the doubt,' she said gently, 'as my friend.'

Henry nodded. *As my friend*. 'Of course,' he said. 'No more bad blood between us.'

Verity smiled and hugged her friend once again. He felt reassuringly solid. 'I don't know what I'd do without you,' she said.

Henry grinned. His eyes were pale in this light. 'You'd be devastated, I'm sure.'

It didn't take many minutes more for Verity to clamber back up to ground level and fall into the arms of Martha. Together the two girls jumped around, holding each other excitedly.

'We've got it,' shouted Martha. 'We've really got the Bloodstone. Everything's going to be all right.'

Verity giggled.

Jeb grinned as he helped Henry up from the well. Then he offered his hand.

Henry shook it in reply. 'Thank you,' he said sincerely, 'for helping Verity.'

Jeb pulled on his scruffy grey jumper. 'You'd've done the same, I know,' he said.

Verity glanced across the kitchen garden to see Rafe running towards them with Jasper at his side. Rafe's flowing silver hair was distinctly awry and he was still wearing a navy smoking jacket. 'Jasper's told me everything. You've found the Bloodstone? What on earth was that teacher up to? And that *blasted* well,' he ranted, looking terribly worried. He pulled Verity towards him and gave her a hug.

Verity rested her head on his chest. Slowly it was dawning on her what a narrow escape she'd had.

'I'm fine,' she said, trying to reassure him, and herself.

'What will your parents say?' Rafe said.

Verity blanched. Her mother did always make such a fuss about things. She felt a wave of tiredness wash over her.

'Perhaps Verity could stay at the Manor tonight?' said Martha. 'It might be safer . . .'

Rafe patted Martha appreciatively on the arm.

'There seems no sense in worrying them unnecessarily,' he said.

'That would be lovely,' said Verity. She looked around the kitchen garden. It seemed a lifetime since she'd last seen it. She wasn't sure anywhere felt safe at the moment. But at least here she wouldn't have to explain the morning's events to her parents.

'Quite extraordinary: the Bloodstone being in this well all these years,' said Rafe, shaking his head.

'Can we see it?' asked Martha.

Jeb took the cloth bag from his pocket and dropped the Bloodstone onto the lawn. They all crouched down in a circle to peer at the vivid red stone, the size of a large fist, nestling amongst the lush green grass. It looked exactly like a heart.

None of them said a word, not even Henry.

'How can we keep it safe?' asked Verity eventually.

'We'll put it in my study, under lock and key,' said Rafe.

'But Povl could come back at any time,' said Verity anxiously.

'I will arrange for the Manor to be guarded,' said her grandfather.

'Once the *Storm* returns,' said Jasper, 'Abednego and I can take it away.'

'How can you hide it?' asked Verity. Now that the Earth Witch didn't have the Mistress holding her back it was a ticking time bomb. Jasper said nothing, obviously reluctant to be drawn.

'No one's mind works quite like Jasper's,' said Henry. 'I'm sure he's got a plan. He had a solution for the Storm Bringer, and that was nearly as dangerous, in a different way.'

But the Storm Bringer hadn't been someone's heart once. Verity felt a pang of sympathy for the Earth Witch: doomed to spend her years scattered around the world as sand. She yawned, her vision swirling.

'Let's get you back indoors,' said Rafe to Verity, taking her by the arm, 'and I will contact Tom.'

Rafe arranged for Verity to be put in the room that overlooked the garden, above his study. And for once Verity decided to do nothing for the rest of the

365

day. Instead she read on her own: a reward to herself. Just like old times, she thought to herself with a smile, remembering her life before Henry.

In the evening she ate a tea of boiled eggs and toast at a table in her temporary bedroom, enjoying the silence and feeling safe in this quiet room. Rafe wouldn't eat until much later.

Just as she was finishing, the door opened. It was her grandfather. 'Now, are you comfortable for the night?' he asked.

'Very,' said Verity.

'Good, good,' he replied, walking towards the bed.

'Grandfather,' she said. 'I think Brother Povl can be quite determined.' She tried to push the worst memories of her persistent enemy to one side. Panicking wouldn't help.

Rafe took her hand and led her to the bedroom window. They were at the front of the house with a view across the lawn to the cliff edge and sea beyond. Below them, to the right, were two men standing near the front door. She recognized one of them from around the town. A third was doing a circuit of the building. All were dressed in casual, but warm, clothes – as if they intended to be there for some time.

'There are three more guarding the other side of the building, and a further two in the stables. Plus Jasper of course.'

Verity breathed heavily. She felt better. The scented early evening air was fragrant. She smiled appreciatively at Rafe.

Her grandfather rubbed her head in reply. 'No more adventures for a while,' he said.

Verity laughed. 'No,' she agreed, then turned to walk, with a lighter heart, to her bed. Rafe helped her straighten the covers, and gave her a kiss good night.

As her grandfather left the room, closing the door behind him, Verity reached for a book, but a few moments later there was a soft knock. Rafe must have forgotten something, Verity thought to herself with a smile. She answered cheerily, telling him to come in.

It was Jeb, looking pensive.

His long brown hair was tied back, as usual. His

green eyes looked brighter against the shadows underneath. 'Rafe said it was all right to visit,' he said.

Verity clammed up. In spite of her conversation with Henry, she didn't know what to say to Jeb. First he ignored her, and then he dived down a well to rescue her.

Jeb flushed. 'Good, I – that's good.' He stared at the floor.

Verity could hear a group of ravens squabbling in the grounds. She couldn't bear it any longer. 'Why have you changed? You're awkward with me, have I done something?' she asked.

'I'm not, you haven't—'

'Don't lie,' she interrupted crossly.

Jeb looked at her: at the way her long brown hair flowed over her shoulders and onto the pillow. 'I'm not good enough for you,' he said.

'*Not good enough?*' Verity looked stunned. 'So you do like me?' she said.

'Yes. But you could do better.'

She frowned. 'Have you any idea how patronizing that sounds?' she said.

Jeb took a step back.

Verity pulled herself up and looked him squarely in the eye. She hadn't felt so *furious* in a long time. 'If I've enough judgement to help fight the Earth Witch, I think I'm quite capable of deciding who I should get involved with romantically. Which won't be you, by the way.'

Jeb laughed. 'That's the Gallant spirit, all right,' he said.

Verity glared at him, incensed.

'I don't blame you for being angry,' he said. He sat down on the chair next to her bed. A ray of evening sun glanced through the window. It caught his hair and lit his strong handsome face. 'I was so worried about whether I'm good enough for you, I forgot you're perfectly capable of deciding that yourself.' He looked dejected.

Verity smiled. 'Well, more fool you,' she said. Then she leaned forward and kissed him.

# Chapter Eighteen

That night, the dark streets of Wellow shone under a watchful heaven. Above the cliffs and climbing houses, the velvet sky seemed to have grown larger: it looked in danger of swallowing the world.

In the quiet garden room at the Manor, Verity slept. A silver crescent moon stole through a gap in the heavy cream curtains.

In her dreams she was not floating above the world now: she was deep within it. She was every particle of existence. She was bodiless, but saw every moment, felt every movement. She drifted from her room, through the wood of the door itself and down the grand stairs of the Manor.

The house was silent, save for the odd tick and

creak of a building at rest. The panelled walls whispered to her. She remembered their former lives: from hopeful acorns to stoic oaks. The flagstones told her of their time deep in the hearts of long-cold volcanoes.

The downstairs hall was swathed in moonlit sand. It ebbed and flowed in spectral waves. Verity glided to the front door and opened it. The carved angels watched in sombre contemplation.

Povl stood before her, his clothes damp and more soiled than ever. At his feet lay two of the guards. They were covered in delicate white sand. It crept over them with a silken movement.

Verity did not flinch. This was a dream. She stood aside and Povl drifted past her, into the Manor, pausing only to take her hand. She gave it calmly. The sand followed them, trailing between their feet. It caressed Povl's ghostly face and puckered mauve lips.

Verity sighed in her sleep. He had loved the Earth Witch, she was sure of it. It was her loss that turned him.

Povl led Verity to Rafe's study. Rafe was

slumped on the floor, unconscious, but Verity didn't trouble herself. He was unthreatened here. The sand ignored him, now.

Povl floated towards Rafe, and crouched over him, reaching into his jacket to take a key from an inner pocket.

Verity drifted to the ornate gilt mirror hanging above the fireplace. She stared dispassionately at her reflection. The waxing moon lit her face. The pale white sand of the Earth Witch's body crawled over her features. It poured in and out of her nostrils, her eyeballs, her ears. It scurried and swirled across her vision.

Unconcerned, Verity held out a hand. It was coated in a fine mist of sand. She saw trails of it wandering under her skin. She felt it in every part of her. But she was cocooned by it: protected.

Povl appeared behind her. 'You are one with my mistress,' he said.

The sand scratched around Verity's brain in approval. It buzzed and darted between her eyes. Yes, they were united.

Povl reached for a heavy green piece of tapestry

that hung on the wall. He pulled it back. Behind it was a safe. Povl used the key. The metal bolts snapped back. Povl swung open the thick door. There was the Bloodstone. He picked it up, without convulsing. 'You will come with us.'

Verity followed passively as Povl led her out of the Manor. She felt the cool of the flagstones on the soles of her feet. In the garden, the grass was frozen crisp.

Povl stopped at a shed, and opened its door. It was filled with maintenance tools. He stepped inside and chose a pickaxe.

They left the Manor grounds and flowed through the streets. The tall thin man who was dressed like a tramp, and the young girl whose dark hair cascaded over her white nightgown: both solemn as the grave.

They followed a route that crossed the top of the town and traversed the park. A path Verity knew like the back of her hand. They emerged on the other side of the grounds, standing flank by flank. In front of them, Priory Bay kept its silent guard. Its gothic towers cast terrible shadows in the dark.

Povl led her through the school's wrought iron gates. The buildings were still and soundless. He surged towards the chemistry wing and smashed the glass window of his former classroom door. Verity drifted in after him.

Povl lifted the pickaxe above his head. The world held its breath. With a single blow he struck the floor. It cracked. He swung again. The noise of metal on stone ricocheted around the room.

As the dust clouded, Povl cleared a space in the rubble. And when he had finished, Verity dropped with him into the damp hole that lay below.

The tunnel was ancient. It was dank and foul. Nothing that breathed had been here for centuries. Verity waited for her eyes to become accustomed to the dark, hearing just the drip and splash of underground water. But in her mind she could feel the myriad crawl of millipedes, earwigs and woodlice as they busied themselves in the dirt.

Finally her pupils adjusted.

In front of her were the partial remains of a pure white granite statue surrounded by piles of sand. It was of a woman asleep, her clothes draped in folds.

She looked as if she had drifted there: calmly, serenely. Parts of the statue were complete, and in those places her skin shone. Her closed eyes were whole – the curve of her lids enchanting – but her cheek was still unfinished. Her chest was wide open, with a space for her heart: an empty hollow waiting for its beating soul.

Povl lifted up the Bloodstone and placed it in his mistress. 'Now she will be re-formed.'

At his words, sand began pouring into the space. Verity watched. She was a distant observer who stood face to face.

The pale white grains flowed towards the statue. As the sand gathered pace it began to leap and vibrate. Its movement was frantic.

The air was thick and dry. The dust of the Earth Witch's body billowed and boiled in a powerful vortex. Verity coughed and choked. Her eyes streamed, her breath rasped. She held a hand to her chest, wheezing for air. She couldn't see. The noise was terrifying: a howling feral cry of loss.

The white sand, that had cocooned Verity's body, began to pour out of her. It spilled from her eyes, her mouth, her nostrils. She looked down and saw it flowing away: she felt herself emptying of it.

Then all was still.

As the air began to clear, Verity stared around her. Slowly, as if she were waking, the terrible truth dawned on her. Her body shook uncontrollably. In a frenzy she brushed her arms, her face, her eyes: repulsed at the thought of what had consumed her.

*This wasn't a dream. It was real.*

In the corner of her eye, Verity caught the faintest of movements: a glimmer of pearl. She turned. She tried to scream, but the noise wouldn't come out.

The lustrous white statue was standing, no longer lying, in the centre of the tunnel, and it was looking at Verity. Its chest began to rise and fall. It slowly blinked.

The statue was alive: the Earth Witch was alive.

The Keeper was not merely white: she was the purest, most translucent shade of frosted snow. Her pale skin glowed. Her delicate wrists and ankles led to perfectly turned arms and calves. Her hair ran in immaculate curls over her shoulders and down her back. Her cheeks and lips were flawless: firmly shaped and without blemish. But her almond eyes were terrifyingly opaque: as white and solid as bone.

'Free from my sister's prison at last,' she said, in a voice that was as rich as loam, as deep as the earth itself. She clasped her limbs through her loose clothes; gripping her arms, her shoulders, her thighs in reassurance. 'So many years with only consciousness.'

Verity stared, shuddering with fear.

A moan of rapture escaped Povl. Verity tore her eyes from the Earth Witch. Povl was kneeling on the floor, gazing at his mistress in adoration. Then he stood up, swaying slightly. 'My Queen,' he said. His eyes glittered.

She walked towards him, her stride feminine and confident: her posture perfect. She stroked his temple. He swooned at her touch.

'You brought me my heart,' she said.

'They thought mere mortals could protect it.' He smiled, a lunatic grin. 'They were fools.'

She reached out a lush arm. 'Shall we begin?'

Povl clasped her hand eagerly, his face pathetic with adoration. Both of them seemed oblivious to Verity. 'Our revenge will start here,' he said.

The Earth Witch closed her eyes to summon up her power. In a split-second a low, deep noise pulsed from far below. Verity could feel it throbbing through her. The walls around them began to shake. She realized what the Earth Witch was doing. 'Please don't—'

The Keeper of the Earth turned to Verity, her tombstone eyes filled with hate. Verity shrank back.

'Is this the girl?' she asked Povl.

'Yes,' he said. 'This is the thief.'

The Earth Witch walked slowly towards Verity, who stood completely still: too petrified to move. The ground continued to reverberate. Reaching out, the Earth Witch pulled Verity to her with both hands.

For the smallest moment Verity's world stopped. In the midst of her terror she marvelled at the Keeper's flawless complexion: her fine arched brows, the generous curve of every delicate white lash.

The Keeper tore apart the neck of Verity's night-gown and held up the boat charm. 'How did you get this?' she demanded.

Verity's breath skidded to a halt. Her heart was pounding, her mouth too dry to speak, but she knew she must. 'A friend made it for me,' she choked.

The Earth Witch's face creased with disdain. 'Not the wooden trinket: the chain.' She ran an elegant finger along it.

'You stole *my* necklace from *my* servant,' the Earth Witch roared. The walls shook. 'My most precious belonging: the charm I gave to my lover. And you have tainted it forever. You will pay for that.'

'But I—' Verity's hand flew to her neck. The chain that held Jeb's carved wooden boat was the plaited hair of the Earth Witch; the necklace from the story. An image of the Keeper with long tresses of precious metal flashed through Verity's mind.

Povl smiled nastily. 'Kill her, Mistress,' he said.

The Earth Witch ignored him. 'I have felt you

wearing it since you dropped into the sea,' said the Earth Witch. 'Povl told me you stole it.'

So he *did* talk to her, somehow. Verity's head ached. This was too much.

'From that moment my hatred for you was fierce,' said the Earth Witch.

Verity glanced at Povl. The teacher smirked.

'You will come with us,' said the Earth Witch.

From nowhere, an avalanche of earth raged through the tunnel, warping and writhing like a giant serpent. It snatched Verity up, and swept her along, holding her in its heavy grip. She screamed, clawing for purchase as the crumbling deluge engulfed her.

Povl shrieked with joy. 'We shall punish the world. We will reign together.'

The Earth Witch's beauty was distorted by the power coursing through her. Her perfect white face was a mask of grim satisfaction.

The three of them surged through the tunnels, driven along by the avalanche. Verity gagged and gasped for air, her nose filled with the rich scent of clay, and soil and dirt. Everything was blackness and a terrifying roar. She was entombed. The earth squeezed her chest like a dried flower pressed in a book. The remnant of Povl's cackling laughter echoed in her head.

Above the tunnels, the streets of Wellow shook with gathering intensity. Buildings quivered, plates and cutlery spilled from tables, chairs rattled across the room, floors rolled and jolted. Dust filled the air in choking clouds. A formidable, bass groan of noise rumbled through every thing. Screams and shouts rang out from houses as light after light flicker-ed on.

Then, just as suddenly, it stopped.

# Chapter Nineteen

The avalanche finally spewed Verity out. She lay in the dirt, gasping for breath, coughing and heaving. She pushed herself up just enough to spit the soil from her mouth.

Verity looked around her. She and the Earth Witch and Povl were in a room, of sorts, or an underground cave. The walls were paddled clay. It was fresher than the tunnel they'd first entered, but it was still a dank and stale hole in which Verity was trapped. She could be anywhere. No one would find her here.

Povl took a match from his pocket and lit a torch on the wall. Behind him was a wooden door, heavy and bleached from a whitewash that had long since flaked off. It was strengthened with bars of iron.

The Earth Witch strode about the space: a look of fierce exhilaration on her face.

Verity crawled to her, grabbing at her elegant white robes. 'Please don't do this,' she begged. 'If you destroy all the happy stories, the world will descend into chaos.'

The Earth Witch's angelic face was at once demonic with anger. 'How dare you speak to me in such a way,' she snarled, brushing Verity's hand away.

Povl leapt on Verity, dragging her violently across the floor. He was more deranged than ever. 'You will show respect,' he screeched.

The Earth Witch smiled in approval, her eyes still dead. 'You understand, my dear Povl.'

'I have missed you so,' he breathed, gazing at her with adoration. 'Every day was torture. But now we are together.'

'All shall know our pain,' she replied bitterly.

'Yes,' he said eagerly. 'Shall we start with her?'

'Soon,' she said. 'The others have arrived.'

\* \* \*

Verity heard footsteps. The door swung open. A light shone in her face. She squinted, holding a hand to her eyes, then gasped: it was Henry, Martha, Jasper and Jeb, each in their nightwear.

But as she jumped up to greet them Verity realized something was terribly wrong. Her friends marched into the room, then formed a neat line and stood silently, as though controlled by the Earth Witch. Pale white sand swirled over them, swathing their bodies.

It was too cruel. Verity ran from one to the next grabbing each in turn; pleading with Henry and Martha to hear her, shaking Jasper by the arms of his nightgown, but their faces were expressionless and their eyes shut. Jeb frowned and sighed at the sound of her voice. None of them woke.

'What have you done to them?' she cried, turning to the Earth Witch, the words spilling from her mouth.

'They dream,' said the Earth Witch with satisfaction. 'They helped you preserve the stories and must be punished. We are beneath your precious library: under the room in which you defied me. The stories will not survive much longer.'

Verity clenched her fists in resolve: there was no time for fear. 'Think of all the innocent people who don't deserve this,' she said, running to the Keeper. 'You were happy and in love once. Can't you remember?'

The three stood in a wretched triangle at the centre of the dim space. Verity and the Earth Witch gazing fiercely at each other, Povl lurking by the side of his mistress.

'I protected the world, and it stood by, while my sister stole the man I loved,' said the Earth Witch.

Verity gazed helplessly at the vengeful Keeper and tears sprang to her eyes.

The Earth Witch frowned. Was there just the tiniest flicker of doubt on her face? 'You have no right to question me,' she said.

'She is a Keeper,' said Povl.

Verity seized her opportunity. 'So was the Mistress,' she said. 'Was everything *she* did unquestionable?'

Hate rippled across the Earth Witch's face. 'My

sister could not bear to see happiness without feeling the need to extinguish it,' she said. 'And I paid the price for that.'

'And now every living creature has to suffer? Surely that makes you as bad as her?' said Verity, her stomach churning with fear.

The Keeper looked furious. 'It is time to deal with you,' she growled, 'the thief first, then her helpers.'

Povl clapped his hands.

'I didn't steal—' Verity began.

'Do not lie to me,' the Earth Witch roared. 'Only *my* hair could make a chain of that kind.' She stamped her foot. Such a small movement, but the blow threw Verity to the side of the room.

A low, growling boom rumbled from the depths of the earth. The ground shook, more violently this time. The torchlight flickered manically. Verity felt her body being jerked back and forth: like a mouse in a cat's jaw. She saw her friends topple to the ground, unable to protect themselves.

The walls rippled like water. Dirt filled the air, clods of soil dropped from the ceiling. The ground in the middle of the room began to tear. The creaking and splitting was deafening. The earth opened up, revealing its delicate strata. The centre of the room was now a chasm.

As the shock subsided, the Earth Witch took hold of Verity and dragged her towards the exposed hole. Verity shrieked and struggled, but the Earth Witch was inhumanly strong. In one swift movement she plucked Verity from the ground and swung her upside down.

Verity screamed. The Earth Witch held her over the abyss. The space stretched into the dark. As Verity's eyes grew more accustomed to the black she realized something was glowing.

'Lava,' said the Earth Witch. 'No more than you deserve for taking the property of a Keeper.'

Verity gripped onto her. 'I didn't steal the necklace,' she begged. 'My friend gave it to me: his godfather gave it to him. Povl is lying: he hates me.'

Povl stood watching. He smiled but only Verity could see that. Her head roared with blood. There were her friends: all so close, but oblivious to what was happening.

The Earth Witch began to shake Verity loose. 'Take that cursed necklace with you.'

Povl's ashen face was rapt. 'Destroy it,' he cheered. 'He never loved you as I did.'

*He never loved you as I did.*

Verity twisted round, still upside-down, still held tightly in the Earth Witch's grip, to stare in shock at the grotesque inverted image of her teacher's face. There had been another, of course, who stood to gain if the Keeper lost her lover.

She remembered reading the words on the story hidden in Alice's diary:

'. . . *when you helped me steal a lock of her hair,*' *said the Wind Witch with scorn.*

'*No one will ever know the depth of my feelings for her,*' she heard Povl say to her in the well.

'. . . *it were the original, not the copy . . .*' she heard Jeb telling her as he made her keep the necklace.

'There were two necklaces,' she screamed at the top of her voice to the Earth Witch, 'Jeb said there were two.'

Povl jumped.

Verity began to shout every thought, every word she could field in her defence. 'What if the Mistress made a copy of your necklace? What if *that's* what she held up as proof that your sweetheart didn't love you? Povl could have helped her steal your hair. I think he was terrified of losing you. You must have known how much he loved you. He didn't like your love, did he?'

The Earth Witch stopped and dropped Verity to the floor where she lay on the ground in a heap, fighting for breath. The Keeper turned to face her servant.

Povl swallowed, his frame twitching anxiously. 'The girl lies,' he stuttered.

The Earth Witch stood perfectly still, her divine face rapt in concentration. 'There is a part of your mind hidden,' she muttered at last. 'What could you wish to keep secret?'

'Mistress, be reasonable: I must have some privacy,' Povl pleaded. 'I learned to keep some minor thoughts from you: that is all.' A pang of guilt darted across his face.

The Earth Witch stared at her servant intently.

'There is nothing for you to know,' Povl insisted, 'nothing you need search my mind for.'

But the Earth Witch was plainly ignoring his request. Seconds later she gasped. Slowly she advanced towards her servant, holding his gaze with a look of bitter hurt and betrayal. Povl's body hunched ever lower, but he could not break away from her reproachful eyes.

Finally she stood in front of him. Povl's hands flew up, but the Keeper caught hold of her servant and reached into the polo neck of his mud-stained jumper. Slowly, agonizingly, she pulled out a necklace. It was identical to Verity's: a woven plait of finest gold.

Verity stared at the two of them in astonishment. The Mistress had really done it. She'd cheated her sister: tricked her and her sweetheart into believing the other didn't love them, after all those years of waiting.

The Earth Witch pulled the necklace from Povl in horror. She held it up. The delicate chain shone against her pale white skin. 'How could you?' she asked. Her voice was weak. 'I trusted you to guard me while I slept. And you stole my hair for *her*.'

Povl's spine hunched. 'Your sister used every wile to persuade me,' he said. He hung his head.

'She showed me this other necklace, to make me believe he did not love me any more,' the Earth Witch said. Her voice cracked.

'He was going to take you away from me,' said Povl, his eyes wild. 'I couldn't bear it.'

'He still loved me?' she asked.

'His love would have faded,' said Povl quickly. 'He was not good enough for you. I will never desert you.'

The Earth Witch dropped to the floor. Her face flickered with pain. 'I cried until I was white,' she said. 'Thinking I had lost him broke my heart.' Her beautiful face crumpled with loss. She began to sob: terrible, silent, heaves of sorrow. 'And he didn't leave with my sister: he loved me still.'

Verity's eyes stung but she stayed where she was. The Earth Witch's grief was too raw.

Eventually the Keeper stopped. She looked calm. The discovery seemed to have taken all the anger from her: like a boat that is robbed of wind. 'I will not punish the world,' she said. 'It was my sister who caused my suffering: not my bondage to the elements. Aure always took everything she wanted. I will not be the same.'

Verity sagged with relief.

'I will deal with you presently,' the Keeper said to her servant.

Povl stared at his mistress, the words sinking in. After a moment his face switched to a scowl of fury. '*I dedicated my life to you*,' he screamed. 'I acted only out of love.' He lunged at Verity, grabbing her by the hair. She gagged at his dank stench.

'I have had enough of this girl's interference. Kill her, and the story will die with her,' he said wild-eyed, dragging her towards the pit.

'Let go of the child,' said the Earth Witch, her voice deep.

'You must be avenged,' insisted Povl.

The Earth Witch gazed at her servant. 'You will come with me,' she said.

Povl scarcely glanced up. 'I will follow you, of course. But first let me kill her.'

'No,' the Earth Witch corrected, pointing imperiously. 'The child will live.'

With the speed and power of a volcano, she threw Verity to safety and gripped Povl in both granite hands. Then she flung herself, and her devoted disciple, into the open chasm. They screamed together: a primeval wail of loss, and fear, and pain.

Verity pulled herself up to peer over the hole. She could still make out Povl's flailing arms, the terrified look of panic on his face. But the Earth Witch was completely serene in her descent.

Verity looked into her eyes. *'He loved me still.'* The thought echoed in her mind.

She heard a groan from the other side of the room. Her friends. Verity ran to them. All four lay on the floor, tangled amongst each other. Her heart in her mouth, she began shaking them.

Henry was the first to wake: coming to with a start and looking around the cave in horror, his clear blue eyes damp. 'It wasn't a dream: I could see you, and I couldn't help . . .' He grabbed her tightly. She held him back, her eyes shut. She could feel his heart pounding in his chest.

They stood up.

Her friend recovered himself and sniffed. 'You really must stop having run-ins with mad witches like this,' he said.

Verity wiped her face, half-laughing, and half-sobbing, in reply.

Martha began to stir, staring about the room in silent disbelief. They pulled her up. Verity dusted down her hair and pyjamas. 'Nothing hurt?' she asked. Her friend just shook her head and grabbed both of them. The three children rocked silently together.

Finally Jeb woke. He watched from the ground for a moment then stood up. 'Are you all right?' he asked Verity.

Somehow his gentle tone made it worse. Verity's lip wobbled. She couldn't trust herself to speak.

Jeb offered a hand. She took it. And this time, she believed it was over.

## Chapter Twenty

Verity felt fully recovered several weeks before she could get anyone to agree that this was the case. Even her friends sided with the grown-ups this time. But eventually she was pronounced well enough for a day of sailing.

She woke in the morning, giddy with anticipation, her mind skidding from one plan to the next. Spring was here, and across Wellow blowsy daffodils were reaching the end of their bloom. As she pushed up the sash of her window, the air was already warm and fragrant.

Olivia toddled into the room, book in hand. She had just learnt to walk. Without saying a word, she began to look for a comfortable place to sit and be read to, quite certain no one was going to argue with her plan.

Verity picked her baby sister up with a grin and placed her on the bed, against one of her pillows, then sat next to her, flicking to the front of the book.

Poppy appeared at the door and jumped under the covers to join them. 'Olivia's very talented for her age,' she said proudly, wriggling to get comfortable.

'She knows all the farmyard noises already,' Verity agreed. 'What do cows say, Olivia?'

'Moo,' their little sister replied seriously, pointing to a picture of a Friesian.

Both girls leaned to kiss her.

'Now do you think you can manage to stay out of trouble for two minutes?' asked Poppy, who had eventually winkled the whole story out of her sister. 'Can we trust Verity near the library?' she asked Olivia, shaking her head.

'No,' said Olivia, shaking hers back, which just made Poppy giggle even more.

'I blame that flibbertigibbet Miss Cameron,' said Poppy solemnly.

Verity smiled, but inside she felt sad. She knew there had been no message from the librarian: she'd checked with Martha each time she visited. Yet again she wondered why there was still no word from her friend.

'*They're here*,' Poppy shouted at last, running out of her mother and father's bedroom. She and Verity had been taking it in turns since breakfast had finished to watch from the window for the appearance of Henry, Martha, Jeb, Percy and Will.

Verity leapt down the stairs at breakneck speed, her sailing gear already on.

'Not so fast,' said her father with a smile, appearing from his study.

'Do try to be careful,' Mrs Gallant fretted while Verity hurriedly kissed them all goodbye and opened the front door to her friends. 'Don't do anything I wouldn't.'

'We were thinking about a spot of light sewing, followed by some knitting,' said Henry on the front doorstep.

Verity gave him a shove as she stepped outside.

She smiled at Jeb. They hadn't had a chance to be alone together since that evening at the Manor.

Percy and Will were waiting outside on the street, leaning against the front wall. She hugged them both, which they accepted with good humour.

'I'm slightly alarmed to see you up and about,' said Percy. 'You can cause less damage in bed.'

'I'm surprised the town doesn't insist you come with a health warning,' said Will.

'And the one bit of good you do – trashing a chemistry classroom – is fixed by your grandfather,' said Percy, shaking his head in disgust.

Verity shrugged apologetically. Rafe had arranged for the science wing to be restored with minimum fuss.

'Where was he when you were dragging us all to the library each day?' asked Will. 'Didn't feel the need to help out there, did he?'

Verity laughed and gave her family one last wave goodbye while Martha promised that yes, they would take very good care of their friend.

Then all six of them began to walk down the street together.

'I brought a picnic,' said Martha, pushing to the front, 'not as delicious as one of Mrs Twogood's, but hopefully it will do. Sailing gives me a huge appetite, so I'm terrified there won't be enough for this lot.'

Percy and Will held up two gigantic picnic hampers. Verity had wondered what they were for. 'These are fine for us,' said Will, 'but I'm not sure what you're all going to eat.'

'Are we borrowing a yacht?' asked Henry, 'because I don't know how we're going to fit all that on two dinghies.'

'Better lighten the load before we leave,' said Percy.

They hadn't made any plans about where to go, which was exactly as Verity preferred it. She felt the breeze play around her face. Her stomach tingled.

They strode down through Wellow, all excitedly chatting and laughing. Verity looked around with interest. Most traces of the damage caused by the Earth Witch had been fixed. She could still spot the occasional smashed tile on the ground, or the odd piece of loosened masonry, but much of the town had been restored, as if it wanted to heal quickly.

Before long they were at the upper cliff of the harbour. 'Can we stop at the library?' Verity asked hesitantly.

Even Martha groaned in response.

'Have you *seen* the weather?' asked Henry.

'We don't have to stay long,' said Verity. 'I'd just like to see Jasper, that's all.'

'Come on then,' said Will. 'But no lingering.'

The main hall was still and cool when they burst in through the red double doors. Jasper hurried to greet them, looking fully restored to his normal self. The buttons on his uniform gleamed.

'I wondered if you might say hello,' he admitted.

Verity grinned. She hadn't seen Jasper since the appearance of the Earth Witch. As Henry had pointed out during her convalescence, there was really no good way to explain to either Gallant parent why a customs officer was suddenly taking such a keen interest in their daughter's welfare.

Jasper picked up a stack of books from the entrance desk and then put them back down again uncertainly. 'Do you have time for a cup of tea?' he asked hopefully.

Verity looked pleadingly at her friends. 'Just one, for old time's sake,' she said.

'It's your day,' said Henry, affecting stoical resignation.

'Don't forget there are so many things I haven't had the answer to yet,' Verity added.

'Us too,' said Martha. 'Everyone's been busy, especially Jeb: helping Isaac and Rafe in their work to restore the town.'

'It's this sort of behaviour that goes a long way to explaining your unpopularity with witches and the like,' said Percy, ushering Verity magnanimously into the reading room.

'I don't suppose there's any shortbread knocking around?' asked Will.

It didn't take long for Jasper to rustle up a kettle of boiling water together with some tea and cups, while Martha fished around in the copious hampers and retrieved teacakes, butterscotch and milk.

'Got the place looking spick and span,' said Will as he stretched out in a wingback chair.

If anything the library seemed cleaner than ever. Verity was certain all the surfaces looked more polished. And there was definitely less dust. She wondered whether Miss Cameron would like it when she returned. Surely it couldn't be long now until she did.

'Since the Twogoods helped clear away the main debris I found time to tidy up,' said Jasper. 'There have been very few visitors recently.'

'I suppose the entrance to the hidden cave is blocked again?' said Verity, stirring her tea.

Jasper nodded. 'It is not a space Miss Cameron would want made public,' he said. 'I closed it off as quickly as possible.'

'Presumably Brother Povl got a job at Priory Bay because the Earth Witch was beneath it. But how did he manage that?' said Verity.

'Probably best not to dwell on it,' said Henry, cutting another slice of cake. 'To think you used to feel sorry for him.'

Verity smiled wryly. How could she possibly

have once thought he and Jasper might be friends? She jumped up and gave the customs man an unsolicited hug. It caught him completely unawares but his smile was genuine.

'I'm sorry I was so rude to you, when you arrived,' she said. 'I think you've done Miss Cameron proud.'

Two tiny spots of pink appeared in Jasper's cheeks. 'To work with a member of the Gallant family for the *Bibliothecary* is an honour,' he said.

'Jeb. I can't bear it any longer. How did you get the Earth Witch's necklace?' asked Martha.

'From my godfather,' said Jeb quietly. 'He gave it to me on Christmas morning and died later that day, with Isaac at his side. Told me it belonged to a girl he loved. Waited a long time for her, he reckoned, and just when he thought they were to be together, she disappeared. Her sister told him she were gone.'

'And you gave the necklace to Verity?' asked Martha.

Jeb flushed. 'He told me I should pass it on,' he said awkwardly, 'to the right person.'

Martha couldn't resist a knowing smile.

'He said the necklace was a charm?' said Verity.

Jeb nodded. 'Isaac always reckoned it might be something to do with the Keepers. He lived a long time, did my godfather: longer than he should've by rights.' Jeb looked simply at Verity. 'I thought it might keep you safe. What a fool.'

'It saved us in the end,' said Verity, reaching for his hand. Jeb smiled.

'And your godfather knew there was a copy?' asked Jasper.

'Told me there might be a second one, just like it, made by her servant, who couldn't be trusted.'

'How could he have worked that out?' asked Percy.

Jeb looked uncertain. 'I asked Isaac,' he said. 'He reckons that if you knew Povl, and the Mistress, and had a long life to ponder on it, you might wonder if that's what they brewed up between 'em.'

'So the Mistress cheated her own sister,' said Martha.

'She wanted my godfather for herself, but he couldn't get the sweetheart out of his mind,' said Jeb.

'Never took the necklace off till he gave it to me.'

'Who *was* your godfather?' asked Henry.

'Thomas Heartsease,' said Jeb.

Martha gasped. 'The man who made the Heartsease Cup,' she said.

''S'right,' said Jeb. 'Reckon we'll never know if he realized it held his own lover's heart.'

Verity wiped an eye with her sleeve. What a pointless, tragic waste.

'Tom always said the servant were a weaselly kind of feller,' Jeb added reflectively.

Verity smiled. 'That has to be the understatement of the year.'


The sun was hot and high in the sky by the time they left.

'It's been such a long time since we've been sailing,' Martha said to Verity. The two friends grinned. Grabbing each other's hands, they ran down the cliff-top path to the quay below.

Shaking Jasper by the hand, in thanks for the tea, Percy and Will followed.

The moored boats bobbed and clinked in the

breeze. The sea was clear, and green, with not a trace of pale white sand.

'She really is gone,' said Martha. The two girls stopped at a jetty and hugged each other.

Above them still, at the library door, Jeb caught Henry's arm. The young Twogood boy paused, but his body strained forward impatiently.

Jeb glanced at the ground. 'Verity would be lost without you,' he said. 'I wouldn't like to stand in the way of that. But I'm not backing off this time. We're not likely to end up friends, but perhaps we can get along well enough, for her sake.'

Henry stared into the middle distance. The sun shone in his eyes. 'She obviously likes you too,' he said eventually.

Verity and Martha waved in the distance.

'Why are you two dawdling?' shouted Will.

'Shall we go to Soul Bay?' Jeb yelled back.

Verity beamed. 'That would be lovely.'

*Book Four*

# Spring

## Epilogue

From the top of the downs, above Soul Bay, you can see the coast of Wellow stretching out like a promise of things to come.

Cross the narrow track and climb over the stile. When you reach the sandy path that leads to the beach, the noise of the ocean is dimmed. The bank of grass that veers up to your right protects you from the wind. As you round the corner you reach the precarious wooden steps, put there many lifetimes before us.

You can stand on that timber staircase, at the top of the cliff, and gaze across the emerald sea to the melting horizon beyond. There is divinity in that view.

On the shore, far below, a girl walks hand in

hand with a boy. Tall for her age, her long brown hair flows in the wind. She is wearing a red cotton sundress. It suits her figure.

The boy is lithe and strong, with bright green eyes. He bends over to pick a shell for her and places it in her palm. She smiles. Her charcoal eyes sparkle. She looks radiantly happy.

Out on the water a sandy-haired boy sails past. He is racing his dinghy as fast as she will go: sitting his weight out to level the red-sailed boat for speed. The salt spray splashes his face. It mixes with the tears streaming down his cheeks.

The sky is cloudless. It is warm today. Summer is coming, and this year the weather will be hot.